THE PUMPKIN-EATERS

The
Pumpkin-Eaters

LOIS BRAUN

I.C.C. LIBRARY

TURNSTONE PRESS

Turnstone Press
607-100 Arthur Street
Winnipeg, Manitoba
Canada   R3B 1H3

Turnstone Press gratefully acknowledges the assistance of
the Manitoba Arts Council and the Canada Council in the
publication of this book.

Cover illustration and design: David Morrow

This book was printed by Hignell Printing Limited for
Turnstone Press.

Printed and bound in Canada.

Some of these stories have previously appeared in the
following publications: "No Cats in Heaven" in *Western
Living*, "Sahara" in *Prairie Fire*, "The Pumpkin-Eaters" in the
Journey Prize Anthology (McClelland and Stewart) and "Still
Lonely in Wawa" in *Paper Rainbows*. A dramatic version of
"Still Lonely in Wawa" has been aired on CBC Radio's
"Speaking Volumes" and "Aircraft."

Canadian Cataloguing in Publication Data
Braun, Lois, 1949-
    The pumpkin-eaters
    ISBN 0-88801-148-2
I. Title.
PS8553.R36P85 1990   C813'.54   C90-097046-4
PR9199.3.B73P85 1990

For Joe

CONTENTS

THE RIGHT COMPANY

Loretta and Washbottle were up front, and Suzy in the back had just loaded the Permac when Mr. Hoople came in with the stranger. The stranger wore his socks pulled up over his pants bottoms and amber-yellow glass in his spectacles. Loretta thought at first he was a customer, from the railway crew maybe, come to buy a morning mickey. That was her first impression of the stranger.

The Pinehaven Dry Cleaners and the Pinehaven Liquor Vendor and the Pinehaven Videomart were all in the same cinderblock bungalow, right across from the Pinehaven Post Office. The three businesses were all owned by the same man, Arby Hoople, and he hired three full-time workers and three part-timers to run them. The shops were all connected with doors, the liquor vendor and dry cleaning shared a cash register.

In the videomart, Washbottle was spread-eagled against a wall with the curling corners of a new poster pinned under his spidery fingers. Suzy had Tina Lewycki's peach jumpsuit in her hands. She found the invoice in its pocket, where Loretta had put it, and snapped the slip of paper onto one of the several mousetraps Mr. Hoople had mounted on a beam near the sorting table. After stapling a red tag to the label in the collar, Suzy checked the jumpsuit to see if any spots needed special attention. She found a cigarette burn on the cuff of one pantleg, and grass stains on the rear end, plus something that could have been tar or oil. Just as Mr. Hoople and the stranger walked past Loretta's counter, Suzy yelled through the curtain, "Looks like Tina Maria's been sliding her rump around Lovers' Lane again. You'd think if she was going to lie down in a pasture she'd stay away from peach."

"Suzy's cocker spaniel," Loretta explained to Mr. Hoople, still unaware that the other man was not a liquor customer but in company with her employer. "Peach is her neighbour's lhasa apso." But Loretta could tell he'd never heard of a lhasa apso.

"That shipment come in yesterday?"

"Yes sir." It came in every Wednesday.

Mr. Hoople walked through the curtain into the dry cleaning room where Suzy was working, and to Loretta's surprise the second man, with the khaki work pants tucked into his wool socks, followed Mr. Hoople. But the man paused to smile at Loretta, as though he were telling her he'd be back.

Suzy shook the jumpsuit once or twice to make sure no loose grass was tucked into the folds. Then she laid it on the spotting board. She was startled when Mr. Hoople's voice cut into the tumult of the air-conditioner, exhaust fans, Permac, dryers.

"Two machines, two storage racks. Sorting and folding table. Sewing machine. Suzy does mending and patching on request. Perchlorethylene comes by truck. It's stored in a tank outside. This gizmo is called a susan."

Who is this, some sort of relative? Suzy wondered. While Mr. Hoople demonstrated the susan for the stranger, she finished treating Tina Maria's grass stains. With furtive glances at the stranger's face, she examined the edge of Big Angie's sixty-dollar K-Mart quilt for chocolate spots. She found traces of grease all along the hem. "Buttered popcorn," she muttered to herself. The men headed for the back door leading to the alley. Before he went out, the second man smiled at her.

Washbottle had blushed when he'd heard Suzy's comment about Tina Lewycki's grass stains. He'd felt himself blush, even though no one was there to see it. Suzy and Loretta irritated him so. He felt lucky to have them working right next to him, because he liked listening to them chatter and giggle and talk about the customers in those brief intervals when no customers were in either store. But when the women made fun of him, he went to the farthest corner of the videomart and straightened out the cassette boxes on the shelves. Of course, they went right on talking. If a customer came into the liquor store, Loretta usually said a very loud "HIII!" as a signal to Suzy behind the curtain to shut up. When someone came into the videomart, a bell rang over the door. Washbottle did not need a bell—the door was always within his view. Suzy and Loretta needed a bell.

When he'd first been hired by Mr. Hoople to work there, the women had called him Martin and had left him alone. But it hadn't taken long for the guys to come in to rent some movies. "Washbottle! Yah! You work here, man? No shit! Not bad! You get to take the skin-flicks home every night, eh?" Washbottle didn't have a tape machine at home. His mother wouldn't allow it. "Maybe you have to preview them, eh? Man, oh man, Washbottle, you're lucky, man!"

Loretta and Suzy had both stood at the connecting door, watching what was going on. Loretta had mouthed "Washbottle" at him with her big pink lips when he'd happened to glance in her direction. His friends had noticed the two women, too: one in her late thirties, five feet tall, chubby and blonde, with very bright, friendly eyes; the other tall, red-haired, strong looking, with a large mouth painted a virginal pink colour. The boys had nudged each other and whispered, and rolled their eyes at

3

Washbottle, who was trying to get them over to the Horror section. "Cute," he'd heard Suzy say in a loud whisper.

"Dumb bananas," Loretta had said, louder. But by then the boys were looking at a movie box that had a picture of a skull with a dragon coming out of one of its eye sockets.

Suzy and Loretta didn't know that the boys were not really Washbottle's friends. He was not allowed to bring friends to his house. If he disobeyed, his mother and stepfather found clever ways to punish him—with a hot clothes iron, or a splintery two-by-four, or darning needles that were never used for darning.

"Washbottle, Washbottle, where'd you get that unfortunate name?" Loretta had asked him. "You know, you're young. Me and Suzy didn't realize you were that young. Maybe we can help ease you out of it, Schnooky."

As soon as Suzy had weighed the next load, she parted the curtain and said to Loretta, who was dusting bottles, "Who he?"

"Dunno. Gave me the creeps."

"Hoople introduced him to all the equipment in here."

"Brother, maybe?"

They both laughed. "Adopted, maybe," said Suzy.

"Hey, Washbottle," Loretta yelled. "Mr. Hoople was here with some guy. You know who it might be?"

Washbottle had a blob of sticky-tack at the end of each finger for putting up the poster. SILK INTERLUDE, *a story of lust and danger and love.* "I didn't see him, but I heard Mr. Hoople's selling this place."

"Who told you?" said Suzy with sudden anger.

"They want to turn it into a chicken place."

"Oh my god, Loretta. A chicken place. We'll have to wear paper-boat hats and get spattered with grease all day."

"Sssh!" cautioned Loretta. She wondered if Washbottle was having them on. But he'd never joshed them before.

"I won't do it! Oh my god! I'll have to move to the city. There are no more jobs in this town. I don't want to move away!"

"They might come back in. You better get back to work, Suzy."

About twenty minutes later, Loretta heard Suzy call, "You still got that lump in your armpit, Loretta?" Suzy'd wanted to ask Loretta that for a couple of days, to her face, but she had trouble looking at Loretta eye to eye when serious things needed to be said. They talked about serious things through the curtain.

"I don't know. I haven't checked for a couple of weeks. You still got yours? HIII!"

Suzy knew Loretta was referring to Vernon, Suzy's ex, who'd come back to town after an interlude in the city working for a fly-by-night enterprise that made hot-dog relish. He said he would stay with her until he found a job, a few weeks, and if he didn't have work by then, he'd head back to the bright lights. A month had passed, and Suzy was having trouble evicting him.

She heard the whirring of the cash register up front, then the snap of the cash drawer closing. It didn't take long for small-town drinkers to make a selection at the Pinehaven Liquor Vendor. "My lump?" Suzy yelled. "You'd need a shoe horn to get him in and out, he's getting so fat." If she lost her job at the dry cleaners and was forced to move to the city, she'd never shake Vernon.

The bell rang in the videomart.

Washbottle looked up from the computer. Arby Hoople came in with the man wearing amber-tinted glasses. "One-and-a-half employees, Martin here's the one," Mr. Hoople was saying. "How many titles now, Martin? Nine hundred and sixty-three? Multiple copies of some. A few are retired every month. 'Course, we're always buying. Low overhead, though. What's our membership at now, Martin? He keeps all the records on computer."

Arby Hoople and the stranger meandered around the display

shelves. They whispered in a corner for awhile, Mr. Hoople gesturing to the counter where Washbottle was checking returns that had come in that morning. Washbottle knew they were talking about "the blues," as Mr. Hoople called them, the movies the Rev. Darcy Janz called pornography, and Suzy called erotica, which were kept under the counter.

In his hands, Washbottle held THE MARTYRDOM OF SHEILA, *the true story of a suburban miracle. The story of a housewife's tragedy.* The renter had watched about half of it, and it wasn't rewound.

Mondays were always slow for liquor buying and dry cleaning. Summers were slow for the Pinehaven Dry Cleaners. They didn't do silks. Silks went to the city. Slow Mondays Loretta and Suzy sat on the sill of the rear door to have their lunch. They looked into a grass alley, and across the alley into the rear entrance of Pinehaven's funeral parlour. Its double doors at ground level were always tightly closed. Jimmy Schuppert slipped in and out as though he had whores hiding inside. Today, as most days, his hearse was parked in the carport next to the doors. The women could see a fine film of dust on its polished fender.

"Fun Cap hasn't had much business lately," said Suzy. "You'd think in a town this size somebody'd die every day. I'd like to see Jimmy bring in a stiff someday. I've only ever gone in the front door of the Fun Cap."

A few years earlier, on Hallowe'en, tricksters had vandalized the facade of Schuppert's Funeral Chapel. They'd stolen letters from the white clapboard beneath the fake stained-glass window, and in the morning Pinehaven's citizens read, 'Schuppert's Fun   C ap   .' Loretta had been disgusted with the prank. "They could have done something more creative," she said to her husband John. "Like, why didn't they make it say, 'Pet Funeral Chapel'? Someone new in town might even have brought in a dead goldfish or a collie or something. Or how about this—'Upper Fur Ape.' 'Fun Cap' doesn't make any sense."

The sun shone on Suzy and Loretta. Suzy's plastic spoon made a dull rattle in her empty yogurt cup as she waggled it idly back and forth. Loretta chewed on a piece of cold pizza.

"You know," said Suzy, "I always think that dying starts when your body goes through those doors. Like, you're not dead in the hospital, or in your smashed-up car or whatever—you're kind of in a coma, and then when the undertaker takes you in, then you start to die. And you know what he's doing to you and everything, and when he's finished, you're dead. He's the one who puts the screws to you."

One of the double doors across the alley opened slightly for just a moment, then closed again.

Loretta said, "I used to think people would stay all nice and neat in their coffins until Judgment Day, and then when the Lord came down from a big cloud, they'd tunnel up through the ground somehow, and no matter what you dressed them in when you buried them, they'd all have white angel clothes on, and they'd float up to the cloud with Jesus."

"Yeah, I thought that, too," said Suzy.

Jimmy Schuppert came out of the Fun Cap. He locked the door carefully and walked down the alley to his house half a block away.

Loretta went inside to get coffee from the pot they kept going in the back. When she came out with two mugs she said, "Jimmy always pretends to be so mournful and respectful and he's so careful not to let anyone know what's going on inside his la-BOR-atory, but I happen to know, when he's at the coffee shop, he tells plenty, in the right company."

"What's the right company?" Suzy blew into her cup. "Is this de-caf?"

"And I also happen to know he has shown his friends

corpses, before he's worked on them, if they're bashed up real good, and decapitated or something."

Suzy made a bad face. "Eeew, it is that de-caf crap. I don't think anybody's ever been decapitated around here, Loretta."

Loretta leaned back. "Washbottle! You ever heard of anyone's head coming off in an accident lately? Around here?"

Suzy said, "What's the right company? Does Jimmy Schuppert have any friends?"

The side of the building the videomart was on had a rear door, too. When Washbottle heard Loretta's voice, he put down his movie catalogue and went to that door and unlocked it and swung it open. He leaned out. He saw the women squinting at him in the bright sunlight.

They just kept squinting and staring at him. Finally he said, "What?"

"He speaks," said Loretta.

"We're going to make a date for you with Tina Maria," said Suzy. "She'll help you get rid of that green stuff growing at the ends of your fingers."

Washbottle looked at his hands. But there wasn't any sticky-tack on his fingertips. He'd rubbed it off with his thumbs. Suzy and Loretta were always telling him they were going to get Tina Lewycki to teach him about life. Life was all around him in the pictures on the video boxes. Nine hundred and sixty-three pictures of life. And more kept being added. Sex was on the front of the boxes under the counter.

Suzy said, "You want to touch Tina's jumpsuit? It's peach."

Washbottle had thought they wanted to ask him something interesting. He ducked back inside and closed the door.

"If they turn this into a chicken place," said Loretta, "I gotta quit. And if I do that, John will take his mom out of that nursing home and bring her to live with us. And when he's on night shift, me and the old lady'll have to keep quiet all day. I'll go crazy."

"Can you picture Washbottle as a busboy cleaning up chicken bones?"

"Suzy," Loretta said, "I'm scared to see if those lumps are still under my arm."

"Lumps, now. . . ."

The following Monday, Suzy came to work excited. She came through the back door at eight-thirty and waited impatiently for Loretta, who always came through the front door just before nine. The weather was turning warmer and warmer, and Suzy decided to get the steam press going so she could get the hottest part of her job finished early in the day.

When Loretta did arrive, a customer came in with her, a well-dressed woman wearing sunglasses and a wide belt of woven straw. She bought sloe gin. Imagine starting in on that junk first thing in the morning, Loretta thought as she put the bottle in a brown paper bag. She didn't know the woman, although she'd seen her before. A lot of people came in from smaller neighbouring towns.

As soon as the customer left, Suzy began talking behind the curtain. "Loretta, I went to church yesterday. I took Willy to Sunday school and decided to stay for the service. So I'm sitting on the pew there waiting for it to start, and I look around at all the people coming in, coming down the aisles. I wasn't even wearing a Sunday dress. . . ."

TING! The bell rang in the videomart. Suzy fell silent. When it rang again, Suzy said, "Loretta?"

"Yeah."

"Mr. and Mrs. Hoople came in. I gawked and gawked, it was so weird."

"It's weird to see the Hooples in church?"

"Have you seen Mrs. Hoople lately, Loretta? I tried not to stare. . . ."

"HIII!"

"Busy day," said Suzy to herself. "Loretta?"

"Yeah."

"Well, you know how Mrs. Hoople, even though she's ancient, always wore her make-up so nice, and dressed so elegant, and strutted around like a fashion model. I mean, she lived to look good, right? Well, she came down the aisle, and I mean, her make-up was ALL OVER HER FACE! In the wrong places. And crooked and lopsided. I figured she must have been drunk when she put on her face this morning. Rouge was up there on one side, down there on the other. . . ."

TING!

". . . bumpy edges on her eye shadow, thick patches of face powder. . . . And her lipstick!"

"Suzy, how'd you get close enough to see bumpy edges on her eye shadow?"

"I went up to them after the service and said good morning. If it hadn't been so sad it would have been funny. But then, you know what? Mrs. Riediger beside me in the pew, she knows I work for Mr. Hoople, she asked me if I knew that Mrs. Hoople was losing her eyesight. She can't see straight in front of her, only around the outside. Isn't that awful? Loretta?"

"It's ironic," said Loretta through the curtain. She'd liked looking for ironic things ever since she'd gone to the high school play last winter, and during intermission had eavesdropped on the lawyer and his wife talking about irony this and irony that. "It's so ironic that all her life Mrs. Hoople's calling was to shop for clothes, and look like a million dollars, and pluck her eyebrows, and go to make-up demonstrations. . . ."

"Oh, her eyebrows . . . !"

"And now. . . ."

"Mrs. Riediger told me," Suzy said, "that the Hooples want to move away, see if they can find a cure."

"Going with the silks to the city," said Loretta.

Suzy smoothed a polyethylene bag over the creamy rayon

shirtwaist dress she'd cleaned on Saturday. She pulled an invoice out of one of the mousetraps overhead and impaled it on the hook of the wire hanger. As she watched her own hands work, she wondered how Mrs. Hoople trimmed her fingernails. "I guess going blind isn't the worst thing that can happen to you when you get old," she called. "I guess there are worse things."

For awhile, everything was quiet in the Pinehaven Dry Cleaners-Liquor Vendor-Videomart. Suzy bagged another dress. She turned on the air-conditioner, she sorted the items that needed to be done that day.

Then she saw Loretta's face poking through the curtain. Loretta's eyes were large and wet, and her big pink mouth drooped at the corners. "Suzy," she whimpered, "those lumps are still there, under my arm. I have to go see a doctor. Don't I?"

Before Suzy could say anything, the back door opened and Mr. Hoople appeared, wearing his straw fedora tilted back on his damp, thin hair, and Suzy was caught between them with a pair of pin-striped pants in her hand.

Loretta ducked back from the curtain before Mr. Hoople saw her head between the drapes. She stood facing the curtain for a minute or two, working the muscles of her face and blinking to keep the tears from spilling. When she did turn around Washbottle was standing in the connecting doorway, leaning in with his slender hands propped above his head on either side of the door-frame. He had a worried look on his face, and Loretta thought he was going to try to say something nice to her. But his hands slipped down the frame and he said, "Got any nickels?"

After Mr. Hoople left, Loretta opened the curtains wide and helped Suzy tag and bag suits and quilts and sleeping bags.

"How's your mother-in-law?" said Suzy.

Loretta felt drained, as though she'd been crying for a long time, even though she'd only come very close to crying. She felt dead and listless. She said, "That old lady crawled over the bed-railing in the middle of the night and fell flat on her face on a hard floor. The nurses didn't notice until who knows when. She's got a big cut all stitched up on her eyebrow. It happened Friday."

"I don't think I want to get old," said Suzy, and Loretta wondered if she was saying that to make her, Loretta, feel better about the terrifying lumps in her armpit.

"I don't think you'll have much choice. Anyway, the cut isn't the worst thing. Last night when we went to see her, her whole face and her neck were completely black."

"BLACK?"

"Well, sort of dark navy blue. Bruised, for cripe's sake. I told her she looked like a boxer. And she lost."

"You told your mother-in-law that? Was that supposed to make her feel better?"

Loretta shrugged. "I thought she might laugh."

"Did she?"

"She smiled. Half of her smiled." Loretta rubbed the arch of her own eyebrow, thinking about what it would feel like to have a scar, a dent in the thin padding over the skull.

"We both had face stories today," said Suzy. "Old faces. Things going wrong when you get old."

"It's ironic," said Loretta.

A woman came into the liquor vendor and walked past the shelves of bottles right up to the counter. A dry-cleaning customer. She'd come to pick up her white linen slacks. When Loretta took the claim check to the rack to find them, she noticed that Tina Lewycki's jumpsuit was still hanging there, cleaned, mended, and neatly embalmed in sanitized plastic.

Washbottle's mother never cried. He was curious about Loretta's tears, even though they had stayed inside her eyelids. She had seemed to him that moment to be a mother of some sort. The synopsis on the back of one of the movie boxes told about an unhappy boy who'd been adopted and went looking for his natural mother, and when he found her, the caption said, she cried for joy, and the boy told her, "You will never be my real mother until you've cried as many tears as I have. And you will have to cry into eternity to do that. Or, just one tear of true sorrow."

Washbottle had not heard what had happened between Suzy and Loretta after Suzy told the story about Mr. Hoople's wife. He didn't know why Loretta had cried. But he'd caught a glimpse of something beyond her thick, pink lips.

Where was the movie about the boy and the tears? Washbottle walked up and down the displays until he found the box he'd been thinking about. He read the back of it again, the part about the boy looking for his natural mother. But there was nothing on the back of the box about tears. Perhaps he'd seen it on the poster when the movie first came in. Of course, the poster was long gone.

A week later, Suzy left the Pinehaven Dry Cleaners just before noon and came back with a small bag containing paper plates and plastic forks and a package of paper napkins. She also had a square box. "I ordered it Saturday," she said to Loretta as they sat down on the door sill to eat their lunches. "I told them I wanted it for noon today." She opened the box in the sunshine.

Loretta watched spiritlessly.

"It's a Black Forest cake," Suzy said. "Real whipped cream."

Loretta had been depressed throughout the past week. She said her mother-in-law's condition was getting her down—the old lady's mind seemed to have been fuzzed up by the fall. Loretta had told Suzy, "She keeps talking about butterscotch pudding. 'Don't burn the butterscotch pudding.' John says he doesn't remember ever having butterscotch pudding when he was growing up."

But Suzy knew Loretta was waiting for the lumps to go away. Suzy had bought the cake to cheer her up.

They admired the fancy piping on the top of the cake. Maraschino cherries had been pressed into cream around the edge, and three more were embedded in the centre. "Three cherries in the middle," said Suzy. "Let's call Washbottle to have a piece."

But Washbottle didn't come when they called him. Loretta had to go and get him while Suzy cut the cake with a big knife she'd brought in her handbag. "Does he have a customer?" she asked when Loretta came back alone.

"Nah. He's coming. Just sittin' at his stupid computer. Do you think he's scared of us?"

Suzy cut three wedges and laid them on the little plates. The whipped cream softened and oozed in the heat.

Washbottle didn't say anything, except thank you, when Suzy handed him his plate and fork.

"Not a bad cake, for that stupid little bakery," said Loretta. "I wonder why it's called Black Forest."

Suzy noticed that Loretta was eating with more enthusiasm than she'd shown lately. She acted as if she were really enjoying the cake.

They all had seconds, smaller pieces, and Suzy was just going to take the cake inside when Jimmy Schuppert came walking along the alley towards the rear of the Fun Cap. He nodded to them without breaking his stride or showing any interest in their picnic.

Suzy looked at his shiny brown shoes and stood up on the cinder block that formed a step down to ground level and said, "Mr. Schuppert, would you like a piece of this Black Forest cake? It was made fresh this morning, and it's got real whipped cream."

Jimmy Schuppert, with his key in his hand, hesitated at the mortuary door. He turned his head, and started to answer, and because his key reached for the lock Suzy knew he was going to say no.

14

"We have lots here," she said, "and nowhere to keep it fresh for the rest of the afternoon. The cream will go bad."

"Oh my god," Loretta muttered. "He'll think she wants to keep it cold on a slab in his morgue. 'Jane Doe's Black Forest cake.' "

Washbottle wanted to laugh, but covered up by wiping the whipped cream away from the corners of his mouth with his fingers. Loretta gave him a napkin. Washbottle touched her hand when he took it.

"Is it someone's birthday?" Jimmy Schuppert asked seriously, as though that would determine whether or not he'd have the cake.

"No," Suzy replied. "It's just Monday."

The man put the key back in his pocket and started towards them. Suzy yanked another plate out of the paper bag and sank her knife into the gooey topping. She cut him a big piece.

"Warm out here," said Jimmy.

"Coffee?" said Suzy.

"This is very, very good cake. Did you make it?" A white border began to form around Jimmy's lips. He ate quickly, almost sloppily, as if he'd never had cake before.

"Nah," said Suzy. "I got it at the bakery."

"Nice," said Jimmy.

Suzy introduced everybody. She called Washbottle *Martin*. Jimmy Schuppert, while his tongue flicked out at the mess around his mouth, said he knew who they were. He said he'd known Martin's dad. It occurred to Suzy that he'd had dealings with the dead relatives of pretty well everyone in town. "Mr. Schuppert, I'd like to ask you a question." She took his plate and began to cut another piece of cake. "Do you like your work?"

"Well," Jimmy began, "I like parts of it."

"Parts?"

"I like doing the funerals. I like to think I can make the bereaved feel comfortable with their grief."

"Comfortable. Wow," said Loretta.

"The rest is science. Chemistry mostly. And of course cosmetics."

A fly tried to get a taste of the sweet, melted cream in the corner of Jimmy Schuppert's mouth. He swept it away with his immaculate fingers. "My clients are simply mannequins which I must repair and dress for presentation. Very beautiful mannequins. The right attitude is important in my job."

"Too bad you have to bury 'em," said Loretta.

Jimmy stayed a little longer, but he did not have anything more to say. A mask took the place of his real face, and he stood peacefully among them, holding his empty plate while Suzy offered everyone coffee.

Finally she plopped the wedge of cake she'd cut earlier onto Jimmy's plate.

"Impossible," he murmured through his mask.

"Have it later," said Suzy. "Or take it home for supper."

Jimmy Schuppert held the plate before him with both hands and crossed the alley to the double doors beside the hearse. He opened one of them just a crack and slipped through as though he were a flat sheet of paper.

Washbottle liked to keep boxes in order. It was important to have them in order in case anyone came in asking for a certain title, or when he needed to put RESERVED stickers on them. But the rows of pictures also made stories. The rows of titles made stories in Washbottle's mind. Some nights he dreamed about the movie boxes. The figures and colours came alive and oozed among those that were from real life. Mostly the colours. In Washbottle's dreams, the colours could make stories.

A few days after the cake luncheon, Washbottle was rearranging the displays when he heard Loretta's "HIII" and then, "We thought you forgot all about it."

And then, "I've been busy" in a voice that had smoked many

cigarettes and had slept till noon more than just on weekends. A voice familiar to Washbottle, followed by that low, quick laugh.

"Busy ain't we all?" said Loretta.

Washbottle turned and saw the peach jumpsuit lying on the counter between the two women, along with a five-dollar bill. Tina Lewycki had on a bright turquoise T-shirt with matching earrings. He couldn't see the bottom half of her because of the counter.

"I want to wear it to a party on Saturday. My sister's coming home from the hospital. She had a double mastectomy."

Washbottle saw Loretta's hand pause as it came out of the till.

"Double? How old is your sister?"

"Forty-three. She's a lot older than I am." The laugh again, a bit more nervous now. Washbottle turned back to the wall display. His eyes hunted among the pictures.

"Double. Forty-three," said Loretta. "Wow. And she's having a party?"

"She's got a good attitude. Don't worry. We'll make sure she's in the right company."

Washbottle found the box with the turquoise woman on the front. ANJELICA, *true story of the mystical, magical, and the mysterious.*

Loretta said, "Meaning what?"

"Women. Just women. We're going to squeeze her new boobs."

"What's her—you know, her prognosis?"

"About the same as yours and mine, I guess." Tina slid the jumpsuit over the counter and left.

Loretta disappeared and through the curtain Washbottle heard her and Suzy talking, but he couldn't hear what they were saying.

A customer came into the videomart. He was around Washbottle's age. After searching up and down the aisles for several minutes he asked Washbottle what he would recommend. Washbottle gave him *Anjelica,* though, of course, Washbottle himself had never seen it.

"I fried Vernon's eggs on the cement driveway this morning. Cripes, it's hot!" Suzy fiddled with all the dials on the air-conditioner, as she'd done the other days during Pinehaven's heat wave. Adjusting the controls on the air-conditioner didn't seem to make any difference—the blast was feeble, the air only faintly cool. Suzy suspected that Mr. Hoople had preset the machine, and that the dials were dummies. "Tits on a bull," she muttered as she turned the knobs back and forth and waited to hear some kind of click that would trigger a stronger, icier wind.

"What are you feeding that clod eggs for?" yelled Loretta. "Pretty soon you'll have to hire a truck to take him to collect his pogey. Not to mention what it's doing to his heart."

"End of the month," said Suzy. "He's leaving at the end of the month."

They'd heard nothing more about the sale of the Pinehaven Liquor Vendor-Dry Cleaners-Videomart.

Loretta hadn't talked to Suzy for a long time about the lumps, and to Suzy it seemed that Loretta had simply put them out of her mind, just put the worry away. Tucked it into some crevasse where it was barely noticeable. On the other hand, maybe the lumps weren't there anymore. Suzy did know that Loretta had not been visiting her mother-in-law much lately.

"Storm's coming," said Loretta. "I can hear the thunder." She had the front door propped open with a stack of cardboard flaps from the cartons the liquor came in.

"I can't hear it," said Suzy, giving one final, sharp blow to the air-conditioner.

"Open the back door."

Washbottle had no air-conditioning on his side of the building, and he didn't have the front door propped open. He wore a shirt with long sleeves to cover the wedge-shaped burns in the crooks of his elbows. TOY BOAT SUMMER, *it's cool and peaceful at the lake, but love and murder are lurking in the pines.*

The storm rolled before it a mass of heavy, damp heat as it approached. Suzy and Loretta and Washbottle sweated as they worked: sorting, weighing, and pressing garments; unpacking cartons of thick-glassed bottles; showing customers to the movies they couldn't find and filling out the rental forms. Just before closing time, they felt and smelled a giant spark from the low, rumbling nimbus above the town, followed instantly by a loud snap and sizzle, and then tumultuous thunder echoing through the skies. In a moment the streets and sidewalks clattered with rain.

"Oh beauty," murmured Suzy as she watched through the open curtain and the open front door.

Loretta and Washbottle locked up their shops. Loretta and Suzy went to the back door and stood on the threshold and took in the sweetening air. After a few minutes, the rear door of the videomart opened slowly, and Washbottle, too, stood and watched. The grass in the alley absorbed the rain, and the sound was softer there. A few houses down, the large drops drummed on a child's wagon left out in the yard.

Headlights came up the alley at the same time as the storm began to diminish. Jimmy Schuppert's hearse rolled towards them through what was now a drizzle. Its windshield wipers clicked and squeaked across the curved glass and the tires made a muddy trail on the grass.

"I guess there was a funeral this afternoon," said Suzy.

"No," said Loretta. "Look—he hasn't got his undertaker suit on." They could see him through the windshield, still wearing his mask.

The hearse turned towards the dry cleaners, stopped, then backed up carefully to the double doors of the Fun Cap. The three onlookers were riveted to the shiny wet car and the figure of Jimmy at the steering-wheel. "Loading or unloading?" breathed Suzy.

The rain stopped. A wind came up.

Jimmy Schuppert got out of the hearse and stood for a moment beside the car door, looking now at Loretta and Suzy and Washbottle, now at the back of the hearse. He crossed the alley. "Would you like to see?" he asked them, cautiously, with just a hint of a smile.

"Who is it?" blurted Loretta.

Jimmy Schuppert shrugged and replied, "His car collided with an oil truck."

"Oh my god," gasped Suzy. "Did his—?" She made a cutting motion across her throat with her finger.

"Explosion," whispered Jimmy, shaking his head. "He's not from town. Burned."

Loretta and Suzy looked at each other. Suzy said, "Well, I'm no chicken." They stepped down together from the door sill and followed Jimmy Schuppert through the tunnel of cool wind.

Jimmy walked to the back of the hearse, between the hearse and the mortuary. He opened the two sloping doors with hardly a sound—they were kept well oiled. Suzy and Loretta came nearer, and Jimmy folded back a white shroud. The smell of ash mingled with the dampness and the lingering traces of ozone created by the lightning. Out of the corners of their eyes, Jimmy and Suzy and Loretta saw Washbottle slowly crossing the alley.

Without speaking, they stared at the body. Washbottle came and stared with them, and rubbed the crooks of his elbows with his long, slender thumbs.

"He looks like a stick of charcoal," said Suzy. Then she clapped her hand over her mouth, remembering that he wasn't yet dead—not until he'd passed through Jimmy's doors.

No one else said anything. The blackened face was unrecognizable. Loretta's eyes looked right through the charred corpse.

She did not even seem to be aware of Washbottle pressing closer and closer to her, almost leaning on her.

"He wasn't wearing these when it happened," said Jimmy Schuppert. He picked up an object lying beside the body. "These were found on the car seat, folded up."

On Jimmy's open hand lay a pair of metal-framed eyeglasses. He had cleaned the soot off them. The lenses were tinted an amber shade of yellow.

"They're prescription," said Jimmy. "Thick glasses, fairly strong. He should have been wearing them. Quite mysterious."

Suzy said, "I guess Mr. Hoople won't be going with the silks for awhile yet."

Loretta pushed her way past Washbottle and started back across the alley. Suzy caught up with her and whispered, "Gee, thanks, Jimmy."

"That's another thing I like," Jimmy Schuppert called after them. "The mysteries. The little mysteries."

"Gee, thanks, Jimmy."

Loretta stood behind the cash register and totalled up the day's receipts. When she was finished, she sorted the cash and stuffed it into the deposit envelope. Her hands trembled. Every movement of her arm reminded her of the deformities growing in her body. She thought the lumps were getting bigger. She thought she could feel them when she held her arm close to her side. And she thought she'd found more such swellings in her neck now. *Little mysteries.*

Loretta checked her watch. Five-fifteen. Would someone still be answering the telephone at the clinic? She reached under the counter for the telephone and dialled the clinic, and cancelled the appointment she had for Monday afternoon.

Washbottle closed his till. Three cassettes were left on the counter to be filed on the library shelves behind him. He opened the cases to make sure they were all rewound. He was still shaking. The cases reminded him of coffins. He knew whose face he'd wanted to see in Jimmy Schuppert's hearse. Even when Jimmy had said, "He's not from town," Washbottle had known whose face he'd wanted to see there. He looked through the connecting door at Loretta, working at her counter. He found the sight of her comforting.

It's ironic, Suzy thought as she turned off the air-conditioner and the coffee machine. I buy a cake to cheer up my friend, to make her not worry so much about death, and we give a piece of that cake to a weird undertaker, and he repays us by showing us what death looks like. And the dead guy turns out to be the guy who was going to take our jobs away.

Suzy kept her handbag by a small, rectangular mirror propped up on an old school desk. She took out her lipstick and stroked her lips with it. She was careful to make the colour arch exactly right, to make it exactly even. With a moistened fingertip she smoothed her eyebrows.

"Isn't it ironic?" Suzy shouted to Loretta. Suzy stuck her head through the curtain. The light beyond the door was still grey and dim. "Isn't it ironic," Suzy said again, as Loretta hung up the telephone, "that we turned out to be the right company?"

STILL LONELY IN WAWA

6:38 P.M., Christmas Day

The night is as sharp as morning ice. A moon is up there—we see it above the swath cut through the trees. The CBC fades out, snagged in the Lake Superior spruce trees. A blizzard is coming in from the southwest. A Colorado low. Brian and I have decided to leave for Toronto right after Christmas dinner at his half-brother's house, to get ahead of the storm. Christmas dinner was a hard duck with something black and garlicky for sauce.

We left when Jennifer Laverne began throwing china off her high-chair tray, and her mother and father told everyone at the table to lift their feet and not walk around at all until they'd found every single teensy-weensy fragment of Royal Albert. Mom's Christmas will be quiet. Cheryl won't be there.

11:03 P.M.

Brian finds a filling station that has remained open for Christmas travellers. We're not hungry, but we buy coffee from a cashier wearing a neck brace. We pour the coffee out on the shoulder a little further on because it is a nuisance to have the cooled, half-filled cups in the car. Neither of us has said much so far—driving late at night on Christmas Day has put a spell on us. But when we get back into the rhythm of driving, I start talking about how good it will be to be in Toronto with my brother and sister and Mom. I don't say anything about the distances between our families—we've gone over that many times before. And I don't say how the missing sister will not be missed this once. Except by my mother, who never admits that one of her children might be a quirk. Brian does not have much to say—he does not want to admit it, either. The oddballs in his family are even more outrageous than Cheryl, but he is protective.

He keeps his eye on the moon. When it disappears, the snow will begin to fall. How far will we get?

2:45 A.M., December 26

We find a Super8 south of Sudbury. We've never stayed at a Super8. It's not a bad room. Brian eats the shortbread his sister-in-law gave him from the tray of Christmas baking, I take a vitamin and a swallow of Pepsi I brought from home.

Just as I am falling asleep, a loud cracking sound from just above our bed frightens me so much, I jolt and turn rigid under the bedsheet. Brian sleeps. I worry that a beam is giving way and the room will collapse. The second time the cracking occurs, I get up onto my knees and without switching on the light I look at the wall above the bed. A picture hangs on that wall. I test it. It feels secure. In fact, it is bolted into the plaster.

But now I cannot fall asleep.

No one in my family is left in Toronto anymore, besides Mom. Cheryl, Coral, and Rick all left the city before I did. I was the last to go. The rest of them thought I would stay and look after our mother. But it didn't work out that way, and I had as much right to leave as the others. She tells me she is not lonely. I miss her.

The wall snaps again about ten minutes later, just as I am

drifting off. I remember a trip to Florida when I was a little girl. We made a mistake one night and chose a motel that was a little run-down. In the morning when I sat up in bed and looked into the dresser mirror in front of me, I saw a cockroach come out from behind the picture above the bed I was sharing with Coral. I begin to think there is a cockroach behind the picture now, hiding, and warning me. What was on the picture? In the dark, I couldn't tell.

7:42 A.M.

In the monochrome of an overcast dawn I see that snow covers the cars in the Super8 parking-lot. By the time we've put on our clothes, we can see the large flakes floating outside our second-storey window. Out on the highway, wind turns the snow into long streamers in the open areas. But we make good progress. Mom is not expecting us this early—it will be fun to surprise her.

Rick and Coral and I have decided that she should sell the condo and move into a home. Some sort of home.

11:58 A.M.

I play shave-and-a-haircut on the security buzzer. She's usually at the intercom in a flash. But we wait and wait and stare at the names on the tenant registry, names we've seen there all these years, names that never change, all beginning with a single initial. Then I press the buzzer loud and long, thinking she might be sleeping, or talking on the phone. She wouldn't have gone anywhere in this storm. Finally I press the button beside M. Barlow. We know Mary Barlow, but will she be there?

Mary lets us in without even asking who we are. As we are coming down the corridor, Mom's door opens, and she is standing there with a shower-head in her hand. She is wearing her leopard-print neckerchief—leopard print is her trademark.

When we hug, the corroded nozzle of the shower-head crackles against my neck hairs.

"I was in the guest bathroom," Mom tells us. "The shower started leaking yesterday, and I was awake all night listening to it, even though I couldn't hear it. I see you finally have a watch, Diane."

"Brian's family had digitals as their Christmas box theme this year."

Mary's door opens a crack.

12:15 P.M.

We tell her that the shower was leaking when she moved in. She is angry that we never told her, that no one ever told her. "I don't go into that room, except to get it ready for you guys," meaning Coral and Rick and Cheryl and me. We've already made caesars and are sitting in our usual spots at the kitchen counter: Mom on a step-stool—she has one heel hooked on a rung beneath her—I on the low telephone table at the end of the counter with one foot on the same rung. Brian sits further off at the dinette table. Mom has placed a large monkey-wrench in front of Brian. She tells us how she found it in the old cabinet in the underground parking garage. The cabinet's door faced the cement wall and she had to turn the cabinet around to get at it. A man happened by and helped her. She doesn't know his name, but she's seen him before. I am thinking, she always finds a man to help her, easily. They always happen by at the right time. The wrench is rusty and far too big for the job. Brian is probably remembering how after my father died, my mother never called us over, except when she wanted Brian to repair something. It hasn't happened for such a long time, though, that Brian will probably be glad to fix the leak, for old time's sake. Mom picked up a new shower-head this morning—went out in a storm to get it, even though she's told us time and time again that she never goes out in bad weather.

12:47 P.M.

Mom tries to sell us the old shower-head for five dollars. We tell her we'll take it, but not for five dollars. Brian has put the new one on, but it doesn't stop the leak. We tell her she'll have to get the maintenance man to shut off the water so she can hire a plumber to fix the leak.

2:10 P.M.

Mom's found an American football game on cable. She and Brian are watching it with such intensity, you'd think it meant something to them. I sit and read the Christmas mail she's received from all her friends and sisters, cards and letters she's kept in a box instead of standing them up or hanging them up the way other people do. She makes me read all the verses in the cards.

3:00 P.M.

In the blizzard outside, a tumbleweed comes rolling across the courtyard that my mom's patio doors look out into. The tumbleweed catches in a drift of snow, and for a few moments it shivers in the wind like a cold rabbit.

"Oh, the poor thing!" my mother cries. "Isn't it sweet!"

We are well aware that my mom has wanted a cat or a dog for a long time. But the condo doesn't allow pets. Just birds and fish and things. Mom has a bird. Has had many birds. The one she has now doesn't do much. Mom watches the tumbleweed for a long time, giving a running commentary on its movements while Brian watches the football players on the field.

3:12 P.M.

Mom informs us that all football players wear padding in their bums to give them a nice shape. "It's foam rubber," she says. "Men don't have such perfect butts."

We argue with her but it is useless. We tell her that Coral's husband Mike will straighten her out when he gets here. He's a fitness instructor. But she probably won't believe him, either. I wonder why it matters to us so much.

3:27 P.M.

Mom glances out the patio door and sees that the tumble-weed has rolled right up to it. It sits shivering at the window. Mom runs to the door and slides it open and scoops up the prickly weed. "It's a sign," she says. "It wanted to get in. Into my house. Isn't it darling?"

She puts it into a crystal vase and places it behind the crèche that's set up on a table in a corner of the living-room, so that it becomes a tree growing behind the stable and spreading over the manger scene. I am almost convinced that it is a sign of some sort, since it looks as though it really is growing there.

5:30 P.M.

The storm has let up. We decide to go to a nearby restaurant for dinner, Gordie's, which is a steak-house we've been to before. We make reservations. The place is almost booked up even though it's been storming for twelve hours. Before we go we have another round of drinks.

6:46 P.M.

In the bar before dinner, Mom tells us how many times she and my father had sex when they were in Europe in 1965—only twice, because they were always too tired and they were travelling with a large group and they had a large itinerary. She says they were itineraried right out of their libidos.

Brian thinks it is kooky of my mother to talk with her children about sex, and he says, "So how did you find the time?"

A couple of business executives next to us are watching the bartender do bartender-magic tricks with coins and brandy snifters and olives, but I think they are listening to every word my mother says. She does not have a quiet voice.

"Once he went to a museum without me. One evening. I don't remember what kind of museum. It may not even have been a museum. It was in Hamburg. A few people went. I was too tired. But when he came back, I was hot. And so was he, surprisingly. He didn't get hot as often as I did.

"The other time was the last night we were in Europe. Paris."

Of course.

"We went to the Folies Bergere."

I am surprised that she remembers the name, Folies Bergere. How often has she heard the term since then? But then I remember she is a couch potato and hears plenty on the TV every day.

"We had a lot of champagne. I guess they do that on purpose, so that you have a memorable last night in Europe. The only trouble is, the champagne is cheap, and everyone gets carried away, and what kind of shape are you in the next morning when you're supposed to catch your plane?"

The business executives are definitely listening. The bartender is concentrating on making his dime disappear. She wouldn't be talking about those things if Coral was here—Coral and Mike are parents of young children. In her mind, that makes them innocent by association.

"Neither of us could remember the name of the airport when we got into the taxi in the morning. Early morning. And nobody from our group was around to help us."

"How did you get to the right place?" Brian asks.

"I don't remember. We were both hung over. I don't even remember much about the sex."

8:28 P.M.

Mom doesn't eat her entrée. She is a little drunk and seems to want to stay that way.

9:30 P.M.

Driving home from Gordie's, Mom sings Christmas carols in the back seat of the car. Brian is driving her car, a white 1972 Cadillac. She loves her car, and insisted that we take it to the restaurant. It would look nice in the fresh snow, she told us. First she sings "O du fröhliche," then "Kling Glöckchen," and then "O Tannenbaum." Brian and I join in when we can.

8:45 A.M., December 27

Mom makes us admire the Christmas tree. She thinks it is the most perfect tree ever. Brian comments that the trunk is bent. (The tree really is quite perfect, and you can barely see that the trunk is a little bent.) She points out to us that it is not dropping any needles, and asks us over and over again why. "How come that tree doesn't lose its needles like Christmas trees usually do? I can't figure it out."

Then she tells us which are her favourite decorations and kisses each one.

9:34 A.M.

We plan our day. The malls are open, so we can shop. I need to buy something for Rick's kids, even though I won't be seeing them. And wrapping paper and ribbons will be on sale. Brian rolls his eyes and asks if there are any more football games on TV.

Mom informs us that the first happy hour will be at eleven-thirty. She'll put the goose in at eleven. We'll go shopping after lunch (cold barbecued chicken and bean salad from the deli at the supermarket).

10:20 A.M.

I try to make friends with the budgie. Mom says forget it, even she has not been able to make friends with it. I tell her she should have named it Onan, like Dorothy Parker did, because it scatters its seed on the ground. She says she's heard of Dorothy Parker but not Onan. I am too embarrassed to explain it to her.

2:25 P.M.

A tree in the mall is covered with red bows. Mom tells us she is tired of her Christmas tree decorations and wants to buy all new ones. Her tree has wooden drummer boys and grotesque elves and china Rudolphs and capricious Santas and doves made of real feathers. They are not decorations she had when we were little—she collected them somehow after we'd all left home, probably at post-Christmas sales. But it doesn't matter— they represent to me her life after Father, a life she designed for herself. Brian and I take her away from the tree in the corridor and remind her about how she had kissed her own ornaments just that morning.

3:09 P.M.

Mom sees a plush toy cat in a store window. The cat is life-sized and has a long floppy tail. At first, we don't notice that she is not with us. And then we see her in the window cuddling the cat and talking to the sales clerk. The clerk flips over the price tag, reads it, and says something to Mom. But Mom is waving to us and stroking the cat and does not hear what the clerk says. I wave back. Brian moves over to a candy-store window. The clerk repeats herself and Mom puts the cat back on the shelf with a frozen smile and comes back out into the corridor. "If anyone gives me money for Christmas, I'm going to buy that cat. It'll be more lively than that stupid bird."

5:26 P.M.

Coral arrives. Mike gives my mom an athletic hug and she makes flirtatious remarks about his moustache. Coral hustles and bustles around the tiny kitchen, ready to cook even before she has her coat off. Her boys stand in the living-room with their hands in their pockets and look at the tree in the corner. They probably don't notice the bent trunk. What they do see are the little white envelopes with their names on them—Grandma's Christmas presents. Cash.

5:45 P.M.

Mom lifts the lid on the roaster to see how the goose is doing. Its skin has split down the middle and shrunk away, and all we can see is a bare, dry, grey breastbone, no meat in sight. She looks at me with a mischievous smile, a smile that I have always loved because it has always meant, all my life, that a joke is in the vicinity. That a goose with no meat at Christmas is funny. One time when Father was still alive and wigs were a women's fad, my mother, wearing a new platinum blonde, entertained some of her higher-classed friends at a dinner party. She opened the oven to take out broiled filet mignon and the nylon wig melted and shrivelled up. She thought it hilarious and paraded the mess in front of her dinner guests.

Now she whispers to me over the naked carcass between us, "It's a Christmas miracle."

I worry about how we will feed everyone. Mike has a huge appetite. So does Brian. Brian is on a diet, but Mom's Christmas goose is his favourite holiday meal.

"Good thing the kids are vegetarian," she says.

"The boys are vegetarian?"

"Well, they don't like meat particularly. Coral feeds them beans to make up."

"What does Coral do?" says Coral. She's just finished unpacking. We had to move to a hotel after the shopping trip earlier. It is their turn to stay in the spare bedroom.

Mom puts the lid back on the roaster. "I was just telling Diane that the boys don't care much for meat. She was worried that there wouldn't be enough."

"Actually, they're over that. They love fowl."

"There'll be plenty," Mom coos, the way she always does when things look grim.

Coral pours us all weak rye and waters. "I see you got a new shower-head in the guest bathroom. Did the leak stop?"

"Why didn't any of you tell me about that leak?" Mom waves a turkey baster at her. I mouth a 'no' over Mom's head.

"We thought you knew."

6:06 P.M.

Mom and Coral and I peel potatoes. Coral is angry at Rick because he has put his daughters in a French school. "Sherry can't even read properly, and Laura wets her bed. They don't need any more stress."

"Oh, don't get excited," says Mom. "It'll all work itself out."

"All that whispering," Coral pouts. "Who's Cheryl skiing with now?"

"I think he's Austrian. Or Italian. From Montreal."

"Or maybe he's not Austrian or Italian," I breathe.

"She thinks they might get married out there."

Coral and I stop peeling and stare at our mother, who calmly puts a slice of potato in her mouth. We can hear her crunching on it as our gazes shift to the pile of parings in the sink.

"Did you know about this?" Coral accuses me. She's always worried that I might know more of our mother's secrets than she does.

"No," I answer. "I'm just glad she's not here." There, I've said it.

The door buzzer goes. Mike and Brian are back from the liquor store getting wine.

"Hush," says Mom. "Keep peeling."

6:21 P.M.

The telephone rings while Coral and I are arguing over how to fold the napkins. She is nearer the phone than I am, so she answers it, expecting to hear Rick's voice. She says hello in a merry, false sort of tone, a tone she uses only with Rick and Lana because she doesn't connect with their spirituality. But the tone becomes cautious when she hears a stranger on the other end of the line. She passes the receiver to Mom and makes a face at me. "It's a man," she says to me without moving her lips.

Suddenly we are each folding the napkins our own way without thinking about what we are doing. Mom speaks to her caller in the same false cheery voice Coral had started out with, telling him that her family is here from out of town, telling him we'd be here for a week, which is not true, wishing him a nice holiday. She is holding a cole-slaw knife in the same hand as the telephone receiver. Her other hand is wrapped around the rye and water.

A few months ago when I was visiting my mother by myself, the telephone rang in the middle of the night in her bedroom. Her voice was low for several minutes, and then in the morning nothing was said about it. I wanted to ask her if she got a lot of crank calls in the middle of the night, but she had talked to that person for a few minutes—not a long time, but longer than you would speak to an intruder. She did not want me to know about it, so I didn't ask anything. But it scared me. She wasn't safe.

Now she says three or four times, "Have a nice holiday," before the caller hangs up. "One of the men from church," she says to us. "A lonely old widower." She opens the whisky bottle and splashes some into her drink.

"Men often admit they're lonely more readily than women," says Coral.

"I've never heard him say that he's lonely," Mom says. "But there are signs."

"You should date him," Coral says, getting right to the point.

6:50 P.M.

Coral's boys come into the kitchen and ask their grandma why there is a weed in the crèche.

6:55 P.M.

Mom gets the mixer from the hallway closet and asks Coral if she will mash the potatoes while I open the tin of cranberry jelly. Mom volunteers to make the gravy. She is a good gravy-maker, and we are happy with our assignments.

"Make them lumpy!" Mom cries over the electric whine of Coral's mixer. The off-switch on the mixer does not work. It starts as soon as you plug it in. The cord is so twisted it is shorter than it was meant to be.

Coral turns up the speed. "Cheryl's the one who likes them lumpy!"

"And she's not here!" we chime.

"She's skiing in Vanderbortenkirchenspeise with her thirteenth gigolo!" I shout.

"Gigolo and gigolette!" says Coral. "How do you like your potatoes, Diane?"

"NOT lumpy. But not too creamy. We like them DRY. Dry and NOT lumpy."

The telephone rings again. Probably Rick, but this time we are not sure, so we let Mom answer it. The telephone cord tangles with the electric mixer cord.

At first she does not say anything, but looks puzzled. Then her face clears and she sits back and waits. After a few seconds, a broad smile bursts, and she says, "Hi, sweetheart! How's it going?"

"Rick," Coral and I mouth to each other. Coral unplugs the mixer.

"No, what?—You're pulling my leg!—We were just talking about you!"

Cheryl.

Coral and I busy ourselves putting food into the oven to keep hot while Cheryl spans the ocean with her voice. We notice that the goose is still in the oven on a platter, full of stuffing, uncarved. In our haste to make the potatoes unlumpy, we'd forgotten to unstuff the goose.

"That's marvellous, darling! Just marvellous!" Now she is talking like Katherine Hepburn in a thirties movie. "Would you like to speak to the girls?"

Coral and I are juggling the platter and bowls of vegetables and pot holders. We both shake our heads at Mom.

"Say hi!" I say.

I scoop out the stuffing while Coral sharpens the knife.

"Why don't you let the men do that?" says Mom to Coral, with the mouthpiece of the phone to her neck. "Yes, we are very excited," she says to Cheryl. "The girls made the potatoes lumpy, just the way you like them!"

I plug in the mixer and turn up the speed.

6:59 P.M.

Mom insists that one of us talk to Cheryl. I take the receiver from my mother and say hello.

She is wearing fur, probably white. Her hair is wild, unbrushed, arranged with casual strokes of perfectly manicured fingertips. She is holding a glass of milk in her right hand—she always pours herself milk when she needs to do something serious in between parties. Somewhere nearby will be a leather-bound address book, well worn, much like the one I used to steal to read in the bathroom early in the morning, when she was still asleep. Also nearby, the Pooh-bear, her third since she was a baby. Her face changes with each moment that passes: first her eyes sparkle with joy, dimples deepen; then comes that tentative look, a sudden fear that the person she is talking with does not love her quite as much as she wants to be loved.

The first thing she asks me is if I'm still lonely out there in Wawa.

7:14 P.M.

We toast Christmas and the new year and Mom, and begin passing dishes of fifteen-minute-old vegetables around the table. Coral found meat on the goose, despite a dull carving knife, actually quite a lot of meat, and once I've tasted everything in quick little forkfuls, I am satisfied that the dinner is as good as ever. I put Cheryl's call out of my mind for awhile. Mom got on the line again and talked until the conversation was cut off by what she called "the sound of ocean waves." The boys speculate what kind of a sea creature would chew through a transatlantic telephone cable, and Brian and Mike talk about American football between mouthfuls of potatoes and gravy.

Then I start thinking about how Cheryl is so different from the rest of us, being such a risk-taker, following whim and instinct like an over-grown fairy.

"Actually, Cheryl hasn't got much of an imagination, when you really think about it," I say out loud. And I say it louder than I had planned. "I mean, marrying an Austrian skier—it's like a Cary Grant movie or something."

"Well, is he really a skier," says Mike, because he is always practical, "or does he earn a living at something—"

"Normal?" I say.

Mom has filled her plate but isn't really eating. She holds her wineglass in both her hands. "I haven't got a clue. She never mentioned a thing about where he gets his money from. They're going to live in Montreal. She said that."

I look at Coral. She is staring at me. "We don't like normal for Cheryl, do we?" she says.

"Mike," says Brian through a balled-up napkin, "tell Mom what football players wear on their tushes."

8:32 P.M.

The boys remind us that we have gifts to open. They can hardly wait to have Grandma's money in their hands, to count it and begin planning how they will spend it. They already know they will buy something with it in Toronto, and not back in Kingston, since their friends will envy anything bought in Toronto.

Mom's gotten thermoses for Mike and Brian, "for when they go to hockey games or football games," even though neither of them goes much to hockey or football games. Coral gets shrimp forks, because she asked for them, I get a red silk blouse which is of noticeably higher value than the other presents. "I feel a little sorry for you," Mom whispers. "You don't have children to give you presents at Christmas, and you don't have very many friends yet in Wawa."

I put the blouse back in its box without trying it on.

Mom opens her gifts. No one has given her money.

9:00 P.M.

The boys want to swim in our hotel pool before it closes. We hurry and rinse the dishes and scrape the leftovers out of the serving bowls into margarine containers for Mom to eat after we're gone.

Mom and I leave the apartment last. Someone has to stay back with her when everyone else is trekking to the car or else she never comes. She thinks of hundreds of things to do at the last minute, and without someone pushing her, sometimes doesn't show up at the car for several minutes. Now she covers the budgie cage and coos to the bird through the cage-cover while I stand and wait at the door with her coat. "The boys are impatient to get to the hotel. The pool closes at ten."

She seems a little unsteady. She had a lot of wine and not very much food. "Good-bye, sweetie!" she calls to the budgie as she closes the apartment door. "Dumbbell."

9:15 P.M.

The women and Coral's kids drive to the hotel in Mike and Coral's car. Brian and Mike take ours. Mom sings German Christmas carols. Coral knows all the words and sings along.

9:25 P.M.

The boys change into their swimming trunks in the bathroom of our hotel room. Brian and Mike say they need to stretch their legs after the goose and go for a stroll around the hotel.

Outside the room, Coral and I stand at the railing that overlooks the pool six floors below. Two teen-aged boys are showing off their diving for a group of girls sitting at the edge of the pool. "Did you talk to her about selling the condo?" Coral asks.

"No, not yet. I'm not sure it's the right thing to do."

"Are you kidding?"

"She took off that shower-head by herself with a rusty pipe-wrench."

Coral says, "Her mind is going, and she's lonely as hell. I mean, her drinking—is that a sign, or what?"

We hear our mother scream inside the room. When we rush inside, we see her looking at us with large eyes. Her mouth is open and she is pointing to the television.

She's been fiddling with the dials and has found some sort of X-rated adult channel. Coral and I see unclad squirming bodies surrounded by leopard skins. I reach for the controls, to turn away from the orgy, but Mom puts her hand on my arm. "I didn't know they had things like this on TV," says Mom. "Think of the children in this hotel. Do you mean that they can turn on the television and watch stuff like this?"

"No, no, Mother," says Coral. "They turn off the connections at the front desk if you register with kids."

Mother's eyes are glued to the set.

"Really, they do."

"I can't get any sound," says Mom.

The boys come out of the bathroom dressed in their trunks. Coral leans over and turns off the television.

"My Christmas is ruined," says Mom. "I have to try not to think about this." She does look troubled. I am a little surprised, because of the stories she told us at Gordie's last night.

Her shock does not last long. While the boys swim, she banters with the young guys in bikini trunks Coral and I watched earlier from the railing six floors up.

7:53 A.M., December 28

The telephone rings in our hotel room. Brian rolls over and answers it and passes the receiver to me.

"Rick and Lana called last night when we got back. They'd been trying for awhile. They're all sick."

I don't say much. It's still dark outside.

"Coral isn't up yet. Nobody's up. Even the boys."

I think of something to say. "Did you put the leftover goose in the fridge last night?"

"No. I had some when I got up. It's a pretty good goose, isn't it?"

Leaving fowl on the counter overnight and eating it the next day and the next was a big problem I had with my mother. She hadn't ever gotten sick from it so far, but at her age she couldn't afford to take the risk.

"Come for breakfast," she says. "Soon."

I don't say anything.

"Okay?"

10:10 P.M.

I sit down on the floor in my mother's living-room, beside the table with the crèche. The boys have gone to bed on the hide-away in the den, and the rest of us are spending our last evening together just talking, planning the next visit.

Coral has taken it upon herself to sound Mom out about selling the apartment and moving to a senior citizens' complex. Mom thinks it is a joke, and Coral does not get any support from me. We are not ready for it.

I look at the tumbleweed behind the stable. It looks natural and very much alive there. I don't know what kind of plant a tumbleweed is, or how one happens to be in Toronto. But I do know that it stays alive a long time after it has cut itself away from its roots.

Coral has given me a k.d. lang tape for Christmas. Now I put it on my mom's stereo and turn up the volume. "Mom, do you want to dance?"

We dance to "Big-boned Gal." We hold each other tight. My mom's body is soft and feels the way my eyes always say it will feel.

10:19 A.M., December 29

Brian and I stand in the front hallway of the apartment. Our bags are packed and the car is loaded and ready to go back to Wawa. We've said good-bye to Coral and Mike, who are staying another day, and now Mom stands in front of us holding the shower-head in an old Birks box she found in her closet. She saves boxes. She phoned me once just to tell me she found a nice big box in the incinerator room in which she could keep all her smaller boxes.

"Remember years ago when Dad was still alive, he and I went to a night-club to see Sandler and Young?" she says. "We talked to them after the show. I think it was New Year's Eve. Sandler fell in love with me. He kept coming back to our table and kissing me. I mean, everybody was kissing. But he always came back to me." She sighs—not a romantic sigh, more a tired, nostalgic sigh—and gazes up at the light fixture on the ceiling. "Tony Sandler is going to be singing at the O'Keefe this New Year's

Eve, in the foyer. They're having some sort of party in the foyer. Do you think I should go?" She looks at me. "Do you think he'd remember me?"

"I think you should go, but don't expect him to remember you." Coral would be outraged.

"Did I tell you I had a check-up the other day? I don't think I did."

She is quiet.

"How did it go?" I ask.

"Oh, the doctor says my cholesterol level is up."

"Oh?" My mother has always prided herself on her good health.

"Way up. I have to cut down on some things."

My throat tightens. Three of her sisters have heart problems. A fourth one died a year ago of heart disease. "Did you tell Coral?" I ask.

"No." Mom waves the idea away with the Birks box. The shower-head rattles inside. "I can get it down again easily. I've been eating a lot of cheese and crackers lately. You know, it's so handy, instead of cooking myself a big meal."

She stares down at the carpeting on the condo floor. Then she smiles up at me, the way she did when she saw the split skin of the goose. "I asked the doctor if alcohol had cholesterol. 'No,' he said. 'Thank God,' I said."

Between the phone calls we make to each other, my mom makes lists of all the things she wants to tell me and ask me. I make lists in my head, but when we talk, or when I visit her, nothing gets settled. I don't ask the questions I need to ask her, and I don't get to tell her things I want her to know.

All that's left is to hug. She is good at hugging. I am always stiff and a little distant. How do you get good at hugging?

She walks with us to the main entrance. "Make sure you send Cheryl a present. And call me, okay?"

I looked at the picture on the wall over our bed in the Super8 the morning it started to snow. It was of children and parents and a dog strung out along a beach. They were all wading in the edge of the water, each in a different place, none of them touching.

Snow has started to fall again. I don't know if we'll make it all the way back to Wawa. It's a long ride.

THE PUMPKIN-EATERS

White bubbles seep along the shiny lip of Aunt Ruby's new pot. The lid lifts and falls like breathing, like Grandy's sunken lips when he sleeps on the crocheted cushion. His lips part and touch, part and touch, though the skin on his cheeks has stretched so tight from his jaw to the bone under his eye that his cheeks do not puff out with the breath passing through.

Now the white foam is all around the edge of the pot and the lid dances in multiple breaths. Foam trickles down the side of the bright metal to the red-black spiral beneath it. Cats' hisses explode from the dribbles hitting the spiral and the foam splits into tiny beads that do their own dance, then disappear like angels speeding back to heaven.

And now it is gushing from the pot. A mass of glossy bubbles that flow together and spill and spill and spill and begin to roar in my ears.

I have heard of rice. They eat it in China. But when Aunt Ruby gave me the box and I poured it into the new pot, I loved the little milky pearls that looked like they could have flowed from a mother's breast, and I would have liked to scoop them up in my hands. "Be polite at Ruby's," my mother said before I left. "Be polite," said my sister Callie when she and Jakie Martens dropped me off in the Buick, though she didn't get out of the car, and I saw them kissing even before they were out of the yard. And so, out of politeness, I did not touch the rice.

"Cook it in here with some water," Aunt Ruby said, "at 11:30," and she pointed to the big black switch on the electric stove and left the room. She and Mary are raking up everything that's dead in the big garden in the sunny corner of the farmyard. She did not tell me how much rice to put in the pot, but the box is half empty and I use up what's left. While it heated up I thought about Grandy upstairs. He has no kitchen. My grandma left thousands of jars of canning in the pantry when she died, and Grandy eats the canning right out of the jars, with bread from the store, and cheese. He eats hundreds of store-bought cookies a day. Aunt Ruby and Mary live in the basement, where the big kitchen is, and two bedrooms, and the pantry with the dresser and the mirror and the cot and the jars of canning. Grandy never eats with us. And I never see him come down here. I don't know how he gets the jars up to his elegant oak dining table. But he does. I've seen him eating it, and I've eaten with him. Yesterday we had crabapples and red beets and he told me about the dog and the brick.

When Grandy was small, he had a dog named Looky. Grandy and his brother taught Looky how to catch a rubber ball high in the air. Looky would jump high, high, high, and catch the ball. One day some other children came to watch. The ball flew back and forth and Looky caught it every time. Then one of the other children picked up a piece of brick. "Jump, Looky!" yelled the child, and he threw the brick. Looky jumped and broke his teeth. And all the children laughed. I think Grandy probably laughed, too, but now he says it was a bad thing to do. "They were bad children," he said and shook his head. He doesn't wear teeth. His chin sticks out like Popeye.

I want to hide from the slithering rivers of sticky rice-milk. I want to run outside to the shed where Grandy keeps the car he never drives. But I remember that Aunt Ruby showed off her new pot that she got when she bought herself the electric stove, and I think, it will be ruined. It will turn black like a witch's cauldron and they'll tell Mama and her milk will dry up and she won't be able to feed Dickie. I use my skirt hem bunched up to take the handle. A little well under the hot spiral is filled with burning, blistering juices, so I turn the black switch to OFF. I find another, older pot and start again on a new element. But I know I won't be able to eat the rice. I would like to forget rice and eat pickled watermelon with Grandy.

A scorched smell hangs as heavy as a wet towel in the basement kitchen. I hear them coming to the door. Through a wilted vine I see their boots pass the window that looks into the yard if you're tall enough. I feel trapped. With a hundred aching strokes of the pump I bury the new pot in a sinkful of cold water.

When Callie said, "Be polite," I was looking at the tree beside the driveway. A tree full of hard, red apples. A reaching-fingers sort of tree that draped over the road like a warning or a spell. Every autumn the tree looked just like that—hardly any leaves on it, but bright with fruit. This time I was here without Mama, though, and I looked long at the apple tree to make sure it was exactly the same.

No one met me in front of the boxy house Grandy built for Grandma. I stood holding a shopping bag stuffed with my nightgown and my Sunday dress and fresh stockings and bloomers and an extra sweater while Jakie's Buick chugged away. Far off, voices sang, like in the evenings at home in town when our neighbour Beaner Redekopp turned his radio on and we could hear it through open windows. I felt embarrassed about standing and listening like a spy, but I couldn't just plunk myself down in the house, so I put the Eaton's bag inside the door and set out to find Ruby and Grandy and Mary.

Grandy does not have a dog anymore. After Grandma died, Ruby told Jump the drayman to shoot Robb because the dog was old and useless. But he wasn't that old. He couldn't have been too old because he bit Aunt Ruby in the back of the leg, hard, and then disappeared, and Jump made Aunt Ruby give him fifty cents anyway to pay for him coming, even though he couldn't find anything to shoot, though Ruby did look for something to shoot so the fifty cents wouldn't be wasted.

As I got nearer the voices, I could tell they were angry. I stopped. They were behind the hen-house where the chickens had a fence. I heard the tapping of Grandy's hammer, and Aunt Ruby's sentences coming very fast and short, the way she talked when she was mad.

If only Robb had been there. I could have romped with him into their view and pretended I'd been having too much fun with the dog to pay attention to the arguing. If a butterfly had happened by, I would have chased that all around the yard until they noticed. But it was too late for butterflies. I would have to stand at the edge of their quarrelling until it was over and then shout, "Where is everybody? I'm here!" Only I'd gone a little too far. I could make out words now. Aunt Ruby's.

"Why do you think she left the farm to me? She knew what an ungrateful old man you are! What a miser you are! I do your wash every Monday, those stinking socks, but you don't bathe, and you complain about the darning in the heels! I will not darn for you again! And the mud on the steps . . . !"

Tap-tap-tap. Grandy's weaker voice. I move closer. Just a little closer.

"Hah! Money?" It is Ruby again. "All you do is drive that truck all day. What a waste. Gas bills, this high. Do you even have a picture of Mother up there somewhere? No. . . ."

"You stay out of my house. . . ."

Tap-tap-tap.

"It's time to kill these chickens! Here you are mending their fence. They're skinny and probably too tough already. At least I could make soup. . . ."

"Who fed them? I fed them!"

"With my feed!"

"What is mine, then?"

"Nothing!"

Far off, in the corner of my eye, Mary came at me, carrying two pails. She'd been feeding the pigs. I waved and tried to smile.

When Mary moved in with Aunt Ruby, I asked my mother, "Why isn't Mary *Aunt* Mary? And why don't they have husbands and children?"

"They're both virgins," said Mama, and she laughed and laughed while her steel brush shushed against the hard metal of the woodstove.

I didn't know what virgins meant. I thought it might be something like cousins or stepsisters.

Mama said, "Something to do with their church. Prayer sisters is how it started. Mary was jilted by a city man and had a breakdown. Ruby's counselling her." And she laughed some more.

But when Mary came to me with the pails, came across the wide, grassy space between the hen-house and the pigsty, I heard only Aunt Ruby's cry ringing in my ears. *My* house! *My* house! *My* house! Grandy built it for Grandma and Ruby and Mama a long time ago, before I was born. How could it have become hers? If only Grandy could make it disappear the way he made Robb disappear before Jump got there with the gun. . . .

First, Aunt Ruby's feet in men's socks at the top of the stairs, followed by the bottom of her skirt and then the edge of the wine-coloured cardigan Mama gave to Grandy once for his birthday, but which Aunt Ruby wears in fall and spring to do chores. Mary's feet are submerged in large wool socks, too, but she wears men's pants, or maybe boys', she is so small and child-bodied, and she takes the steps lightly, elf-like, while Aunt Ruby comes down like the cows being unloaded at the CN in town.

When finally their faces show, I am trying so hard to hold their gaze away from the rim of the pot not quite under the surface of the water, their heads seem to float disconnected from their bodies. The faces float down, down, Aunt Ruby looks down at the stairs and her socks on them, Mary looks at me with her deer eyes. . . .

"Rose-hips," says Aunt Ruby, and she lowers a syrup pail to the floor beside the larger pail that holds the kitchen garbage. She reaches into the larger pail and takes out the empty rice box. "Good tea with honey," she says, and her eyes fly to the electric stove where the old pot is beginning to sigh. Her eyes flutter around the room, searching. I see her necklace with the cross glittering in the V of Grandy's sweater.

"Can I take Grandy some? He loves rose-hip tea and says it's very medicinal." I stop pumping. I've drowned the new pot. A black stain eats at the metal even in the cold well-water bath.

"No," says Aunt Ruby. "He does not like rose-hips anymore. Besides, he nearly mowed those roses down last summer. Very nearly."

Mary puts a stem of rose-hips into a crystal vase, the one Grandma used for buds in springtime. The smooth orange-red balls remind me of apples.

Aunt Ruby rolls a heavy sock down her ankle and along the length of her foot. "You'll need boiling water and soap to soak it properly," she says, but she is looking at Mary and her mouth is lifted in one corner in a funny kind of smile. "I'll do it."

Mary looks at Aunt Ruby's arched foot and undoes the buttons of her own coat.

"Is it ruined, Aunt Ruby?"

"No, Violet, it's better than ever."

"Has it happened to you?"

"Lots of times." She laughs the way Mama laughed.

I ask Mary, "Has it happened to you?"

She nods.

"And now it happened to me! Does that mean we're all—like sisters?" I want to say *virgins*, but I am too afraid.

We eat. I am surprised at how the rice has swollen and softened. I am used to potatoes that stay the same size when they cook. I eat as much as I can, but the pot hardly goes down. "We'll have it with milk and sugar and cinnamon tomorrow morning before we go to church," says Aunt Ruby.

Aunt Ruby is the only one I know who has cinnamon. Upstairs, Grandy's fork tinkles in a jar of dill pickles.

Across the mud-rut road from Grandy's lives the lame girl Amelia. More than lame. Twisted and crooked somehow. I can't quite picture it, though Grandy has tried to describe it for me. I wonder if she has to go to school. I don't have to go until Mama and Dickie are used to each other and Mama is over her depression. I have wanted to catch Amelia in her yard whenever we've driven by, but Mama tells me not to stare, so I haven't seen her, though my eyes strain in their corners every time we pass. Aunt Ruby once said she would ask her to come for a visit sometime when I was here, but I said, before I could think, "No! I wouldn't know how to play with her!" What can a lame girl do? Can she lock arms with you and run a hop-skip along a packed road or a sidewalk? Can she climb the fence to watch the pigs toss muskmelon shells in the mud? Can she chase a butterfly through the grass or roll down a snowhill? I only wanted to see her.

A boy in school, Benno, has tiny crooked little fingers on one hand. He says he caught them in a mangle when he was small.

When I was younger, I used to imagine Amelia pulled by her hair into the mangle while her mother pressed the bedsheets, her whole soft body going through and coming out with everything out of place. The idea still comes to mind when I think about Amelia, or when I see Grandma's mangle, which stands against the wall in the basement kitchen.

Today is Amelia's birthday. Grandy took them eggs for a cake early in the morning. Her aunts and uncles and cousins will be there. I walk along the driveway to the road, and then into the flat fall grass beside it and to the apple tree, and no sooner am I there than one of the big black curved automobiles Mama calls Easter-egg cars bounces by in the ruts and turns into Amelia's yard. I see a man with a hat in the driver's seat, and a boy's face staring at me out the rear window. "Don't stare," I say out loud, but his eyes are glued to me under the tree.

I hear a bluebottle. This morning Mary caught a moth against a window pane and let it out the back door. Indian summer, warm in the sun. A good day for Amelia to come out.

A hawk lifts straight up from the ground across the road and not too far from Amelia's yard, and I am reminded that a ditch runs down that way. It is filled with brown grasses and brittle weeds, but I can get nearer to her if I belly through it up to a spot where I will be even with the back of her house, where the relatives might sit in a circle of chairs on such a nice afternoon. Grandy will not miss me, he is taking his nap, and Aunt Ruby and Mary allow me to slip away because they are girls, too, and know about secret hours alone.

I want to take off my stockings, it's warm enough, but the dry thistle and dead twigs would scratch as I crawl. As it is, they snag the wool and pinch my dress. Sometimes I crouch and walk on my feet like a duck, and it does not take long to get to a place where I can see through a grove of bare maples to the back of Amelia's house.

A three-legged cat hop-skips across the swept dirt yard. A

bicycle with a ribbon tied around its handlebars leans against the side of the barn.

A hand presses against my throat. I have been dreaming about Benno's withered fingers. He is able to wrap them tightly around my neck and I awaken gasping and coughing. Where has the sun gone, which warmed me to sleep? The air is white and crackles.

Someone is standing at the edge of the ditch. Through the smoke I see a hat pulled low, a hanky tied around nose and mouth, a pitchfork with its tines pointed to the invisible sky. And then I see short, crisp flames rising from the bottom of the ditch. Grandy is burning off the old, dead grass and the weeds with their full heads of brown seeds.

Without taking a breath, I run along the ditch away from the flames, but when I get to the edge of the choking cloud, I find I cannot breathe. Just as Grandy takes my arm, I see through the smoke the yellow bow and the bicycle in Amelia's yard. The heat from the fire billows upward and twists the rider's body this way and that. The bicycle melts under the thrusting of her crooked legs. She is separated from the ground, and seems to be flying, like an angel riding to heaven on Grandy's flames.

When I tell Aunt Ruby about the fire she says a curse about Grandy and I laugh and tell her he didn't know I was there, it was not his fault, but she pumps harder than she needs to, to get me water for my hot, dry throat. The new pot stands polished and silver on the new stove. Mary bites her lip and strokes my head. They have me sitting on the one parlour chair that is in the basement kitchen, a velvety armchair with Grandma's doilies on the headrest and the arms. When I look up at Mary, I see a tiny white feather caught in her hair.

"I don't believe in war, see, Vi? But my uncle fought in the Boer War, in Africa. That was a long time ago. His picture is in this encyclopedia book right here. Do you think that's a uniform he's wearing there? His people didn't turn Anabaptist like mine did. He went to war, ended up like a general-type. We don't believe in it. Turn the other cheek."

Grandy keeps his encyclopedia books in this funny room attached to the pigpen. The room is like his office. The floor and the workbench are darkened with oils and waxes and spilled feed, and windows are so coated with grime that, except for one, the fat barn spiders have abandoned the webs in which they usually drowse during autumn months. But stacks of paper and neat rows of books on a wooden table make it an office. Carpenters' pencils lie helter-skelter like pick-up-sticks. Grandy does not believe in coffee, either, so he has poured us tin cups full of hot rose-hip tea which he brewed in his old forge. He got the hips from wild roses earlier in the fall. "Better than any other kind," he says as he pours it. But I know what he means. And Amelia's mother gave him wild honey in trade for the eggs, and we put the honey into the tea and stir it with screwdrivers. My throat still hurts and I can't stop coughing.

"Is he dead?" I ask.

"Oh yes, he's dead."

"Did he get killed in the Buhr War?"

"No, he did not. I don't know how he died. But he was famous. Got into the encyclopedia. See? '1856 to 1909.' "

Grandy keeps his finger under the dates on the page. The words are in German. "Things aren't ending right for me here," he says to the spider in the window. "I won't be able to die at ease and I won't die with the history of a general."

"You won't die at all, Grandy."

"She'll be all gone, the whole shebang." He scrapes his boot hard on the oily floor and stares at the spot his leather sole has erased. "I should be able to end my days on my own territory. I'd forgotten I'd deeded it to her, you see. Just forgot. She kept the books. Didn't even know she had a will. I don't have a will.

"I built it myself. She was eighteen. Built the house in one year, here on the land the government gave us to farm. Gave it to her."

But where did Looky break his teeth? Was it not here? I thought it was here.

"I didn't think things had much changed over all those years. And then she ups and deeds it over to Ruby. Maybe things didn't change enough. That must be it. Didn't change enough." He closes the book.

"Maybe Aunt Ruby will get married and have a baby," I say to him. "And move to a new house. And let you have this one back."

"No sign of that. No sign of that. She's nearly past prime." He leans forward and pokes a finger into the web. But the spider sleeps. "It'll be left to the spiders. They will inherit my kingdom."

I try to sort it out. I hold the warm tea in my mouth as I think about the puzzle Grandy has ravelled up here in the dim shed. I don't know much about generals, but with the pitchfork in his hand earlier this afternoon, and the smoke all around, and the hat pulled over his eyes. . . .

A commotion breaks out among the snuffling pigs next door. I jump up from my chair and run outside. Grandy follows slowly. "That's just the young boar tryin' out his parts on Esther," he says.

The big pig I've named Dorothy has draped herself over Esther and forced her down on her knees. It is not play. Esther's squeals are angry and she is trying to get away.

"Little Esther there's a virgin," Grandy laughs.

"Get away Dorothy!" I shout, and I pick up a branch and try to poke her through the spaces in the fence. Dorothy doesn't notice. "Get-away-Dorothy!"

Grandy watches me and smiles with his lips shut tight, so his gums don't show, and from the back of his throat comes a choked laugh.

As Dorothy and Grandy laugh, I throw the branch away and walk to the rickety gate at the corner. I raise the cracked leather loop from the fencepost and lift the bottom of the gatepost from its groove in the dirt. But I don't step into the pen right away because the floor of it is deep with rotted vegetables and fruit and manure and mud and dirty straw. Grandy comes along and without saying anything puts the gate back and loops it in his slow, careful way. Esther has escaped to the opposite corner of the pen. Dorothy puffs and oinks softly in the middle.

"Vi," says Grandy, "Vi, she's not a Dorothy. She's not a Dorothy, see?"

Something is going on here that is part of grown-ups' secrets. Like virgins and prayer sisters, and Aunt Ruby's socks, and Grandy eating alone, and Ma having Dickie, and rice, and. . . .

"I can't believe you don't know what them walloping pigs were doing just now, Vi. Jiminy, you must have cats in town and stray dogs, and—and—you know, the kids in school and your sisters and such to tell you about these goings-on." He stares at the dead grass and shakes his head. "I know your mother won't tell you. I know we didn't tell her. But she found out somehow, and in time, too. Ruby, she got it wrong somehow. It's not a man's place to tell a girl, so Vi, you gotta keep your eyes and your ears open! Aw, damn, your ma should tell you. It's not up to me. Well, where did you think your little Dickie came from?"

"Not from pigs!" I spit the words into the mud and the limp pumpkin shells, even though I know that is not what he is trying to say. But I do not want to hear.

" 'Course not from pigs, dummy! All I'll say is, they're making babies and Dorothy's not a girl, she's a boy. A big walloping boar. And Esther's a female and she's doing her duty, and there's nothing you can do to change that, little Violet!"

He stomps off to the black truck parked under a naked elm. Robb's doghouse is on the back of the truck.

"And don't go asking Ruby questions about it, either!" he shouts before he gets in. "She got it wrong, somehow!"

He jolts off in the dusty black truck. He has meant to bring that old doghouse to the dump for years, but he never gets around to driving the five miles and dropping it off, though he drives around enough day after day.

I'd forgotten it was Hallowe'en. Mama never lets us go out on Hallowe'en night, and she always turns the porch light off with a loud click as soon as the Beaner Redekopps have brought their children over to show us the wonderful costumes Mrs. Redekopp has made for them. Mama does not believe in Hallowe'en, but she gives the bratty heathen Redekopps each a cookie, because, she says, they're neighbours, and it's polite, and then she switches off the porch light so no other begging heathens will come to the door expecting candy. I love the costumes Mrs. Redekopp makes, but I forgot it was Hallowe'en today, and I won't see them this year.

So I am surprised at first to see Mary straddling the short wooden bench in front of the house, doing something to a bright, large pumpkin. Pie comes to my mind first, but Thanksgiving is over. Second comes Mama expecting Dickie any minute, and Callie saying, "Ma, did you swallow that pie pumpkin out in the garden *whole*? Didn't you know you were supposed to scooooop out the seeds"—Callie pretends she's scooping with her long thin hands—"and then chaaaawp it up"—she chops—"and then cook-it-all-to-mush, and then scooooop up the meat from the shell, and then make pie? And here you swallow it all in one piece." She shakes her finger in Mama's tired face. "We're gonna have to call you Peter pretty soon. One of these days you're gonna have a big surprise when that pumpkin wants to get out of there!" I do not think that is very polite of Callie, but Mama laughs till the tears run out of the corners of her eyes. As soon as Dickie was born last week I thought of him as a pumpkin.

Third to my mind comes Hallowe'en. I'd forgotten about it for awhile because the days have been so warm.

Mary is singing. She is singing the Peter, Peter, pumpkin-eater verse to a sad tune I've never heard. She sings it a few times, and then sings Mary, Mary, quite contrary to the same tune. Her voice is sweet and high and clear and she sings the songs slowly.

"Are you making a—" I begin. Mama and Grandy have told me that Hallowe'en is the worship of the devil.

"Jack-o'-lantern," Mary says, still scooping out the seeds with a yellowed hand. She drops them into a basin beside the bench, along with the soft strings attached to them. I sit down on Grandy's home-made mud-scraper and watch her. She keeps humming and singing.

Then I say, "Are you and Aunt Ruby prayer sisters?"

"Oooh yes," Mary answers.

How can Grandy and Mama say that Hallowe'en is heathen and bad, and Aunt Ruby allow Mary to make a jack-o'-lantern? I say, "My mother doesn't believe in Hallowe'en."

"Oh?"

"Grandy doesn't neither."

Mary reaches for the knife lying next to the basin among dry caragana leaves that have rolled onto the walk during the night breezes. Then with the knife in one hand she sits and stares at the blank pumpkin face for a long time, just frozen there. She does not even blink her eyelids.

"Oh no!" I've just thought of it. "Hallowe'en and Amelia's birthday! They're on the same day!" A child born on the devil's night. How anxious must her mother have been, trying to hold the baby in until past the midnight hour! Dickie was very close to being a Hallowe'en baby, I realize. I try to keep out the thought that Amelia was born twisted because of Satan's power, or that her body is twisted because her mother tried to keep her inside too long, till the clock had struck twelve. "How awful to be born on Hallowe'en," I say out loud. But Mary has begun to carve.

Perhaps it would be fun to dress up in frills and lace for a birthday party while other children were disguised. Tonight Amelia will wear frills and lace, surrounded by pretty ribbons from all her gifts, while witches and cowboys and clowns stream by her lighted windows.

The knife is sharp and Mary moves it easily through the flesh. "He has a hard time here," she says as the hollow pumpkin murmurs through the mouth she's begun to carve. "Your grandfather. Not because he doesn't believe in things, but because he and Ruby are the same people. He is her ghost, haunting her before she's had a chance to live or die. His spirit has separated itself and one part of it hovers above and watches quietly."

I could see Grandy at his table above Aunt Ruby's table, eating his ghostly canning.

"She can't make her mistakes and try on new skins without him there, her old self, wearing still the old skins."

Such odd things Mary says, she does not talk very much, ever, but odd things like that could bother Grandy, I am thinking. And I do not think she is telling the truth.

"And he is haunted by the ghost of your grandmother, who shares Ruby's body. He can't stand to see his beloved, with whom he failed, and whom he abandoned, except for his bodily presence, can't stand to see her living in the heart of his daughter."

The caragana leaves click on the cement path as a wind stirs in the corner where we sit. I can't believe that Mary, who walks and talks so quietly and whose hand caresses Esther's and Dorothy's heads when she brings them their slop, could speak of evil. But haunting and ghosts and putting on new skins sound like witchcraft. The part about failing is such a surprise to me. I must forget she said that.

She sends me inside for the candle. The air in Aunt Ruby's kitchen is rich with parsley and sage from Mary's herb garden.

"Candles," says Aunt Ruby. "You know, Violet, I think they are upstairs in one of the drawers of the oak buffet. We have no candles down here. Bring a bunch for our drawer."

Grandy's part of the house smells like old things. It smells especially of vinegar and stale pickles, but beneath that is sweat and old pee in a chamber-pot. The candles are beside his Bible.

The sun is painting the horizon red by the time Mary has put the candle into the pumpkin-head and has fastened it and lit it and put the stem back on top. She sets it on the bench facing the road and the driveway and the apple tree, and we run to the road to see how it looks from there. The face has sad eyes and a stupid laughing smile. I wonder as we walk back to the house if Amelia can see it. I think it is a very good jack-o'-lantern. The evening is quiet. We hear only Esther and Dorothy making pig night-sounds.

I am in the pantry putting on my wool slippers when I first hear the angry cracked cries coming along the walk. At first I think it is trick-or-treaters from town trying to scare the farmers.

"Whores! Sinners! Witches! Thieves! You've gone too far now!" Grandy is at the top of the steps. He bangs the screen door so hard many things rattle all over the house. I hear jars in the pantry, the empty jars upstairs, the metal ring on the kitchen window blind, silver in Grandma's buffet, unknown glass things in the bedrooms, all clinking and rattling with the slam of the door, and some of them keep on their fearful calling as Grandy's feet pound on the basement stairs.

I run into the kitchen. Aunt Ruby and Mary look calm, unsurprised. "It's the jack-o'-lantern!" I yell at them. "You shouldn't have! I told you he wouldn't like it!"

"Trespassers!" Grandy takes big steps to the new stove and lifts the steaming kettle by its hot handles, and then takes big steps to the big pail and dumps the pot into it. "Thieves and slaughterers!" he shouts as chicken parts and greasy broth flood over rubbish bits in the pail, flood over the empty rice box whose corner juts like the prow of a ship out of the debris.

"Go outside, Violet," says Aunt Ruby.

"It's the jack-o'-lantern! He doesn't believe in them! Take it away, that's all!"

"Go outside."

"You're tearing me up piece by piece like two wild animals!" I hear Grandy say as I rush up the steps and out into the dark Hallowe'en night.

I kneel and put my lips to the sad eye and am about to blow out the candle when I suddenly know where the quietness is coming from—the chickens make not a sound. Chickens hardly ever make sounds after dark, but I'm remembering the quietness of the late afternoon, when Mary and I carved the pumpkin. That quietness.

I walk a ways into the yard. My feet are cool in the slippers. The voices from the house are faint, and I cannot tell Grandy's from the others. Sometimes for a second or two I hear nothing at all, but then one flares up, followed by another in a different tone. It reminds me of music.

I find the Big Dipper in the sky, and then turn back to face the house. Through the basement kitchen window I see the three heads floating back and forth, one stopping, then bobbing away, another taking its place. The pumpkin-head sits fixed on Mary's little bench and laughs its flickering yellow laugh into the darkness.

When I look from the jack-o'-lantern back to the window, I see Grandy's hands around Mary's throat. I see Aunt Ruby's hands prying at her father's. I see Grandy reach out and take hold of Aunt Ruby's necklace and tear it from her neck. Then all the hands fall away, away, the heads fall away, and I think they have all been struck down by lightning from God.

For a little while I cannot move. I do not know where to go.

Home is too far, but oh, how I wish I were home with Dickie in my arms.

I walk slowly to the house, half expecting to meet death at the door. But when I step inside the porch, it is Grandy's back I see, disappearing through the door leading to his upstairs rooms.

Aunt Ruby is on the telephone at the bottom of the steps. Grandma and Grandy had no telephone, but when Mary moved in, Aunt Ruby had one put up in her kitchen.

"*Now*, please, if that's all right," she says, her lips near the mouthpiece, almost touching it. "Thank you."

I stand at the top of the stairs looking down at her. Mary, sitting, watches me, and Aunt Ruby just stays by the telephone, looking at the floor, her hand resting on the receiver where she has hung it up.

"Come in, Violet," she says without even noticing me with her eyes.

"Where are the chickens?" I stay where I am.

"There were only five."

"It wasn't the jack-o'-lantern, I know that."

"Violet, come in."

"Did you phone Mama or Callie?"

"I phoned the RCMP. They're coming to read the law to your grandfather and take his key away. This is my house and I—we—don't want him here anymore. He is impossible to live with."

"You can't do that!"

"Yes, I can, I have the right."

"He doesn't even have a key! He told me once this door has never been locked."

"It'll be locked from now on."

I hear Grandy behind me. He is carrying Grandma's knitting bag stuffed full of things and a box of store-bought cookies. His eyes have gotten long like Robb's. He looks at me, but not down the stairs, then walks out of the house.

Aunt Ruby shouts, "You wait for the police! Don't you go anywhere!"

But he has vanished like a ghost, and soon all there is left of him is the chugging of the motor of his truck, and yellow headlights cracking the air.

I run out, past the jack-o'-lantern, waving, calling, "Wait, Grandy, where will you go?"

He drives away. For a moment, the lower branches of the tree with its little apples glow and reach, like a warning or a spell.

Where will I go?

He doesn't even have a key. How can they take it away from him?

I have to tell Mama and Callie. How can I ever tell it to Dickie?

Did Amelia see the twisted thing that just happened here?

Where will he sleep tonight?

Grandy is doing what he likes to do, driving his truck. I look into the flickering pumpkin laugh, and there are the years ahead, Grandy with his cookies under his arm, toothless from catching bricks, driving his truck with Robb's old doghouse on the back.

I wonder if Amelia saw.

JOHNNY WINKLER

The woman comes through the parking-lot door of the 24-Karat Saloon holding the hem of her dress in one hand and a soft, partly eaten fudgicle in the other. She is angry and very tall. Beatty watches her stride past the bar towards the Ladies and enjoys her appearance—feathery pale hair, silky clothes, smooth gold-coloured arms.

He keeps his eye on the door of the Ladies while he makes drinks for Robbie to deliver to the few tables occupied tonight. The room is quiet. Hardly anyone speaks. Shuffleboard players click and thump in the corner, next to the flashing lights of the dart game. When the woman comes back five minutes later Beatty asks her if she'd care to stop and have a drink.

"No, I don't care to," she says without really looking at Beatty. Then she stops her long-legged walking and right-angles towards the bar. "Yes. I'll have a soda water."

Beatty pushes a button and fills a glass for her. "Lemon?"

"Lemon. Yes." She slides a thigh onto the bar stool. "And an empty glass, if you'd be so kind."

The new lemon rocks on Beatty's cutting board. He steadies it and makes two incisions with a sharp, curved blade.

When Beatty gives her the empty glass, she lifts the hem of her dress, which is wet from what she's done to it in the Ladies and has a small brown stain on it. She holds it over the empty glass and pours the lemony soda water over the stain. Some of the soda runs off the hem onto the bar. Beatty wonders how she looks from the other side, with her dress pulled up like that, showing her legs.

A man in a black suit comes through the parking-lot door. His eyes flip from table to table until he sees the woman sitting on the bar stool. "C'mon, Glory, we're waiting."

"Pay the man for the soda, Von." She smiles at Beatty with small, even teeth. "See? Almost gone."

"I guess it was the lemon," says Beatty.

"And the fizz," says the woman.

"Johnny's waiting, honey," says the man called Von. He puts a dollar on the counter in front of Beatty.

"I don't want to go all the way to Lloyd tonight. I'm sick of driving, driving, driving." The woman drops her skirt back to her knees and blots the wetness with a napkin. The napkin has jokes on it but she does not read them. "Why can't we just fly to Saskatoon in the morning?"

"Don't make him come in here, Glory."

"He wouldn't. He might be recognized." But there seems to be a joke in what she has said, for she looks around at the dark, empty tables with a smile that is only for herself. "Big place," she says to Beatty.

"Second biggest in Canada," he says.

A car horn sounds outside.

Von slaps his hand on the varnished wood. "Saskatoon tomorrow night, Glory. Let's go." He turns and walks out the door.

Beatty lifts the countertop on its hinges and goes to a window. He raises the blind and looks out into the parking-lot. A Caddy stands idling in front of the door, and in the light from the neon on the pub roof Beatty can read a sign painted across both car doors: MID-WESTERN WORD-OF-GOD EVANGELICAL ASSOCIA-TION. Von has raised the hood and is leaning over the engine with his back rounded so his suit jacket won't hang in the grease.

"Is Johnny coming?" says Glory.

Beatty shakes his head. Glory gets off the bar stool and shimmies her hem down to its proper place below her knees. She smoothes the front of her skirt several times with her splayed hands. Her body straightens and grows taller and she plucks at her dress shoulders to loosen up the drape of the cloth on her breasts.

Beatty says, "Are you a preacher's wife?"

"I don't have half her fun," Glory says. "I'm an organizer for Johnny Winkler. Have you heard of him? 'Heaven Is Near.' We're on a crusade. Just finished up in Three Hills."

Beatty keeps his hand on the cords holding up the blind.

"Big meeting in Saskatoon tomorrow night," the woman continues, "if I'm still alive then. He tried to push me out of the car back there on the highway." She looks down at the place on her skirt where the spot was.

Beatty lets the shade fall. "You'd probably better not go out there then. If he comes back in here I'll question him, lift his nice black shoes off the floor a bit."

"Comes *back*? Oh, you think Von was the one tried to shove me out onto the road. I didn't mean him. I was talking about Johnny. Johnny Winkler." Now she is unsure about walking to the door. Her fingers nibble at her handbag.

Robbie, who has been sitting at one of the tables with two cronies, approaches the bar with a tray of dirty glasses and empty beer cans. He is an old man with a short flat nose and white hair past his shirt collar. Beatty fills the order quickly while Robbie studies Glory. Robbie takes his tray and makes his rounds.

Beatty leans across the bar and looks at Glory with a worried face. "Are evangicles allowed to do that?" he says softly.

She smiles again. "Not most evangelists. Johnny Winkler's divinity gives him special privileges."

Beatty remembers hearing about the crusade. That morning he'd visited his mother and his sister in Hairy Hill. They were canning green-tomato relish and talking about the Three Hills Crusade, and about evangelists. His mother had said there were good evangelists and bad ones. Johnny Winkler was one of the good ones. That morning Beatty had called them evangelists like everyone else. Tonight, after he saw Glory with the drippy fudgicle in her hand, evangicle had just slipped out.

"I could fly you over in the morning," says Beatty. "I'm a pilot."

But Beatty is lying. He used to be a pilot. Just that morning his mother and sister had asked him when he would get his licence reinstated. "You've been on the wagon for six years now," said his mom as she tightened the lids on the sweet green, vinegary relish. "When you going to get back on a plane?"

Glory says, "Don't worry about me." She puts her hand on the bar between Beatty's two hands, which are resting there flat, palms down. Then she walks out through the parking-lot door.

Beatty stares at the space where her hand was. He notices his watch. Gina will be coming in from the dining-room any moment.

Robbie wiggles his tray and makes another batch of empty glasses ring like dime-store bells.

"I told you not to do that," Beatty growls. "It weakens the glass."

"Then pay attention," says Robbie. He was married to Beatty's sister in Hairy Hill, but the vows hadn't held after Robbie tried to burn down their house.

Beatty curses because he has to make one of those slushy margaritas with salt on the rim. He slashes a withered lime with unusual recklessness, and Robbie's thick white eyebrows go up.

Then, just when Gina is supposed to come in through the vendor from the dining-room, Glory comes back from the parking-lot carrying some folded clothes and a train case. "I'm going to change into travelling clothes," she says. "Von's ordering take-out in there." She sets out across the cavernous pub.

Beatty moves over to the blind and slowly raises it with the cord. The interior lights of the Cadillac are on now, and Beatty can see the top of a head through the rear window.

"He's studying the script," Glory calls from the Ladies' Room door.

The people in the bar turn to look at her, and then turn and look at Beatty. He lets the blind down with a rattle.

Beatty unties his apron and goes through the vendor to the dining-room. Gina is sitting at a table in the empty restaurant with the evangicle's driver, Von. Gina is a plain girl with big eyes and straight black hair. Tonight she has on a yellow sun-dress. She and Beatty have a private alcoholics' pact. They know each other from growing up in Hairy Hill, though she is a lot younger than Beatty. They seek each other out on the nights they both work, to raise glasses of tomato juice to a day passed without a drink. The days are like one long staircase they have to climb, though it leads nowhere.

Beatty had planned to ask Gina if she'd want to drive up to Hairy Hill tomorrow night to see the First-of-July fireworks. When Beatty was twelve, his dad took him to the Dominion Day Fair and paid the pilot who was giving rides in a Piper Cub ten dollars to take Beatty up after dark, to watch the fireworks from overhead. That was when Beatty decided to get a flying licence. He saw starbursts splitting the dark hills and doubling in the twisting rivers and lakes, and he felt as if he'd turned life inside out.

Gina has to wait in the dining-room to run up the evangicle's take-out. Von glances over when Beatty comes to the doorway, but Gina doesn't turn around.

Beatty goes back into the saloon. He'd gotten his pilot's licence. He'd never gone to look at fireworks from the air, though he'd always planned to.

Robbie is gazing through the window shade at the big Cadillac out front. "Who was that fella in the suit?" he asks when Beatty comes by.

"Sort of a chauffeur, I guess."

"Somebody making a movie? Is there an actor in there? That woman said something about a script."

"Actor's about right."

"Why don't he come in?"

"Shy type," says Beatty.

"There's something famous about this set-up," says Robbie, still peering between the crooked slats. "She's slick."

"Yeah, it's a nice little car."

"No, I meant the lady. And the car. It's unusual. A chauffeur. And the guy won't come in, even though this place is nearly empty." Robbie looks at Beatty, who is washing glasses. "You think it's Elvis?" Robbie spreads his fingers further apart between the slats. "They say he's still alive."

"Maybe it's him," says Beatty.

"He's got a good cover, that's for sure," says Robbie. "If I see him I'll be famous."

Some patrons leave the 24-Karat Saloon. Beatty polishes the bar and collects dead soldiers from the abandoned tables.

When Glory comes out of the Ladies, she is wearing a T-shirt with a picture of a cartoony-looking man on the front. HEAVEN IS NEAR is spelled in big letters under the picture. The man does not look much like Elvis. To Beatty he looks like Jiminy Cricket.

"Johnny's giving us a little rest period," she says, and puts her dress and her train case on a table close to the bar. "Pour me a soda and I'll drink it." She looks down at the face on her shirt-front. "Can't wash that out with fizz and lemon."

Right after Beatty has poured soda into his tallest glass, a large batch of people comes into the saloon and they are rowdy and all over the room in an instant. They fire their orders at Beatty from scattered points and he gets busy. Some of the orders are fussy drinks, which take time to put together. Beatty files them for last.

Robbie leans on the bar near Glory. He gives the new crowd a quick inspection, then concentrates on her. He does not pay much attention to the picture on her shirt. "You got a mystery man in the Caddy?"

"Yes," she says after a long draw on the barbershop-pole straw Beatty's put in her soda. "Mystery is his game."

"Why don't you invite him in?"

"He doesn't frequent beer parlours. He doesn't like me being in here at all."

"So he's an evangelist?"

"He figures this town is too small for major sinning, I guess. God won't count it if an ordinary Mennonite girl goes into the toilet in a pub to wash a fudgicle stain out of her Sunday dress."

"Where you from?" Robbie asks.

"Manitoba. Johnny's from Toronto. He says Mennonites are good for the image of evangelism."

Robbie shuffles his moccasins on the carpet. "Johnny?"

"Johnny Winkler." Glory stretches out the face stamped on her chest so it is flat and square.

Robbie's forehead wrinkles and he goes back to the window. "Maybe I'll go talk to him," he says, giving Glory's T-shirt another glance.

"He'd love it."

"I thought he might be Elvis."

"Well, he might be." Glory smiles at Robbie. "He's had his sideburns trimmed." Robbie leaves through the parking-lot door.

The noisy drinkers settle in at a table under the moose antlers. Beatty finishes the last Bloody Mary and takes the tray over himself. One of the rowdies moves his chair back just as Beatty comes up behind him, and the tray gets jostled in Beatty's hands. Beatty does not make a mistake like that often—he knows how to approach a tableful of people who are not paying attention. But now he is not paying attention. Not all the drinks are spilled. He slaps the full ones down on the terry cloth and goes back to remake the others and curse Robbie for leaving.

"I've never been in a bar before," says Glory when Beatty has finally finished the round.

"I'm not surprised," says Beatty.

"I hear people turn against their friends in a drinking parlour. That's what Johnny tells us. 'Drink dissolves love like acid,' he says."

"Love's been found in bars. Friends. Even opportunities, sometimes." Beatty has his hands in the disinfecting rinse. Steam warms his chest. "But he's right. Christians best stay out of places like this."

Glory sketches a shape on the countertop with the tip of the straw. "Can you really fly?"

Beatty is not sure how to answer, so he just nods yes. It is not a lie—he can fly.

"What's your plane called?"

Beatty thinks for a moment. "Marvin," he says.

"My Uncle Abe used to give me rides on a funny little plane. You know, with double wings? He lived beside the Red River and raised chinchillas. I used to stick my gum on the wing before we took off to see how long it would stay there."

Another customer calls for a round. Beatty looks for Robbie in the big dim room.

"How many seats does Marvin have?" Glory asks.

But Beatty is pulling beer out of the cooler and setting clean glasses on his tray.

Glory sits very still on the edge of the stool. When Beatty comes back to the till to get his customer's change, she starts to talk in a low voice. Her words are quick and intense. She tells him that the evangelist calls her *slut* and *harlot* when it gets late in the night, and that he accuses her of puckering her lips at the bucket-boys who collect donations at the end of a meeting. He has tried to push her out of the Caddy before.

In her lap she has a small handbag with a pearl clasp. She opens the clasp and takes a package out of the handbag.

Robbie comes in. His eyes are shining.

Beatty encircles the round leathery seat of the bar stool next to Glory with his wide hands and moves the stool closer to her. He straddles the seat. "Tend bar, will you?" he calls over his shoulder to Robbie. "Two seats. It's a two-seater," he tells Glory.

"I think I been saved!" says Robbie as he passes. "I been saved! At least, I think so."

"Here," says Glory to Beatty. She holds out the package.

Beatty opens his hand. She spills a few glossy discs into his palm.

"Blue smarties?" says Beatty.

Glory's eyes are shining like Robbie's. "Blue smarties! Aren't they beautiful and peaceful?"

Beatty says, "A whole package of blue smarties."

"I've been saving them. Always putting the blue ones away so I can have a whole bunch of them at once."

"Have you ever seen fireworks from a plane?"

"You mean while it's flying?"

"Yeah."

"No."

Beatty puts a smartie on his tongue.

"No! No! Put the whole handful in!" Glory lifts his palm to his mouth. "Don't they taste blue?" Her lipstick glistens like a red smartie that's been licked.

Beatty doesn't remember that she was wearing lipstick the first time she came in. He nods, but all he can taste is the chocolate. He says, "When you fly over the top of fireworks near a lake or a winding river, you can see them reflecting in the water. And they cut across the town lights and race with headlights moving along the roads."

Last year, Beatty was on the road on the way to his mom's when the Hairy Hill fireworks started. He got out of his truck to watch, just beside Ridley's Creek. The frogs sang in the mud, high-pitched and steady, and the explosions way up above the distant town were muffled little pops that went off out of sync with the coloured bursts of fire. Just over the low skyline Beatty saw the white bulbs of a silent Ferris wheel arcing.

But another sound joined in with the muffled popping and the frog chorus—Bill Melischuk's Twin Beech dipping and circling, dipping and climbing and doing figure-eights on top of the fireworks. The engine sound was strong and pure. Beatty wished he could be everywhere at once—on the roadside, in the mud beside the creek, up on the Ferris wheel, flying in Bill's Twin Beech.

"You feel like you've turned life inside out," Beatty says to Glory, who is spreading all the blue smarties on top of the bar and counting them. If he could fly her and the evangicle and maybe even Von from place to place, she would not be pushed out of a moving Cadillac on a highway late at night. But then he would need a four-seater for sure.

Beatty stands up and moves two more bar stools behind his and Glory's. "Four seats," he tells her. "Marvin is a four-seater."

Robbie has new energy and moves among the tables spryly, and makes fresh drinks with a kind of reckless joy.

"I like it here," says Glory. "I haven't had anything on my mind for the last year and a half except schedules and lost souls."

Gina drifts up to the bar like a piece of yellow chiffon floating in the air. She folds her bare arms on the cool wood and waits for Robbie to pour her a glass of tomato juice. While Beatty tells Glory how the plains buffalo used to rub their loose hair off on the trees on the hills nearby every spring, Gina sidles over to one of the empty stools behind them and rests against it while she sips her juice.

After awhile, Beatty says, "Looks like we got a passenger. Welcome to Marvin Airlines," he says to Gina. "We're looking at the fireworks. See down there?"

But it is Glory who looks down at the floor and goes, "Wooooo!" Then, "Look out, here's a rocket coming right at us!"

Beatty grabs the imaginary controls with both of his thick fists and veers away from the explosion.

Gina keeps the glass at her chin, tilting it slowly to her straight mouth every once in a while. She is like a slow-motion sequence in a movie. She says, "I'm going to Edmonton to take auto mechanics this fall, Bea. That guy just convinced me."

Glory turns and looks hard at Gina for a moment, then says, "You're a lucky kid," but not in a sarcastic way. She says, "An auto mechanic. That's what I'd like to be. I've always wished I could be Von. You don't just drive a car. You know exactly how it runs and why it runs, and if it doesn't go how you want it to, you get out from behind the wheel and find where it's broken and you fix it. That's how it should be." She starts putting the smarties back in the box, one by one. Her fingernails are long and perfectly shaped. "Do you mechanic your own plane?" she says to Beatty, who is still next to her, steering it.

"Sure," he says.

Gina says nothing, but looks at the back of Beatty's stout neck as though it will explain his lie.

"I guess there are ways," says Glory, "to get nearer to heaven. I listen to Johnny every night, but I still feel quite far away."

As Glory speaks, the door of the 24-Karat Saloon, the door leading to the parking-lot, opens, and a small man with long hands and a large head of hair slips through. He is wearing a grey suit and a white shirt and a dark green bow tie. His head is high and his eyes settle at once on Glory, and he holds her firmly with them.

Gina sees Robbie lift his hand to his brow like a salute, and she twists around to see whom he is greeting in that strange way.

"You want to fly upside-down?" asks Beatty.

"Will it muss my hair?" asks Glory.

Gina takes a sip of tomato juice and watches the light in Robbie's eyes.

Johnny Winkler steps carefully towards the bar like a man walking a minefield. Though Beatty keeps his hands on the controls, he is half aware of a body moving slowly across the room. When Glory feels the touch on her upper arm, the soft long fingers moving like a sudden erection of hair, from her shoulder to her elbow, she does not look around. Her own fingers fidgeting with the smarties box become still, the knuckles sharper.

"It's time to go," Johnny whispers into her ear. He says the words very slowly. His fingers are still on her arm. He smiles a flat evangelical smile at her, even though he is looking at the back of her head. "Glory's a little tired," he says, a bit louder.

Then Glory sits up straighter. "This bartender is flying us to Saskatoon," she says. "That's your seat." She points over her shoulder at the remaining empty stool behind her, beside Gina.

"Von ordered hot chocolate for you. With marshmallow." Johnny Winkler moves forward so he can get a clear view of Beatty. "A pilot." He smiles. "Just like Jesus." His eyes slide back to Glory. "But we'll take the car. We must leave."

Beatty can think of nothing to say.

"We're out of place here. I can't be seen in an establishment like this. Try to make it up to Saskatoon, and then we'll find you some peace for a few days."

At last Glory stands up. In her high-heeled sandals she towers over Johnny Winkler. "I hate road trips," she says.

"Hate is not in our vocabulary, Glory." Johnny smiles again at Beatty.

Glory starts for the table where she'd put her train case and her dress.

Johnny Winkler picks up the box of smarties from the bar.

But Glory does not walk quite up to the table where her train case and her dress are lying. She takes a step towards the bar where Robbie is cutting a lime for yet another margarita. She is very quick. She has planned it in that brief moment that she was moving towards the table.

She is very quick. She slips the knife easily out of Robbie's wet hand and in a motion like a giant wheel turns and brings the slender blade down hard into Johnny Winkler's chest. The jolt of the knife reverberates up into Johnny's hand. Blue smarties scatter through the air like blue sparks and form a pattern on the gold carpet as they land, one by one, in delicate plops. Glory's arm in coming down grazes Gina's breasts, and Gina leaps back. The tomato juice makes a bright wound on her bright yellow dress.

Johnny staggers backward against a table. In the seconds it takes for the table to topple, and for him to fall, he stares at the front of Glory's T-shirt. He sees himself looking back, except that on the shirt he is smiling.

Beatty is surprised at how fast everything happens. It is hardly a speck of time. In fact, it all happens at once: the evangicle picking up Glory's smarties from the bar, Glory grabbing Robbie's citrus knife, the huge, arcing thrust of her arm, the smarties flying through the air, Johnny Winkler falling against the table, and falling to the floor. It all happens exactly at the same time, not in slow motion like in movies, not like watching a plane flying in a far-away sky.

And Robbie is so quickly at Johnny's side, on his knees. He reaches for Johnny Winkler's head, perhaps wanting to hold it, but he just kneels on the floor and cries. The tears are there so quickly. "I told him everything!" Robbie says. "I never told anybody everything before. I thought he was Elvis."

The patrons of the 24-Karat Saloon are all on their feet and looking at Glory and Beatty and Gina and Robbie and the small, well-dressed man on the floor with the citrus knife sticking out of his breastbone. Gina has one of the napkins with the jokes on them in her hand and is clutching it against the blood-coloured stain on her dress.

"Can you fly me away from here now?" says Glory.

I have no plane, Beatty wants to say. The best I can do is the Ferris wheel at the Hairy Hill fair, he wants to tell her.

"He's not dead or anything," announces a girl who'd been playing shuffleboard.

But Beatty cannot speak. All he can think of are the blue smarties. He remembers them in slow motion, scattering through the air like blue sparks.

NO CATS IN HEAVEN

Boy Fehr crawled past the last headstone and rolled into the depression outlined crookedly by a chipped cement crib sunk into the grass. He gasped for breath, for he'd run the two miles from town, first along the railroad track, and then along a middle-road that cut through Billy Schultz's wheat. And he had also laughed the last hundred yards, and his knees had begun to weaken. Laughing, gasping, and crawling, he had arrived at the last headstone at the edge of a barley field. He propped the back of his head up against the weathered granite marker and faced the wind with his eyes closed.

All the graves faced east. The cemetery was a good place to watch the sun coming up over town summer mornings. Old maples bordered three sides, but the east side, the direction all the graves stared, was clear.

Boy spread his arms to let the breeze pass through his shirt. A wind from the east disturbed the June warmth. East winds brought storms, hail, a wrong slant of rain. The young green barley plants rippled up to cemetery grass, which was too short to catch the rhythms of the wind, and only jerked in spasms like

Boy's brown hair. The graveyard was kept as neat as a park, even though no one had been buried there in Boy's lifetime, and he'd never met any of the skeletons below. Every week in summer, Billy Schultz buzzed along the gravel road that cut through Silvercreek on his Turfmaster and turned into the defunct cemetery to trim the grass. In autumn he raked. He never wore his cap when he worked here, or his overalls, like he did when tossing dead chickens out of his barn onto burning heaps of rubbish.

Boy rubbed his eyes. The silver chains on his wrists spun webs of sunlight in the air. Then he remembered the paint on his face. One knuckle shone oily green. Gerbrandt had come to 105 and told him in front of the whole class to go home and wash his face. "If you want to paint half your face green, go join a circus!" Tomorrow, Boy decided, he would paint his whole face green. He'd spent most of the morning at the video arcade where being green was normal in the glow of Cosmic Death Race and Space Duel.

Mary-Mac hadn't cared that he'd showed up in her writing class with his face painted. She had laughed and told him to write about how it felt. He hadn't written anything in her writing class all semester, but she let him talk and talked back. "Anything dead on the road this morning, Boy?" she'd ask. "Two kittens and a bunch of salamanders," he'd answer. (Everybody would make a face and shake their heads.) "How'd they look?" "The salamanders looked like—" And then she'd say, "Write it down," and shove a piece of blank paper under his nose. He would draw pictures instead.

Boy's arms lay brown and slender at his sides. Looking at them, he felt as though they were detached, that his nerves were not connected to them. A tear was beginning in the toe of his runner. He'd painted both his runners with Jiffy Marker on the bus ride to the nuclear plant in Pinawa. When they got off the bus, Purina Christina had said, "Manny, what'd you draw on your shoes?" (She called him Manny because she was his second cousin and all his relatives called him by his real name, even though his parents didn't.) "Dante's Inferno," he'd whispered to her, as though it were something dirty, which was what she expected from him. "This one's Dante, this is Andante." "Oh," she'd said, and he'd seen her stealing glances at his feet as they toured the nuclear station. Purina's such a dog, everybody said. But she wasn't, really.

"Gettin' any vibes today, Cornie Baby?" said Boy into the wind. "Smell the canola factory? East wind. Warm and cool at the same time. Feel it?" The grave next to Boy belonged to Cornie Kehler, who had been four when he died of polio and became the last soul to be laid to rest in Silvercreek Cemetery. No Kehlers lived in Silvercreek anymore. Hardly any Mennonites lived here now—Fehrs, Rempels, Schultzes, and Silent Peter Pankratz. The rest had moved to town or further away, and their places had been taken by smooth-tongued people who changed Silberbach to Silvercreek and called it a bedroom community, which Boy thought was a very sexy label. Little Cornie Kehler's grave was half the size of the adults'. Even his marker was smaller. *Asleep in Jesus,* it said, in English, though the words had faded during the many prairie winters that entombed the stone in ice for months on end. Boy had filled in the letters with Jiffy Marker once, but the weather was already beginning to erase the ink. Boy liked talking about Little Cornie to his friends and teachers, even to his parents. "Little Cornie says death is like lying in the back seat of a car at a drive-in movie." (Had Cornie Kehler ever been to a drive-in movie? He died in 1953.) "Little Cornie told me Silent Peter Pankratz is half in death all the time." "Little Cornie wants new shoes—his feet are cold." Nobody knew whom he was talking about. They thought Little Cornie was a dwarf who hung out at the arcade, or an old man Boy had met at the curling rink. Nobody knew except Purina and Sluddy.

Boy turned over and ran his fingers along the grooves in the headstone behind him. *Selig sind die Toten, die in dem Herrn sterben.* He didn't know much German, the language the Mennos used when they were being formal. But he'd translated some of the slogans with his dad's *Langenscheidts. Happy are the dead who die in the Lord.* ("What are you looking up, Boy?" "German." "German what?" "Verses." "Is it for school?" "For Sunday school." "Oh." His father had been puzzled—he didn't know his son went to Sunday school.) The grave Boy lay on said *Mutter* below the inscription. Her name was Katrina Abrams. She'd died in 1933, and he called her Aunt Katy. The words, as on Little Cornie's grave, were barely legible in the stone. He couldn't tell if she'd been born in 1846 or 1896. If 1896, she would have been as old when she died as his mother was now.

One headstone said, *Mir ist ein schoen Erbteil geworden.* Boy thought it meant, *I have a nice inheritance coming,* but wasn't certain—it sounded as though some whiny old geezer had gone to his grave shouting, "What about my inheritance, you bastards?" His name was Kehler, too, and he lay five away from Little Cornie. Maybe his grandfather.

Wir aber warten eines neuen Himmels und einer neuen Erde. We wait again for a new heaven and a new earth. That was Anna Marie Rempel, who'd lived from 1863 till 1951. Her son, Old Abe, had told Boy's father that she had been addicted to prescription drugs the last ten years of her life. She was probably still waiting, Boy decided—there was nothing new on earth, as far as he could tell. His mother had eight bottles of pills in her panty drawer, and she used all of them. When he was thirteen he'd taken the bottles out of the drawer and sampled them, one of each, one a day, to see how they'd make him feel. Nothing happened. He'd scattered the rest on Anna Marie Rempel's grave. Within a week, eight new bottles nestled among the nylon underthings in his mother's drawer.

Boy looked across the rippling barley at the string of whites and colours and pinnacles two miles away that was town. The sound of the wind changed as he faced straight into it, and he heard its movement in the maples in stereo now, a green rustling and whispering in the leaves. Last November, before the snow, he'd sat exactly here on a calm, colourless day and listened to one dry leaf clicking against a dead branch. It drove him crazy. He found it and climbed up and picked it, and crumpled it in his tattered leather glove.

"Can you see it, Cornie? Close to the end? I can't, quite, but I know where it is. Even with binoculars, I can only see the edge of it. Too many things in the way." The law office. A two-storey brick building with an Old West facade and a flat roof, surrounded by more maples and commercial buildings that were vacant at night. Boy had discovered the hard, flat roof around midnight on a June evening last summer while Police Chief Buhler and Constable Ridd tore up and down streets and alleys in their cruiser car looking for him. Boy had rescued a plaster fawn from someone's front lawn, just lay on his belly and snaked through the grass right under the picture window where, from the street, he had seen a bare-chested man and a knitting woman sitting in front of their television. The plaster fawn trotted off their lawn. But they saw it out of the corners of their eyes, probably because of its white spots, and, after shouting at Boy in the darkness, sent Chief Buhler on the chase. By climbing onto the oil tank at the back of the building, and then up to the rear entrance, and then onto a stocky limb of a maple tree, he could get onto the roof fast. Boy and Sluddy hauled up lawn chairs and cases of beer with rope slung over a branch, and late at night they sat up there and talked and listened to the town sounds, and looked at the moon. They spoke in low voices so people passing on the street below couldn't hear them, although Boy suspected they had been heard sometimes. But down below, you couldn't tell where the voices were coming from. They would sit there for hours and hours, and walk home just before sunrise, if Sluddy didn't have the pick-up. Sometimes Boy's mother was waiting for him with a brown-stained plastic cup in her hand, the one that had *Florida* written in red on the side. Most times she was drugged into sleep.

Mary-Mac had asked Boy once if his parents knew where he was half the time. "My parents? I feel like I'm being raised by robots. Jeeez! They're programmed. They have steel bearings for eyes." (Mary-Mac laughed instead of wrinkling her forehead and turning down the corners of her mouth.) "They have two things they say to me: Deep down there is goodness in you, and Pray for forgiveness. They think I'm a robot. I was born dead."

"They were kids once. Ask them what they did when they were kids."

"They learned Testament verses and hymns. The most fun they had was when crusades came to town and New Year's Eve in church. In church! The Silvercreek Church burnt down when I was little." Boy did not want to hear his father say he had hung out in the cemetery when he was young or played hooky in the pool hall that used to be at the back of the Eaton's mail-order. Boy wouldn't face the possibility that he himself could turn into a robot with a live child.

Boy and Little Cornie looked at the invisible law office for a long time. Boy fell asleep.

Running on gravel. Get away! Get away! He sat up, half in his dream. Running on gravel. He crouched behind Aunt Katy's headstone. The footsteps softened in the cemetery grass. It was Sluddy Wirch. School was over.

"Slud!"

Sluddy had shaved his head after their field trip to the nuclear plant. His hair was just growing back. He reminded Boy of an Auschwitz inmate. "You been here all day, man?" asked Sluddy. He put a red licorice twizzle in his mouth.

"Naw, I played out all my dough at the arcade."

"McCloskey was mad after you left."

"At me?"

"Naw. At Gerby. She almost cried, I think."

"So what."

"Gerby called her out of class. Maybe he canned her."

"Naw. She was quitting anyway. She told me."

"We could do the Co-op store tonight." Sluddy flopped down in Little Cornie's crib.

"Eh-eh . . . " Boy wagged a green finger at Sluddy.

"Sorry." Sluddy came and sat at the feet of Aunt Katy. "It's supposed to storm."

Boy looked east. Blue clouds just above town. Blue almost like sky, but with a clothy sheen, like the satin edge of the blue wool blanket in Sluddy's pick-up. "Maybe," said Boy. He'd been dreaming that Purina Christina was standing on the ground beside the law office, calling up to him. "Emmanuel! Emmanuel!" she called. But he couldn't get down. The tree and the roof and the oil tank had disappeared.

Boy pulled a switch-blade knife out of his pocket and carved a neat deep circle around a dandelion between his legs. "What else happened?"

"Greening gave us a cow's eye left over from 101 Biology. Said he was cleaning out his spare parts freezer for the summer." Sluddy took a red stick of licorice from his shirt pocket and stuck it between Boy's lips. "And Jennifer Loepp said, 'Haven't you got anything sexy in there, like ice-cream?' You know how Greening's got this case on Jennifer Loepp. And he did have ice-cream in there, and they all ate ice-cream. But I dissected the eye."

"What flavour?"

"Cow."

"Moo," said Boy as he flung the white-rooted dandelion plant into the barley.

"Vanilla," said Sluddy.

A half-grown cat leaped straight up out of the barley field

and embraced the dandelion in mid-air, then fell back into the field, where her scuffle with her victim could not be detected in the ripples created by the wind. Sluddy did not see it. She must have been sitting there watching just over the top of the barley, thought Boy. Who had had kittens in Silvercreek this spring? He tried to remember all the pregnant cats.

Sluddy kicked Boy's foot. "So? You wanna do it tonight?"

No, he didn't want to do it tonight. It would be better to wait until Mary-Mac was gone, all gone. And it was better to wait until school was out, anyway. Things like that had a habit of leaking out and seeping around a school. Sluddy was oblivious to details like that. All he wanted was the money, even though they hadn't yet unloaded any of their inventory, as Sluddy called it. They were always waiting for just a little more. "If it storms good," said Boy.

"How come they don't bury anybody here anymore?" asked Sluddy as he counted the granite markers with flicks of his stubby licorice stick.

"No vacancy."

"They could start over. Double 'em up. We could go into business. Used graves."

"I'd like to be buried here," said Boy. He pictured future archaeologists unearthing pairs of skeletons, their bones mingled like underworld lovers. The fossil of Cornie Kehler covered by his own full-grown bones. "They say the world will eventually be crowded with cemeteries. No room for farms or anything. Someday there'll be a law that everybody has to be cremated. Everybody'll have a huge collection of the ashes of their ancestors."

"I wish we'd have cremated Buster. You know before we moved here, when we lived on that farm? We had this schnauzer, Buster. He got run over on the road by a lady driving a Lincoln. My mom took him to the vet, and the vet said his bones weren't broken but he was battered up and there might be internal injuries. So she took him home and she and my sisters took turns holding his head on their laps and my mom gave him a tin of salmon and he wouldn't eat it. In the morning he was dead. Everybody cried like mad. Me and my brother wrapped him up in some red Christmas paper we found in the attic and dug a hole in a field. We had sort of a little funeral and my mom and sisters bawled and then we took turns throwing dirt back into the grave. I think we even put his doggy-bowl in.

"Pretty soon we got a new dog, a lab. And one day we saw him out on the field fooling around with something. Then we remembered that's where Buster's grave was. So we ran like mad out there and that stupid lab was chewing on Buster's leg. We hadn't dug deep enough. He dug him up and chewed away. There were bits of red soggy Christmas paper sticking to his lips." The last nub of licorice disappeared into Sluddy's mouth. "We should have cremated Buster. I don't mind being burnt. The part of you that vaporizes goes to heaven. If they bury you, your spirit gets smothered and that's what haunts the people left alive. Hell, they can cremate me."

"You sure you're goin' to heaven, Slud?" Boy inserted the tip of the switch-blade into the slit in his knee. "Didn't looking at a cow's eye teach you anything? You didn't find her soul in there, did you?"

" 'Course not. She died a long time ago. Who knows how long those science warehouses keep their organs on ice."

"But you mean every time my dad barbecues a steak a piece of cow-soul flies up out of the meat and goes to heaven and hooks onto other pieces of cow-soul that flew up outta, say, Billy Schultz's wife's frying pan?"

"I'm not sure about animals. . . . "

"But if you burn your finger with a match when you're drunk, a tiny little bit of your soul goes to heaven then, too?"

"Why not? Your soul is endless." Sluddy Wirch wasn't a Mennonite. His parents went to the United Church.

"And animals don't have souls? You mean there's no cats in heaven?"

"Well, there are no cats in this graveyard, are there?"

"Maybe cats automatically go to hell," Boy mumbled. "Punishment for cheating God by having spare lives." He watched for the half-grown kitten, to see if it would come out of the field at the cemetery edge. No sign of it.

After Sluddy left, Boy took off his runner, the one with the hole in the toe, and tossed it over the barley. No cat flew up to intercept it. But when Boy walked into the field to look for his shoe, the cat popped up and escaped through the barley, leaping and arcing over the young grain like a dolphin playing in the sea. It crossed a corner of the graveyard and slunk into the underbrush among the maples. Boy followed. He sat down on the grass near where the cat had disappeared and made soft bird-calls and mouse squeaks. A pair of blue-green eyes and flicking ears emerged from a tangle of deadfall.

"Hello, Dante," said Boy.

Jewell Fehr's bacon did not look like the picture of bacon on the cover of the menu of Bruce's Burger Loft, where Boy and Sluddy sometimes had breakfast at 5:00 A.M. She didn't let it lie flat and petrify into a proper rasher. Jewell Fehr stirred bacon as it cooked, so that it came out twisted and curled and buckled like wilted roots. "Goes faster," she told Boy.

Now he sat on the kitchen counter watching their supper bacon heat up in the scarred Teflon pan. He just sat and stared at it, planning to see it turn rigid and flat, like menu bacon. When his mother approached with her cracked wooden spatula, threatening to stir, he held up his hand to stop her. She veered off to her coffee mug and looked through the kitchen window, past the prism shaped like a cross that hung by a piece of fish-line from the frame.

That was when Boy heard the thunder—slow, low-slung

sound-waves penetrating the hollow walls of the Fehr home, chorusing with the bacon popping in its pool of fat.

" 'T's gonna storm," came Jewell's dull voice.

Boy listened to the thunder and thought about the roof of the law office and doing the Co-op store. And he thought about the sounds in the arcade, electronic explosions and ricochets. When his eyes focused again on the bacon, it had twisted and buckled on its own.

"How was school today?" Boy's father had a white noodle nestled in the cleft of his chin. It reminded Boy of a worm.

"I learned a lot." (Boy had wiped the green off his face with vaseline before supper. Not because he'd been told to—his parents had stopped telling him to do this and do that.)

"Good!" said Dave Fehr. Boy watched his father's lips part and the delicately machined teeth appear in a robot smile. "Deep down, you have goodness in you, Boy."

Boy looked at his mother. Her food lay quietly in her plate. She smiled her robot smile at him over her coffee mug and nodded.

A gravel road split Silvercreek in half, and the creek itself intersected that road right in the middle of the village. Roy Steeves, who was the unofficial mayor of Silvercreek because he was on the town school board, had convinced the residents and then the municipality to post a very low speed limit on the gravel street. "We want Silvercreek to be peaceful in all ways," he said. "We want people passing through to hold their breath while they admire this picturesque little bedroom community. They should have to drive so slow they almost stop." Roy Steeves had also declared that the new bridge over the creek bed be wide enough for a footwalk on either side so folks could fish off it in spring.

Normally, Boy heard Sluddy's pick-up truck long before it

was up to the Fehr's driveway. On a calm night, Boy could hear Sluddy start up the truck at the opposite end of the village—a few low growls followed by an irregular clatter. And then Sluddy would try to hit sixty before he got to Boy's place. He frequently overshot the Fehrs' driveway in his desire to make the Big Six-Oh. He called it his freedom ride. Tonight the growling thunder covered the growl and clatter of Sluddy's pick-up truck.

Boy buried his hand in a fold of the blanket on the truck seat. He liked the feel of it, too, under his jeaned buttocks, an old soft feeling, not like the vinyl beneath the blanket. It was the kind of blanket Little Cornie would have been wrapped in when he got his polio fever—a flushed, blond child nestled in blue wool, quiet and lethargic, and unable to move, and then unable to breathe, suddenly dead in his mother's Mennonite arms, like a blue bagful of warm licorice sticks.

"Are you a Christian, Boy?" asked Sluddy.

Boy drew his hand into his lap. "No. . . . But not being a Christian makes it okay to tell lies, so I tell people I am." Laugh, Slud. Laugh and leave it alone.

"Is it because you steal?"

You make a decision to steal, which means you can't be a Christian. You make a choice. Jewell and Dave would say you make a decision not to be a Christian, and the devil recruits you into a life of crime. "No," said Boy. "It's because I—because there's no vacancy."

They passed Purina Christina going the other way. She was with her mother in their Monte Carlo. Boy looked back at them through the rear truck window and he saw her looking back at them between the headrests of the big car. He thought he saw her waving. He heard her calling in his dream. "Emmanuel! Emmanuel!" she called.

One time, when his hair was longer, he'd twisted it into a brown braid at the back of his head, like a pirate, and he'd worn a patch over his eye. He'd met Christina at the arcade and they played Space Duel all night. She'd kissed the patch on his eye and asked him to take her up to the law office roof. She was the only one who knew about the hide-out, but she'd never climbed up. "We could do it up there, Manny," she'd whispered in his unpatched ear. But Boy didn't want to do it with Christina, not because she was his second cousin and called him Manny, and not because everybody said she was such a dog. The self-sacrificing way she offered herself to him made him think of the pills in his mother's drawer.

"Is it because of your old man that you don't want to do the Co-op?" Sluddy asked. Boy's father was the manager of the Co-op store.

"I just wanted to wait until summer holidays."

The storm hit around nine o'clock, well before dark. Sluddy looked out the glass door of the arcade and fretted about the thunder coming too early. Boy destroyed aliens from the planet Vargh.

An hour later Boy began rubbing his eyebrows with his knuckles. "What's happening, Slud?"

"I think they're riding piggy-back. Another one's coming down." He held the door open. The wind was rushing along the wet streets, and thunder was approaching for a second time. Darkness sat behind the neon-fronted stores like a quiet black dog.

At eleven, Boy Fehr and Sluddy Wirch reached under the blue blanket of the truck seat and pulled out two crowbars. Then, as the skies split and thunder exploded on the pavement and against the metal siding of buildings, they strode side by side along the alley to the back of the Co-op store.

Rain got into Boy's eyes. He struck at the padlock with the crowbar, while Sluddy, protected by his baseball cap, made more delicate moves against the lock. They knew they could bang and pry as recklessly as they wanted to. They howled like wolves whenever the lightning showed them the wounds on the padlock. They made more noise than they needed to, and played a game of timing their strikes with the thunderclaps that followed flashes of lightning, although the whole sky now roared.

At last the link broke away from the eye. Boy and Sluddy could not discern the sound it made, but with a gesture of triumph, Sluddy dropped the broken padlock into a black garbage bag he'd concealed behind his shirt.

They crawled on hands and knees along the aisles in Dry Goods, among bedsheets marked *Factory Seconds*, among plastic shower curtains printed with goldfish blowing bubbles, among bolts of polyester and linen. Through Dry Goods, through Appliances, to Home Entertainment, where they crouched and picked tape recorders and radios off the higher shelves by poking their crowbars under the handles and catching them as they slid down. Boy wrapped them in linen from Dry Goods and stashed them in the garbage bag. Tires hissed on the street outside, but Boy and Sluddy hid behind large TV sets.

On their way back through Dry Goods, Boy spotted a sign advertising indelible marking pens for outdoor use. He grabbed a handful and put them in the pocket of his jacket.

Deep sighs of wind shook rain out of the law office tree as Boy and Sluddy prepared to ascend to the roof. Boy went first and Sluddy stayed below to pulley up the bag of linen-wrapped loot. As Boy embraced the garbage bag dangling from the wet rope, he felt as though someone were behind him, watching him. He turned around. A bit of street light spilled onto the roof. There in the corner were other garbage bags, huddled like the old Mennonite women Boy had seen in photos in history books. There were the lawn chairs, folded, leaning against the brick chimney. There was the box of beer, seemingly whole, but probably so soggy that the bottles would fall through if it were lifted. Had something moved just now, in the shadow of the chimney?

Boy took out his knife. The blade sprang open without a sound. A soft grunt from below. "Bark's slippery," said Sluddy. Wet leaves dripped onto the roof as another sigh swept over the town and Sluddy laboured among the last series of handholds and forked limbs.

Skirting the chimney shadow, Boy stared into it, his knife held out in front of him like a candle. "I thought somebody was up here," he said finally, and stepped into the shadow.

"There's nobody up here." Sluddy limped to the lawn chairs and flicked one open. "Banged my shinbone." He wiped the rain from the chair's nylon webbing with the palm of his hand.

Boy and Sluddy leaned back in their chairs and rested their feet on the facade that rose above the level of the roof. The sky was clotted with black masses of cloud, with stars in between. Tomorrow would be clear, though humid, as the rain evaporated from the fields and lawns. The wind had subsided, though the boys sometimes heard a sigh begin at the poplar grove at the west edge of town, and roll along the damp streets, and then ripple over the roof of the law office, deflected by the facade.

"How high you ever been up, Boy?"

"I've been up in a plane. And up in that thing in Calgary. Hell, Eaton's is higher than this, Slud."

"This is the highest you been in town, though."

"No. I went up the Pool elevator once."

"What happened when you were in the plane, Boy? Did you feel different?"

"Yeah. I felt far away from everything." Boy had felt far away from Little Cornie Kehler. And yet he felt close to Little Cornie when he sat here on the roof and could see the whole night sky. "I got myself a cat today, Slud."

"Did you see people playing harps?"

"I named her Dante."

"You mean, you kidnapped a cat."

"I caught her in the graveyard checkin' out the souls trapped underground." Boy again felt the back of his neck tingle. He tried to look behind him without Sluddy noticing. "That's where cats catch new ones."

"You're full of crap."

Cars swished by down below. Footsteps passed beneath. The stars blinked off, and on, and off again, like eyes moving about the sky, watching Boy and Sluddy from different angles. Boy stood up. He went to the black space behind the chimney and looked into it. A week ago he'd seen Mary-Mac's face at the glass door of the arcade. He'd seen it for only a fragment of a second, and then it had disappeared into the darkness. She'd told him earlier that day at school that she was quitting to spend a year in Costa Rica helping some guy replant a tropical forest. It would be volunteer work, she said. "You work harder when you don't get paid." Boy had laughed and laughed. "Well, I don't blame you for wanting to get away from here," he'd told her. Run away, Mary-Mac, run away. And then he'd seen her looking at him through the glass.

Boy noticed something dark and limp coiled on the roof near the garbage bags. He walked over and bent down and touched it, picked it up, and knew what it was. The pirate's eye-patch had not been lying there the last time he was here, he was certain. It had been up here, though. Where?

Then Boy remembered: he'd used it to tie one of the bags closed when he couldn't find the plastic twist-tie. The night he and Sluddy had done the John Deere dealership. "Slud, you been up here without me? 'D'you look in the bag of Deere stuff?"

"No. Why?"

Boy knew Sluddy was telling the truth. Boy knew where Sluddy was every night, and the nights they weren't in town together, they were in Silvercreek together. Boy opened the garbage bag that had had the eye-patch knotted around it for the past month. He reached in. His hand touched cool metal while puddles in the outer folds of the plastic bag trickled into his lap. "How many chain saws we rip off that time?"

"Four."

They were all there. "Slud, somebody opened this bag. I tied it closed real tight."

"Sparrows," said Sluddy. "Look at all the birdshit all over."

"Uh-uh."

Sluddy's voice turned cold. "You tell anyone about this place, Boy?"

Boy wanted to lie. But—"I told Purina Christina."

"What?!"

"It wouldn't be her!"

"But she told someone else!"

Boy remembered Christina's face between the headrests of the Monte Carlo, her large barn-animal eyes, with white showing beneath the irises. She was a girl with longings for passion, for trust. She wanted to trust, and be trusted, not betray.

A cat wailed on the street below.

"I'm keeping her in the tool-shed until she gets used to me feeding her regularly."

"Who?"

"Everybody who's got cats in Silvercreek has lots of cats. They're always glad to get rid of one."

"Are you sure you didn't open that bag?" Sluddy examined the eye-patch. The leather thong was kinked where the knots had been.

Again, the wailing of the cat floated up to the rooftop. Boy could not see the cat, but imagined a thick-necked male with winter-bitten ears and a scarred nose. "A bridegroom for Dante," whispered Boy to the stars.

"We gotta move this stuff offa here tonight," said Sluddy. He dropped the eye-patch and Boy tied it around his own head. "Later. I can back the truck through there. We can take it to Silvercreek somewhere."

Boy fingered the pens from the Co-op Dry Goods in his jacket pocket. He would wait in the cemetery until the sun was rising over town two miles away. The morning would be clear. He could see more and more stars now with his one eye and the black continents of clouds were drifting further and further apart. In the morning, when the sun was turning the head-stones pink, he would fill in the letters carved on Little Cornie's grave with black indelible ink: *Asleep in Jesus*. And he would fill in *Mutter*, too, and *1896*, because he felt sure she had not lived to be old.

The air was suddenly red and seemed to twist and writhe. Boy thought a spaceship had landed nearby. Or there'd been a melt-down at the nuclear station ninety miles away. The wet leaves of the maple tree sparkled dark red. The glow expanded and intensified. Boy took a pen out of his pocket. A scuffling sound came to him as Sluddy clambered off the roof and down the tree. Boy crawled to the place where Sluddy had disappeared and looked over the edge of the roof. Constable Ridd stood on the ground beneath the tree looking up at Sluddy, who was halfway down, splayed against a stocky limb of maple as though impaled there. Boy sunk to the floor.

Unearthly noises on the street mingled with the red glow of the sighing air around the law office. Whirrs and clicks. An hydraulic ladder poked up above the level of the roof. In a moment Chief Buhler's face slid up with it. His lips were parted in a robot smile.

The cat's cries, further away now, joined in with the twisting red air. "Emmanuel! Emmanuel!" they mocked.

Buhler's hand was on his holster at his hip. "Boy? Had to bring the fire department out to get you, Boy." He stamped his foot on the roof. "Leaks. Herman Barnes came up to check it this morning." While Boy was down the street killing Varghnets, watching the reflection of green in the monitor. "He did not find the chain saws useful. Come on down, Boy."

"See you in hell, Dante," whispered Boy Fehr.

The silver chains on his wrists spun webs of fire in the dark as he descended from the roof.

THE SILVERCREEK CEMETERY SOCIETY

In Splinter-Linter's bush, between some bales we'd drug there, was where we kept the tackle box and the funnel, and the bottles—John A. Macdonald vodka and Five Star rye, mostly, or at least, that's what the labels said. It wasn't all John A. Macdonald and Five Star what was in 'em, though—it was mixtures. Whatever me and Lionel could snitch from our mom and dad's cupboards when they weren't looking we funnelled into the bottles until they were full. And we funnelled in whatever Lizzie Schultz brought us, which wasn't much, and whatever Sammy the Clam brought, which wasn't often but when he did was a lot, because his mom and dad had big parties four or five times a year. Early in the morning, Sammy the Clam would empty all the partials left over from the party into canning jars and put them in an apple box and bring them to the bush in his red wagon. We didn't pay Lizzie and Sammy more than a few cents, so they could buy gum and popsicles, and we could have charged a lot more for the bottles when we sold them to Boy Fehr and his friends, and I wish we would have. Lionel was saving up to buy a Lamborghini and I was saving up to leave

Silvercreek and go to university and study languages. My mom said to stay in Silvercreek would be death, and if I learned to be an interpreter, I could travel a lot and earn good money and meet interesting people. I got good grades in school in French, but I didn't particularly like French. Lionel said he didn't mind living in Silvercreek as long as he had a Lamborghini.

It was one Saturday in fall, on a warm afternoon, that we saw the half-circle of chairs in Billy Schultz's garage. Lionel had counted the chairs when he walked past on the road. Twenty-five, he said. We were in the bush trying out Lionel's new funnel. Splinter-Linter's bush is next to Billy Schultz's long new house. The Lindners' house is on the other side of the bush, but it's set way back from the road about half a kilometre from where we had our hide-out. The bush is thick all around our little clearing, but we snuck up to the edge to look at the chairs. We saw a half-circle of chairs, and a card-table and another chair facing them. On a table at the side was a coffee-maker like they have at weddings and funerals.

"A meeting," I said.

"I know that, Nuthy," said Lionel.

"What kind, do you think?"

"Prayer, probably."

"In a garage?"

We watched for awhile but nobody came out, so we went back to fill our bottles.

The new funnel was smaller than the one we had that was from my dad's shop and had been used for gas and oil and stuff. I'd got to the bush first that afternoon. Through the leaves I saw Lionel coming a long way off. His socks were pulled up over his pants bottoms and showed above the tops of his rubber boots. He had two different boots because he lost one at school and snitched Valerie Wirch's left boot while she was outside clapping blackboard erasers. A long way off I could see him carrying a paper bag (with a bottle in it) and the funnel. The one from my dad's shop was washed, of course, but it was big and if it slipped a little while we were pouring, we lost the rye in the dirt.

So after looking at the chairs, Lionel and me admired the new, smaller funnel and tried it out, and Lionel told me somebody gave it to his sister at her shower last night, but it rolled under the piano bench without her noticing while she opened all the other presents. Lionel snitched it when his mom told him to hand out napkins. His sister forgot she'd ever gotten it. We used it to fill up our partials with the shower leftovers. "Some ladies stayed after and drunk whisky," said Lionel. "At the shower they had coffee and tea in my great-grandma's pots. But my mom's friends took off their shoes after everybody left, and drunk. They had fat feet. My mom was running back and forth cleaning up, and she never knew how much was left in the bottle when the ladies went home. I snitched it right then."

The stuff he'd brought was Black Velvet that comes in a nice box which is useless to us, so he didn't bring it along. We sold Boy Fehr a bottle in a Black Velvet box once, and he acted like it was a real treasure and even tipped us a quarter. Only we found that box laying in the ditch next to the old graveyard the next day. It was windy, and I think it blew there from wherever Boy and his friends were doing their drinking. We quit with the fancy boxes after that because I couldn't stand to see them flattened out and dirty in the ditches around Silvercreek. The funnel worked good—it was plastic.

As soon as we screwed the cap back on the Five Star bottle, which was nearly full now, we heard somebody talking on Billy Schultz's driveway. Lionel and me crawled and duck-walked again through the brush and trees until we were at the edge and could see Schultz's house. The chairs were still there, but now a couple of cars were parked on the road out front and ladies and men in clean almost-Sunday clothes were standing talking to Billy. The people were old, except for Billy, and Lionel whispered to me that two of them were his grandma and grandpa. We went back to our clearing, making sure not to make any noise stepping on sticks.

Splinter-Linters knew me and Lionel hung out in their bush, because my mom made me ask them as soon as they moved in. The bush is at the high end of a slough that's got no use. My dad once told me that Billy Schultz had dumped trucks full of dirt on his property before he built his new house, so it wouldn't flood in spring. In our bush, dead trees keep falling, and branches, during storms, and Lindner never comes to clear it out. Getting the bales in was hard. We snitched them off Billy Schultz's field last year to use for tables or seats.

We counted up our inventory and figured we had twenty-five dollars' worth of stuff left, which we had to get rid of over the next couple of weekends, because we'd be closed for business in the winter. We kept the bottles between the bales, and that's where we kept the money, too. It was all covered up with weeds and branches and long grass, and even nettles.

At Christmas time, my mom and dad get sweet stuff called liqueur as presents from their friends. The bottles they come in are sort of Arabian-shaped with long necks, and crystal knobs instead of caps. I saw a show in town once about a lady who had her hair in a French roll (my mom told me it was a French roll). The lady had fur on her nightgown and pretty bottles of different colours of perfume and stuff in front of her dresser mirror. I'm saving up our special liqueur bottles. Washed and with the labels soaked off, they'll look like the ones on the dresser in the show. I'll put water and food colouring in them, and maybe even perfume, and put them on my dresser. Someday I'll buy real stuff. My hair isn't long enough for a French roll, but I'm growing it.

Lionel pulled his dad's rusty old tackle box out of the crack between the bales. We checked it almost every day to make sure nobody'd ripped it off. While I was counting our money, Lionel said, "Let's take two bucks out and pick up some chips and bars and walk to Rosefield."

He meant walk along the tracks. Whenever we went to walk the tracks, we had a choice of walking to town or walking north to Rosefield. Town was closer, but town wasn't too interesting to us, because it was so easy to get to and because we went to school there. So we usually went north to Rosefield. We'd never walked all the way to Rosefield, but we were always walking along the tracks to Rosefield. It was like going down a quiet path through the countryside. Lionel finds pieces of glass, which he puts in his pocket to take home for his collection. Trains only come through once or twice a week. Lionel sometimes says he might move away from Silvercreek to be a mechanic in Rosefield. Not me, I say. I'm going to live in lots of different places in the world. He says, well, this is a place in the world. And I say, and here I am, *now*. But not forever.

I straightened all the bills while I counted, even though they'd been straightened a million times before. "You mean really walk to Rosefield?" I asked.

Lionel said, "Maybe." He always said that.

I gave Lionel two dollars and he put it in his pocket.

Just then, all of a sudden, a whole bunch of people laughed very loud in Billy Schultz's garage, as if somebody'd told a quick joke. Lionel and me nearly flew through the bush to get to the edge. We were a little careless about snapping twigs then.

The chairs were full of people now. Billy Schultz stood in front of the people, facing them. He had a paper in his hand. Even from here in the bush I could see that most of the people were old.

Then just like that I remembered I'd seen a half-circle of chairs like that before.

And then Billy Schultz said, "Well, I guess it's time to get down to serious business. As chairman, I now call the second annual meeting of the Silvercreek Cemetery Society to order. I see new faces out there today. Welcome."

About a year ago, my dad told me to go to Fehrs' house to

bring back a socket set he'd borrowed. I didn't want to do it—everybody said Mrs. Fehr was crazy. My mom said not to be scared of her, she was just a victim and deep down a nice lady. Boy let me in the back door. I wanted just to hand him the socket set and leave, but when I tried to give it to him, he wouldn't take it. He walked back into the kitchen and said, "Come in." So I followed him and put the socket set down on the table. I heard a voice coming from the next room and through a door I saw a half-circle of people in the living-room, sitting in chairs. The voice was somebody reading. I moved to a part of the kitchen where the people in the chairs couldn't see me. The house smelled like coffee and on the kitchen counter was a wooden tray filled with yellow cheese and fig newtons covered with saran wrap. Boy had a tomato sandwich in his hand. "You want one?" he said. I said, "No thank you," and started to leave. Then he pointed to the living-room with his sandwich and said, "Silvercreek Cemetery Society. They're starting a new graveyard, where the church used to be. My dad says there's enough people who call Silvercreek home to be buried here. He wants me to bury him here. I'll get you a Pepsi." And then Boy went into the basement to get a Pepsi even though I said no thank you. In the living-room a man was praying. In between his sentences there was coughing, and people sliding their bums around on the hard dining-room chairs, and the percolator beside the stove saying its own coffee-smelling prayer.

And then Boy came back upstairs and gave me the Pepsi. He whispered something to me right there in the middle of the praying: "Give you five dollars if you snitch a bottle of your dad's rye for me."

Lionel and me sat in the bushes and listened to Billy Schultz lead the meeting. The money from the tackle box was still in my hand. Branches poked us in funny places, and I saw a black beetle crawl up Lionel's knee. "We'll start her off by reading the minutes of last year's meeting, and then we'll have Dave Fehr give the treasurer's report."

The coffee-maker on the side table was bigger than Mrs. Fehr's percolator. A red light was on at the bottom of the coffee-maker, meaning the coffee was done. Beside it were trays covered with shiny saran wrap, probably cheese and cookies, I thought. Not all the people in the Silvercreek Cemetery Society were old. I was surprised to see Valerie Wirch's older sister in one of the chairs. She's nineteen and expecting a baby. There was a live baby there, sitting on a lady's lap. Boy's mom and dad were there, and Mrs. Schultz, and my dad's Aunt Louise. Splinter-Linter Lindner was sitting at the end of the half-circle, facing me and Lionel. We called them Splinter-Linters because when they moved to the village I heard my dad say they belonged to a small, weird church group that had splintered off from the main Mennonite church, and they held their services in the Silvercreek community hall on Sunday mornings when everyone else went to church in town.

Look at the women in this village, Nuthy—hermits, drug addicts, religious fanatics, child abusers. The young girls get pregnant so they can run off with their white knights, who are usually alcoholics. And the ones who aren't hermits, drug addicts, religious fanatics, or child abusers, who consider themselves to be normal, healthy, strong women, get their biggest thrills going to town Saturday nights with their daughters to watch their sons play hockey. To stay in Silvercreek is death.

My mom's a sweater-maker. She used to live in Churchill where she made fancy sweaters for a trading post that sells them to tourists and even sends them mail-order to customers all over the world. She still makes sweaters for Churchill, and says she's gonna go back there to live again someday. She doesn't say what she's gonna do with my dad. But she says the north is a good place for women.

Looking at the ladies sitting in the half-circle of chairs, I didn't think they were nearly all hermits or drug addicts or religious fanatics or child abusers. Of course, I couldn't really know for sure. Sometimes you don't know what's really going on with a person. My mom told me about that, too.

". . . nineteen members last year," Dave Fehr was saying. "Looks like quite a few more this year. At twenty dollars per member, we can pay Peter Pankratz a small honorarium to do the maintenance work at the site. This past year he donated his services. . . . "

Lionel nudged me with his elbow. "Peter Pankratz—does he mean Silent Peter who lives at the other end of the village?"

"They can't mean him," I said. Silent Peter Pankratz lived with his old mom and dad in an old, ramshackle house at the north end of Silvercreek. Lionel had told me that Silent Peter never talked, and never left the house, except to go to the toilet, and even then he kept his face covered with *Country Guide.* Lionel said he never went anywhere without covering his face with *Country Guide,* and no one had ever seen his face. "Maybe Silent Peter's dad's name is Peter," I said. "Maybe they mean him."

"Yeah, must be."

And I thought, not only women are hermits in Silvercreek.

Billy Schultz stood up again. "The paperwork and all the red tape is done, I'm happy to report. We need to make a decision here today as to when to hold a consecration ceremony. Dave Fehr, our secretary, has purchased a record book which will be formally opened, inscribed, and signed at the ceremony."

"I wonder if they'll have food there, too," I said.

"If they do, I'm going," said Lionel. "I thought secretaries were ladies."

"Could we form a committee to provide refreshments at the ceremony?"

A gust of wind flapped the leaves around in the bush and for a few minutes we couldn't hear what anybody was saying.

When it died down, Billy Schultz was saying something about questions.

"Let's go," said Lionel.

"Not yet."

The lady with the baby got up to ask a question, and the baby, who could walk already, toddled away while she was talking. The baby came out onto the lawn between us and the garage. The lady had a very quiet voice and we couldn't hear her question.

Lionel nudged me again. "Look," he said, and he pointed to the field across the road from Schultz's. A dust-devil was corkscrewing across the field towards the garage where the meeting was happening. Those little twisters always remind me of foxes hunting, the way they wander at a quick lope, churning up dust, as if they're hunting. By the time it got to Billy Schultz's, it was just a wind with a little dust, but a pretty good wind. The baby fell down on his rear on the grass. His mom was still talking, but she kept looking at her boy, and finally Joe Splinter-Linter got up from his chair and walked slow and casual over to the baby. Another lady, maybe the baby's grandma, followed him. Mr. Lindner helped the baby up, and then the grandma took him back to the garage.

Lionel and me stayed frozen in the bush. But all of a sudden that Splinter-Linter Lindner was right in front of us, and we knew we couldn't turn and run without making an awful lot of commotion, and besides, he'd see us for sure. But I guess he saw us all along, because he reached into the trees and parted the branches and leaves and said, "Come."

We backed away on our knees. Lionel shook his head. "Come. Come," Lindner said again, in a really dangerous voice, low and quiet. And he stared at us hard with dangerous eyes. And I knew we had to go. I turned my back to him and started to shove the tackle-box money into my jeans pocket, but then that Joe Splinter-Linter Lindner grabbed mine and Lionel's arms, not hard, but sort of pulled us out of the bush. "Come and have lunch with us," he said.

We could see that the meeting part was over and the people were out of their chairs getting coffee, and the saran wrap was off the trays.

"I found some more guests," said Lindner. He had his hands on our backs. We all walked across the lawn to Billy Schultz's garage. Some people said hi. Lionel's grandpa cuffed him on the chin. But most of them there, even my Great-Aunt Louise, didn't pay much attention, they were so busy stuffing their faces—yellow cheese, soda crackers, brownies, puffed-wheat cake. I couldn't see any fig newtons.

Lindner pushed us down on some chairs. I didn't look at Lionel and he didn't look at me. I knew he was thinking we should have gone when he said let's go.

Lindner asked us how we wanted our coffee, and even though it was far too hot for coffee and I would rather have had root beer or lemonade, I said cream and Lionel said cream and sugar, and Lindner brought us each a styrofoam cupful, and gave Lionel four sugar cubes.

Well, this wasn't too bad, sitting and drinking coffee with the Silvercreek Cemetery Society. Lionel really got into it and dunked his sugar cubes into the coffee and sucked on them. I even got up and went to the trays for cheese and puffed-wheat cake. But what kept bothering me was the way Splinter-Linter had looked at us when he called us out of the bush. It hadn't been a friendly invitation. He seemed mad or something. Maybe he was mad because we were spying, even though it wasn't a secret meeting, or even private, if Valerie Wirch's pregnant sister could be here.

While we were sitting there stuffing our faces along with all the rest of them, some standing, some sitting, everybody yapping, but not about graveyards as far as I could tell, Dave Fehr went around with a clipboard and talked to everybody, and they gave him cheques and money, which he put into something like a big wallet, and he wrote things on the paper on the clipboard. Boy Fehr's mom sat on her chair with a melting brownie on a napkin in her lap and kind of stared off across the field like she was waiting for another dust-devil to come hunting.

Lionel finished his sugar cubes, and then he downed the rest of his coffee. "Ready?" he said to me. "Let's go walk to Rosefield."

Just then the baby came waddling to me, waddling like a duck and bubbling spit down his chin. He grabbed my knee and held onto it with his funny fat fingers, and I wiped the spit away with my napkin.

That baby was a real nice kid and I really got into playing with him. After a while I even picked him up and held him on my lap and wiggled the rag doll he'd brought along. I wished I knew his name.

Then Billy Schultz went back to his card-table and said to the group, "Today's business is now complete. Committees have been formed for the various duties for the coming year. . . . "

What kind of duties does a cemetery society have, except to die and be buried?

". . . we have nine new members. Let us close today's meeting with a prayer. Dave?"

All of a sudden, "*Eleven* new members!" somebody yelled. Joe Lindner came from the back of the garage and clapped his hand on mine and Lionel's shoulders. "I think these two visitors would like to be the youngest members of the Silvercreek Cemetery Society!"

He was talking loud. The baby on my lap started to cry and the mother came and got him.

"No thank you," I said.

"No thank you," said Lionel.

But Splinter-Linter kept his hands on us. "I think it would be a wonderful gesture for two of Silvercreek's future citizens and leaders to show their devotion to our community by joining this honourable society today."

I'm not going to die here! I don't want to be buried here! To stay in Silvercreek is death!

"I have to ask my parents," said Lionel.

"Oh, do you?" said Splinter-Linter.

And then I couldn't believe it, he took his hand off Lionel's shoulder and reached down and pulled the tackle-box money right out of my pocket, where I guess it had been sticking out the whole time. "Look!" he yelled. "They brought their membership dues with them!"

"That's ours," said Lionel.

But I knew the jig was up.

"Thirty dollars! A little short, but I think we could give you youngsters a special rate—twenty-five percent off." Splinter-Linter passed the whole wad to Dave Fehr. "Write it down, Dave. You know their names."

Dave Fehr cleared his throat. He smiled at us sort of embarrassed like and said, "Uh—Nuthy? Lionel? Should I put your names down?"

Lionel must have figured it out, too, because he just sat there hanging his head, staring at his knees, so I just nodded and stared at my knees, too. Everybody in the garage was quiet. And then the prayer started, but I didn't feel like praying. I lifted my head and saw that Boy's mom wasn't praying, either. She was watching me with a sad look on her face.

We got to the tracks by walking across Schultz's bale field. Way above, hawks floated on the warm air looking for mice. Ahead of us on the track some little birds went tsip! tsip! and poked around 'mong the pebbles. The track was old. The ties were nearly dust and the rails had wobbles in them. Sometimes we found rusty spikes laying between the crumbly ties. I picked up pebbles—a blue one, a dark green one, one that was red the colour of the seats of the show-hall in town, a royal purple—and rolled them around together in my fist. Sometimes we found bones, the dry, dead bones of pigs and calves that foxes and stray dogs had dropped there.

We didn't have any chips or bars. Even if we hadn't eaten all that puffed-wheat cake in Billy Schultz's garage, we wouldn't have been in the mood for chips and bars. Lionel mostly said two things: we should have gone when he said, and it isn't fair. And I knew he was worrying about his Lamborghini, that he wouldn't have earned it by the time he was eighteen like he dreamed about.

I guess I should have gone when he wanted to both times. But how could I know? How could I know that Splinter-Linter saw us peeking at him out of his bush? How could I know that he'd found the bottles and the funnel and the money and figured everything out?

But it scared me the way everything happened. The way it was all taken away from us just like that, and we had to just sit there and not say anything and stare at our knees like dumb bananas. I knew Splinter-Linter had made a deal with us, making us buy memberships instead of telling our parents. Me, I would rather have my mom and dad find out than be forced to die in Silvercreek.

Lionel didn't pick up any glass, even though we walked further than we ever had before, got closer to Rosefield than we ever had, and saw lots of pieces of glass.

We'd walked quite a long time when Lionel dug into his pocket and pulled out the money we'd saved for chips and bars. "Here's two bucks," he said. "What do you want to blow it on?"

"Save it and start again next summer, somewhere else," I said, even though I knew we probably never would.

So I've been sitting here behind this hedge in my back yard for quite a while now, since we got back from the railroad tracks.

It's getting dark. I'm pretty sure my mom saw me coming down the road—she's almost always sitting at a window, working on her sweaters. She'll call me when it's time. And then, somehow, I'll have to tell her what happened today, about the half-circle of chairs, and about the Silvercreek Cemetery Society.

SAHARA

The summer that the spring grasses turned yellow under a sun that had drawn nearer and a sky that never lowered its lulling curtain of rain was the summer I got Mariechje. An Ethiopia crept through Silvercreek like a gaunt lizard, beginning in Billy Schultz's high pasture at the south end and claiming victory even in the deepest part of the creek bed next to the old cemetery. The folks who walked along the cut of road between Silvercreek's primeval poplars pushed their way against hot winds that swept the silica dust from south to north. Cotton clung thinly to legs and arms as they fought against the wind. Faces stared through wisps of chiffon scarf held by bony hands to keep the sharp-edged dust away from the eyes. Keeping the eyes clear became triumph and salvation in those dry days.

I couldn't keep my fingernails clean. When I changed my clothes, when I drove to town to buy cool green grapes, when I stroked the wretched cat, the crescent of grey-brown dust returned like the tarnish on my silver coffee spoons. My mother loved to manicure my nails when I was a girl. The touching our fingers did those late Saturday afternoons after bath were more reassuring than the hugs before bedtime, far more comforting than my father's awkward palm patting my head when I got a good grade in math or when I remembered to clean the grooves in the tread of my sneakers on muddy days. Sometimes my mother took out her leatherette case and did my hands when she sensed I'd had a bad day at school. Or she'd had a bad day at home. Sparks would fly from the stainless-steel points on those days.

Every night of the dry summer, in the kitchen, I stripped off the heat of day and rinsed my raggish clothes in a big, square washtub I'd found in the old summerhouse. The sound of the water and the way the fabric swam helped cool away the scorching afternoons. I liked the feel of the water on my forearms and the press of the washtub metal against my thighs. I never did it when Robert was around, though. He wasn't home much that summer—the lab at the canola-oil plant in town was air-conditioned, and he worked there most evenings as well as days, leaving me to fend off the siege on my own. My ritual in the kitchen was imperative and secret and silent. I still think about it now when I remember that old cottage in the grove.

Mariechje was from town. "I say meen maun it's not so far. He thinks it's not so close. But we found your hoose not so hard." Mariechje was a Mexican Mennonite. Her mother and father had been born in Canada, but had emigrated with thousands of other Mennonites to Mexico to search for more freedom and more land. But it didn't take long for them to run out of space there, too. The second and third generations slowly trickled back to Canada. Some returned because the snakes scared them. Most came back because they'd heard that Canada was a rich country.

Mariechje and her husband were among the last to migrate to the fertile river valley in which Silvercreek lay. "We been here now seven year. Meen maun he knew your hoosebount's grandpa. Grandpa was old teacher on colony. Yah." Those who remained on the colony would die there, and their offspring would be forced to marry cousins or be absorbed into the Spanish and Indian cultures of Mexico.

Her maun and my hoosebount—they were the men in our lives she could speak about the first time we met. Her man drove a vintage Lincoln Continental and smoked rollies and did not get out of the car when she came the first time to make the deal with me. I never had much to do with him. Sometimes I saw him buying cigarette paper at the Payfair Saturday nights. I'd see the black Lincoln parked out front, and inside at the counter a slim, dark, young-looking man wearing a string tie and a Western shirt with pearl buttons. He'd look at me out of the corner of his eye and nod, and pay for his Black Cats. On his way out, he'd amble past me and with graceful, almost feminine fingers he'd defiantly tuck the dollar bills into his back pocket, instead of putting them into the trucker's wallet on the other hip. While he breathed fire, I cooled my tongue with grapes chilled in a bowl of ice, and waited for strawberry season.

Mariechje was my soldier, fighting the drought for me. All day as I worked at Mullers' Greenhouse showering seedlings and trying to interest despairing gardeners in buying exotic trees for their patios, dust was invading our leaky, ninety-year-old house built by Robert's grandfather when Silvercreek was just a promise. Surrounded now by dirt-drifts and pigweed and thistle, it was no longer a palace of promise nor a fortress of defence. I couldn't bear to sweep up the dust every day. I heard its rasp like a death-rattle under the dishes I set on the table when I laid supper. I felt it under my thumbs when I opened the windows after sunset. It was under my fingernails.

Only the bush rabbits in the shaded perennial garden seemed not to suffer. Their home was underneath the summerhouse. They were abundant, and I loved to watch them frolic around the maple trunks in the evenings.

"We need a good zudda-rain," Mariechje would say when I handed her her weekly cheque. "Slow and long. Yah." Mariechje had seven houses, she was proud of telling me. Eight if you counted her family's tiny, overflowing cottage. Six in town and the one here in Silvercreek. Her daughter Sarah—she pronounced it *Zarra*, richly rolling the r—helped her clean for the upper crust of the big town—a doctor and a lawyer, of course, a couple of corporate farm owners, the president of the canola-oil plant, a retired John Deere dealer. She never talked about their houses, about their possessions, but she liked to talk about their schedules, which were consequently her schedules. She called them by their first names, as though they were her children. "Brenda, she has shower for neighbour daughter next Saturday. Two days I clean next week for her, Thursday and Friday. So I tell Jake and Helen I come there next week Wednesday in the morning, but they don't like that. They have at their house Bible study Friday, and Wednesday is too soon to still be clean Friday. I tell her Saturday morning or Wednesday morning. So. And John and Freda they go Shtates this week, so I have half day off. Yah. See this rink? Last time they go to Shtates they give it me."

Wednesday afternoon was my slot. When I got home from the greenhouse at 4:30, I'd see Mariechje's old white Dodge on the driveway. Sarah would slip into a shadow or into a different room when I walked into the kitchen, which was the last room they did. Sarah was not much more than a shadow herself. She was slender and dark-haired like her father and had his guarded brown eyes. Mariechje was plump and bright-eyed and fair. Her day-clothes were the cast-off summer luncheon dresses of Brenda and Helen and Freda. Sarah wore remnants of past fads which she bought at the second-hand store in town with her share of the cleaning money. The clothes often fit poorly, but Sarah was so much the same, inside those clothes every time I saw her, she reminded me of a mannequin that had been dressed by a destitute shopkeeper—mechanical, expressionless, rigid. She'd look past me when I greeted her and murmur something like hello, but it wasn't quite.

The first time Sarah and I exchanged words was around two o'clock on a Wednesday afternoon. While rearranging marigolds at the greenhouse I tried to decide what kind of cold dish I could make for supper. Robert could not stand to eat hot meals in hot weather. I called Mariechje at my house to ask her if there was a can of tuna in the cupboard. I hated stopping to buy groceries on my way home from work—I was hot and sticky and grimy, and once I was in my air-conditioned car I felt an urgent need to get home as quickly as I could.

"Yah, hallo?"

I hadn't been sure she would answer someone else's telephone. "Mariechje? This is Mrs.—Jane. I want to make tuna salad for supper and I don't want to stop at the store. Could you please see if there's a can of tuna in the cupboard?"

Silence. Then, "Pardon?"

I explained it all again, rearranging the order a little, speaking more slowly, describing the location of the cupboard.

"Just a minute," she said brightly.

I waited a long time. Too long.

A soft, timid, "Hello?" whispered through my receiver. "Hello, my mom? She doesn't really know what you want."

I wanted to hang up. But they might be insulted or embarrassed. "Sarah, I want a can of tuna. You know, fish." *Fesh* was the Low German word. "So you know what to look for?" And I again sketched the map in her ear.

"I think I know."

I waited again, this time not as long.

"Yes, I have it here," said Sarah breathlessly. "Now what should I do?"

The more I saw Mariechje and Sarah work together, the more Sarah became in my mind a robot creature. She took orders immediately and without question or comment. Her expression seldom changed and she never joined in a conversation. She lurked.

Someone else lurked in my starving gardens and on my grey veranda that summer, another shadow. He was an old stooped man, and on sultry days I swear I could smell him before I saw him—a stale, sweet smell, sweat scented with herbs and vitamins, Wonder Oil lingering in a shirt laundered in cheap, decades-old detergent, cloying aftershave freshly splashed, Juicy Fruit gum over raw onions, age-soaked shoe-leather. But most of the time the first I knew of his arrival was the sound of the broom on the veranda. The particles of grey-white dust would swell up in front of the windows looking into the porch, regroup, and settle again within twenty minutes. If the wind came through the poplars, the billowing was more turbulent, and old dust was replaced with new. The old man swept with all the vigour he could muster and I sometimes thought he would fly away in the tumult, like Dorothy in a Kansas tornado.

He never knocked on the door. If I didn't come out at the sound of the broom on the floorboards, he would set the broom in the corner and creep down into the yard, where he might pull some pigweed or pick up a branch that had fallen in the wind.

He would turn at the slam of the screen door. "I didn't mean to disturb you."

"That's what fathers are for."

He despised cynicism. "My, your peonies are beautiful. Mother would have enjoyed them."

The peonies were pathetic, shrivelled and droopy. And my mother's enjoyment of flowers had never been genuine, he'd imposed it on her, had dressed her in flowers like a child dresses a doll.

"Someone has thrown a beer bottle onto your lawn. People are so thoughtless."

We had a stack of empties in the summerhouse, hidden from him and from the cleaning woman, and from Silvercreek in general. I had taken a six-pack out the night before and the box had broken.

"You might wish to dispose of it." He handed me the bottle.

Sometimes I switched to his language. "Perhaps it wasn't someone's thoughtlessness. Perhaps one of the neighbours' dogs went through some trash somewhere and carried it here. I can't believe anyone would deliberately throw it into our yard."

He wagged his pedant's finger beside his ear. "Ah! You may be right. Has it happened before?"

"Well, one morning we found an empty box of fishsticks over there in the bush." Our house was at the edge of a wild grove of maples and willows and Siberian elm several acres big. "Do you think anyone would deliberately throw a box of fishsticks into our bush?"

We watched a sparrow bob along the footpath to where the cat's dish of food pellets nestled near the side of the house. I'd noticed sparrows eating unashamedly from her bowl all spring and thought I should throw crumbs and seeds out for them. The desert provided as little for birds as it did for my soul. But letting them have the cat food took less energy, less sweat.

I knew my father was searching for a way to get around my sarcasm. I wished just once he would confront it, show some anger, allow my anger. He'd tethered my mother, and for a time me as well, to silence and darkened rooms with cruel threads of cotton-candy saintliness.

He continued in his slow, cracked voice like the slow cracks in the dry land that lay between us.

> Even the sparrow finds a home
> And the swallow a nest for herself,
> where she may lay her young,
> at thy altars. . . .

"My, I haven't thought of that verse for a long time. It's a Psalm, eighty-four." He bent over to watch the ants gathering sap from the last peony bud. "I must study it when I get home. It goes on to mention the Baca Valley, which was a very dry valley, and that the pilgrims passing through it brought an unseasonal nourishing rain because of the blessedness of their journey." He smiled at the sparrow, now perched on the edge of the bowl seeking the oldest, softest chunks. "And where are your swallows? Nesting in the porch again?"

"No. They're on the north side under the eaves this year. Away from the hot wind. This is the first time since we've lived here that we haven't had swallows on the veranda. I hate it. I just hate it!" My flat, clay words fell against his Psalm and echoed in the parched creek bed and in the wild grove, and frightened off the sparrow.

"We must try to adjust. The rain will come."

"I'm afraid it won't. Doesn't the sun seem closer? I'm afraid the Earth is beginning to die. It won't rain."

"It will. Someday. You should get Robert to poison the rabbits. They're eating the corn."

On a Wednesday in early June, I came home a little earlier than usual. Business was slow, despite the sale prices. No one wanted to invest in a flower anymore. When I turned into the driveway, I saw Sarah sitting on the ground under a weeping birch tree, painting the back of her hand with the pollen of a tiger-lily. Her knees were spread and her skirt fell between them like a nursery-rhyme petticoat. One of my wide-brimmed hats was on her head. Behind her, a rabbit was frozen against a stand of lavender irises.

Sarah looked a little frightened when I drove up, but she didn't move. "How does your garden grow?" I said to her on my way to the front veranda.

She smiled, and was at once so unlike the robot-Sarah I was used to, I wanted to take her hands in mine and perform a ring-around-the-rosy dance with her right there in the withering grass. The rabbit darted into the thicker bushes beyond the irises.

The kitchen floor was wet. Mariechje was under the table on hands and knees peeling a spot of dried strawberry jam off the linoleum. "Almost finished," she chirped. "Now that takes not so long. The dust is not so much anymore."

"The fields have crops and weeds growing on them now. Keeps the dust down. Sarah found a place in the shade."

"She say she feel sick. I take your hat, I give it her. Is okay?"

"Quite okay," though why she needed the hat to wear in the shade, I wasn't sure. I tiptoed across the room to turn on the big square floor fan. "You can turn this on when you're working," I told Mariechje. "Keep you cool." I sat on the countertop and propped my bare feet on the back of a chair. The calendar on the opposite wall flashed a message. "Oh Lord, Father's Day is in June. What am I going to do with my dad? Do you celebrate Father's Day?"

"We have gathering."

"No presents? Doesn't Sarah buy him a tie or socks or something?" I wanted Mariechje to laugh, to picture her maun receiving a new string tie every year. But her face was stony, and I realized I was getting too personal. "I don't know what to do with my dad. He always gives me back the presents I buy him and tells me to find someone who can really make use of them. He thinks he's being virtuous and self-sacrificing, but actually he's being very unkind to the giver of the gifts."

"What about your mama?"

"She's dead."

"Kencer?"

"No. She took too many sleeping pills. She was seventy-two."

Mariechje clicked her tongue. "Na, na. Sleeping I can do. I never take no pills."

We would not talk about my mama taking the pills on purpose. We would pretend she just wanted very badly to sleep.

121

"Have gathering," said Mariechje. "Maybe is enough."

We would gather up anger, gather forgiveness, or just all the loose ends left untied in the old man's life and present him with an empty package with a nice bow. Because he'd never taken both my hands in his and squeezed them and said, I'm afraid, or, I need you, or even, Jane, I love you. "Maybe I'll give him a dead rabbit," I said.

That set Mariechje giggling, and soon we both laughed across the mottled damp floor while she packed her caddy of rags and cleaners and brushes. "Dead rabbit," she would mutter, and giggle some more.

Sarah came in and put the hat back on the same hook where they'd found it. In Low German, Mariechje gave her a sharp order I could not quite catch. Sarah, her back to us, stiffened, her hand still on the crown of the hat. Mariechje spoke again, louder, and Sarah took the hat and walked quickly across the kitchen floor, skirting the damp spots. She dropped to her knees in front of her mother and reached into the caddy of cleaners. With a bottle of ammonia she dampened a clean rag and began to wipe out the inside of my hat. "Oh, you don't need to do that," I started to say, but Mariechje was pinning Sarah to the task with her stare, and when the girl had finished and had put the cloth and the bottle in their proper places, she hurried back to the entrance and hung the hat on the empty hook. Did her mother think she'd dirtied it, poisoned it? Did she think I had those fears? But it seemed to have nothing to do with either the hat or me. It had to do with Sarah's need to obey.

When they'd left, I sat and watched the floor dry for a long time.

On the way to my father's house in town, I saw one of Silvercreek's setters trotting across a cultivated strip of ground next to the road. Hardly anything was coming out of the ground, just short, spiky pigweed here and there, and when the setter lifted his paws one by one, dust puffed up around them, though the dog was thin and his feet slender. I thought of mustangs crossing the floor of a desert canyon, of camels striding along the crest of a sand dune. But even desert sand did not form the same fine billowy clouds, half dust, half smoke, as dry valley topsoil when it was disturbed. My car roared past and the setter halted with one paw raised. He watched me go by, then began to frolic in the dirt. A young dog, I thought, lost for the day, out for an adventure. The last I saw of him in my mirror he was biting at the dust clouds that his playing raised.

I could not look at the sun, but I was aware of its nearness, its swollen heat poised in the Earth's bleached, ransacked atmosphere. I put on my sunglasses and the sky darkened.

My father's porch was a pre-cast concrete unit of steps—four—and a platform enclosed by a wrought-iron railing. All was immaculate, no broom was in sight. I stood in front of the door for a few seconds and looked down at his tidy geranium beds, which he nurtured with every scrap of water left over from his daily chores and ablutions—cooking water, rinse water, water collected by the dehumidifier in the basement, even the water that ran off his car when he hosed off the dust on Saturdays. He encircled the car with pans and pails so as little as possible would soak uselessly into the crushed rock beneath. The geranium bed was covered with a mulch of dead plants to keep the moisture in. His lawn, like mine, was merely straw.

Before I could knock, he came to the door. On his head was my mother's straw hat, which he wore for only one ritual a year. "Oh! Strawberries? There are strawberries this year?" I could not keep the joy and relief out of my voice.

He waved two baskets and smiled evangelically, squeezing his faded grey eyes so that they wrinkled in the corners. His lips pressed together as they would when he greeted worshippers in a church receiving line. "I heard it on the radio this morning. Picking all day today. I don't know how Henry managed it in this heat wave. One would not wish to think he'd broken watering restrictions. . . ." He stared down at a pink geranium for a moment. Then he looked at me and shrugged. "Well, perhaps the Lord has chosen to bless us with berries during this drought. Would you like to ask me to pick some for you?"

I gave him back his preacher's smile. "No," I said sweetly, though my desire for strawberries nearly robbed my answer of its scorn. "I don't want you to stay out in the heat that long. I just came to get your laundry."

Before he drove away he polished the door handles of my car with his sleeve.

Mother had never quite been able to surrender my old room. I'd taken all my sentimental favourites with me when I'd moved out, but stuffed toys that had never belonged to me as a child perched on the stark spare-bedroom furniture. Teddy bears were out of style when I was little but had made a comeback a few years before she died. The one on the empty wicker basket in the corner sat adorned with the bangles my father had not allowed her to wear and a bright green leprechaun's hat she'd won at a sidewalk sale. A fuzzy poodle that strutted and yapped stood in front of the garish bear. Ancient *Miss Chatelaine*s lay in a neat stack beside them. Two cheap A.Y. Jackson prints on the wall over the spare bed reminded me of my father's futile attempt to pacify my mother with art in her last desperate years, though he did not believe in art, except for useful crafts like quilting and pillowcase embroidery. Other walls held frames and frames of family snapshots, mostly of me.

Two new things had been added to the spare room: a bookcase, my father's, filled with Bible commentaries and paperback testimonials. His own den-bedroom had grown too small for his collection, and my mother's room was precisely as she'd left it. I expected her precious sachets had by now stopped giving off their scents in her deserted drawers. The other new thing in my old room was pails full of hoarded, cloudy water.

The air smelled fetid, swamp-like. They didn't fit. My father was a sanitary man. You never saw a hair in his sink or a smudge or a speck in his kitchen. At this time, when everyone had layers of silt on their windowsills, there was none on his. The pails were not even covered.

Before I left the room to find the laundry bag and search for clues about Father's Day gifts, I looked at the photographs beside the door. In one of them, I was sitting under the weeping birch, now dead, in the back yard, wearing the same hat Sarah had borrowed three days earlier. I'd had dark, nursery-rhyme tresses in those days, too, and if I looked closely, I could almost make out orange pollen stains on my slim, innocent fingers as I pulled on a curl of hair beneath my chin. Only my mother would have taken such a picture, a dream picture of her vision of herself. I was never quite able to reach her after I became an adult, though I have no idea when exactly the bath-time ritual stopped. She was kept apart from me by a barrier of illness and bright red capsules. She lived a fuzzy secret life inside photographs and memories of bears I'd never had.

I looked into the other rooms. My father had nothing, which was everything, which was exactly what he wanted.

Before I pushed open the front door to leave, I saw a fly buzzing around the screen. I let it in for my father to catch in his chloroform jar. He hated to squash things in the house.

"I saw you on the highway last Saturday, in your other car. The whole family hanging out of the windows. What were you doing?" There'd been a child on the roof of the Lincoln, a child on the hood, and several more sitting on the window rims, their heads extending above the roof and swivelling like robots. All the children were blond like their mother, except for Sarah, whose face I saw looking at me through the rear window as I pulled up behind them. Mariechje's husband in his white shirt was at the wheel with his left elbow draped out the open window. The rolled-up sleeves exposed a slender arm, prettily etched, not thickly, with black hair. I passed the Lincoln slowly. From the arm my eyes moved to the man's face. He looked straight ahead and seemed oblivious to the clutter of dishevelled cotton prints and tow-hair and bony limbs around him. His face was much like the one I'd just seen framed in the rear window, except that his was masterful and arrogant, while hers was almost entirely vacant. At first I'd thought they were collecting empty bottles from the ditches, but the ditches were drifted over, and few things came in returnable bottles anymore.

Mariechje was working alone at my house today. Sarah was sick, she said, and so it was taking her longer to finish. Robert would be home from the canola lab soon. "From wheel lets loose—you know what. . . ." She made a dish-like gesture with her hand.

"Hub-cap?"

"Hup-cap. We look for that. Look and look. And Zarra, she have hat like that." Mariechje pointed to mine still in the place Sarah had left it. "Her money, I give it her, and she buy in town hat, something like it. It fly away when we look for hup-cap, so we look for hup-cap and hat, and we find hup-cap. . . ."

"But not *her* cap?"

"Not her cap. So. We find beer bottles. My boys get cash at Payfair, buy cap-guns."

"Why wouldn't you find her hat? It would be easy to see out on the fields."

"It blow into corn."

"The corn is so short and thin, I'll bet she could find it. It wouldn't roll far."

"My boys, they look tomorrow on way to beet-weeding."

When Mariechje had finished wiping the refrigerator, I went and got the crystal bowl of cold grapes and offered her some. She shook her head.

"You have six children?"

"Yah, six."

"Sarah's the oldest?"

She nodded, but her body seemed to stiffen, and her face became passive and secretive, like the week before when I'd asked her about Father's Day.

"No babies at home?" I said.

"John and Freda have also six. It is something to clean there, I say you. Not so hard though. John and Freda take whole bunch to Disneyland next Christmas."

"C'mon, Mariechje, I bet you've got a couple of little ones at home," I teased.

"No babies." She was nervous now, moving around the room like a caged cat, flicking her rag at light switches and door-frames and baseboards. "What you get for Fadder's Day?" she flung out.

"Mariechje, can't you have any more children?"

She drew the mop and pail in from the hallway, nearly upsetting the tepid, soapy water. "Doctor say no."

"Well, that's okay. Six is lots, isn't it?"

"Okay by me. Meen maun . . ." She shook her head.

"He wants more?"

She stopped her cleaning and straightened up and, one hand on her hip, looked at me with impatience in her eyes, and something more than impatience—her face looked as though it were on the verge of grief.

"Oh," I said. "He wants more. . . . Well, there are things you can do about that, aren't there?"

I heard a car door close somewhere. Through the window above the sink I saw my father coming towards the house in his strawberry hat. His arms cradled a bright turquoise bowl of red fruit. While I watched him walk stooped and unhurried along the driveway, I imagined Mariechje's dark and handsome and virulent hoosebount, quietly, in the crowded houseful of children, quietly and forcefully seducing her every night in a hot, white bed.

"So. My Zarra, I give him her."

My father stood on the porch. I turned back to look at Mariechje. Her floor-mop went over and over the same spot of floor, over and over.

Knocking, gentle, careful.

I give him her.

My mind tumbled over other things she'd said like that. "She give it me." "Her money, I give it her."

I give him her. In that crowded houseful of children? Give? And repay her with a cheap sun-hat? A white sleeve rolled up on a hairy forearm, orange pollen staining a sweet childish hand, a graceful curve of chain across a slender, masculine hip. . . . You didn't give! He took her. . . .

My father came in. The strawberries were small and soft and I couldn't find any juice in their white centres.

The smell of her cleaning fluids choked me, made my head ache, my throat burn. The shiny half of floor left behind when she'd slipped out during my father's bestowing of the sickly fruit glared in the late light of sun. I'd run after her and called her, but she and her caddy of rags and her churchy black handbag were gone before I could reach her.

I sat in the kitchen until I couldn't breathe anymore. I had to talk to Robert. I would go to the lab. He might be on his way home, but I did not want to fall apart among the pigweed and the dying flowers, or the kitchen with the smells and the turquoise bowl and the half-washed floor.

The lab at the canola factory held in the worst of the hideous spring—sterile air, blazing naked light from fluorescent tubes, orderly colourless whites. People liked to say that canola oil glowed like champagne, but today it looked like the dead blood of the golden canola flowers that in normal years made rich carpets on the fields around Silvercreek. Many years ago, canola had been called rapeseed. My father when I was little talked about the beautiful fields of rape.

Robert's lab assistant, Tammy, rose from her padded stool at the white arborite counter and told me Robert was in a quality control meeting, had asked her to call me to tell me he'd be late. "I just tried phoning you," she droned. "There was no answer."

I went home and filled the square tub with cool water. My clothes fell away from my body like limp peony petals. I dropped them into the clear water and watched them float, listened to them gasp and drown. The twin faces of Sarah and her father rippled over the floating fabric, vanished, reappeared. I pushed the clothes down with my hands until the gurgling stopped.

Then I ate strawberries until my nails hurt from gouging out the hulls.

As I approached Silvercreek, driving too fast, trailing gravel dust, fish-tailing on the washboard road, I looked for the flash of white among ash and poplar and caragana leaves. I thought I saw it, but as I neared the driveway, it turned into parched lawn grass, which had become whiter and whiter under the assault of pitiless sun and cruel wind.

Her car wasn't here. No Miss Muffet sat in the garden with a tiger-lily in her hand. The kitchen was empty and nothing had been rearranged. Balls of dust collected in the corners, the floor was gritty and stained.

They hadn't come.

Why had Mariechje told me? Apparently, she was able to forget sometimes, to block it out—when she laughed, when she talked about her houses and all the families that belong to them. Perhaps a special female sense had signalled that she could get some sort of help or absolution from me. Or maybe Silvercreek seemed to her like a refuge from town society, from those elite houses, a safe isolated place. Or she might have simply wanted to warn me away from her daughter, away from contamination.

But Mariechje hadn't come back. Her secret lay inert and entangled in the slag of drought in the corners of my kitchen. Was she hoping I would call her, ask her to come back?

But no one answered the telephone, though I tried calling her every day.

On Father's Day, early in the morning, Robert and his brother left for the city to visit their dad in the nursing home. The morning was cloudy, the wind of the day before had sweetened into a breeze, and a faint scent of rain rode the easterly flow. People did not listen to weather forecasts anymore. I never bothered to read the thermometer attached to a north window-frame, though Robert checked it after sunset each night before he drank his beer. He checked it again before he left for work in the morning. But no one liked to look at the thermometer during the heat of the afternoon because the numbers echoed inside sweltering brains and stuck to your skin with the sweat.

By noon the mass of cloud had separated and weakened and burned up in the lower atmosphere. The air became instantly hot with the first beam of sunlight to touch Silvercreek. At one o'clock the telephone rang. I expected every phone call to be Mariechje, telling me why she had not come to clean my house.

I did not recognize the voice at first, a man's. "Jane. I been talking to the town police, they're looking for a fella—"

Billy Schultz was a Silvercreek farmer and the Justice of the Peace. Why would he be calling me on a Sunday right after church?

"—and, uh, his wife I understand did some work for you and, uh, the whole bunch disappeared and someone said you might know where they took off to."

Billy Schultz took Toastmaster's and could speak in proper sentences and used good grammar most of the time.

"Family's name is Paetkau? Wife's name is . . ."

"Mariechje." Something caught in my throat. The air was choking me. "Why do you want him?"

"Well, the daughter there, the oldest girl. . . ."

"Sarah?"

"I don't know her name. Apparently the dad, uh—"

"You said disappeared?" I could scarcely get the word out. My throat burned and my eyes were watering. How dare Billy tell me that. How dare he phone me up on Father's Day with that cruel message. Didn't he have children romping in his kitchen at that very moment?

"They talk to you about heading back to Mexico? Back to the colony?"

"No."

"There's been talk. I guess some of the younger children told somebody that their sister . . ."

"Sarah . . ."

"Yes, Sarah, so, well, I guess they headed back to the colony. House is cleaned out. Don't know if the police in town will report it to the Mexican authorities or not. Probably not. They had no friends here, from what we can tell. All those years and no friends!"

Brenda, Freda, Helen. Jane.

"Figure the old man kept the money away from the family so the wife couldn't run off. Might've beaten up on her, too. Chief Buhler's been talking to social services, you see. They seen cases like this before. Sad case, sad, that's for sure."

I began to cough and could not speak.

"Lot of summer colds going around," said Billy Schultz.

My father burst through the front door. His eyes were wide, moist, and he held a clean white handkerchief to his mouth.

"Happy Father's Day," I gasped, "Dad."

"Girl, there's a fire in the bush. Didn't you notice the smoke? The wind shifted. It's spreading quickly and coming this way."

"Fire?"

"I'm afraid you'll have to leave your house. Here." He held his hanky under the tap and ran cold water through it. "Hold this over your face." He took my soiled dishrag and covered his own mouth and nose with it. Sacrifice. "The fire department from town is in there. It started at the far end. They'll be here soon to try to save your house. I told them I'd help you get out." He took my arm and started leading me out.

"I should take something. . . ."

"You won't know where to begin. Do you wish to take a diary or some letters?"

So odd for my father to talk about wishes. Wishing was pagan, except when done by children. I'd never heard him use the word *wish* except with me, as though fathers were the granters of wishes. I took the hat from the hook near the door. Sarah, I love you.

The whitish smoke was so thick now it erased the sun. I held the damp handkerchief to my face to keep my eyes clear. I could hear cellophane crackling in the distance, and shouting.

Before we drove away, my father bowed his head over the steering-wheel of his Saturday-washed car and silently prayed.

A bit of rain fell that July. We haven't had a spring like that one again. But the climate has changed in our once-fertile valley, changed from what it was when our ancestors began to farm here. The pigweed thrives, dry-land crops have replaced the moisture-loving ones. You have to go north to see the yellow fields of canola.

I never heard from Mariechje or Sarah again. I think about them sometimes and look for their faces on the streets. They could be here somewhere, or in some other Silvercreek.

The bush fire destroyed the house that Sunday afternoon in June. My father is dead now, but I remember his profile in the car before we escaped, I remember the praying. I don't know if he asked for the salvation of the house or for strength for me to endure whatever God had destined for me. Neither was answered.

And though it won the house, the fire did not take our summerhouse. The stack of empties remains hidden, saved by the prayers of rabbits.

SPELLS

At the wooded fringe of Silvercreek, where tidy square yards met virgin oak and willow, one last house reposed in deep snow. Laura-Marie's clock, ticking on her night table, showed 3:22, the middle of the night. But her bedroom was brighter than day, though not a lamp burned in any room. She lay and stared at the ceiling, breathing quick deep breaths like a sleeping animal. She'd awakened thinking morning had come, thinking she and Olivia had both slept one of those long, dead, heavy slumbers she used to have with Willie when he was still here. But the light coming through the windows was an icy light, beyond white, almost green. Like liquid it flowed around objects. It created no shadows. A low hum cradled the house. The hum vibrated in Laura-Marie's breastbone, disturbing the rhythm of the clock, the rhythm of her heart. She felt as though she were pinned to the mattress with a blunt tack.

The hum intensified and changed in pitch, higher, higher. Laura-Marie thought she heard a scream far away. She turned her head at last, to look through the open bedroom door to see if Olivia was somewhere in the hallway or in the kitchen, frightened, but what Laura-Marie saw was the electric fan on the floor near the chair. The fan was there to neutralize the heat required by the old lady in the next room. Now the white blades revolved in slow motion, each one singly visible. The humming sound seemed to be sucking energy from the electrical system as it grew louder and louder.

And then the icy green light dimmed and slid away. As it did, the blades of the fan turned faster and faster, until they were invisible. Laura-Marie feared they would fly off their shaft and cut through the protective wire mask. She twisted her body towards the window beside the bed and, grasping the sill, pulled herself to it. The light moved away through the oak trees beyond her snow-covered driveway. The snow sparkled under the bright moving air as the light hunted among the trees. When Laura-Marie looked back into the bedroom the fan had returned to its normal speed. The clock ticked.

In the other room Olivia was not snoring. Had she seen it? Was she, too, looking through her window at a light retreating in the woods?

At dawn, a feeble white January dawn, the coughing started in the next room, followed by snorting and mumbling, then the sound of a thin stream of water pattering into a metal basin, then gurgling in the drain, then gargling, then silence. Through her open bedroom door Laura-Marie could see the kitchen and a bit of brown skirt along the edge of the door-frame. Sometimes the old lady's whole body hulked past the rectangular opening. And Laura-Marie thought, she's doing everything normally—maybe nothing has changed. Or maybe the light was a dream.

She put on her Cryla-tex No. 7-purple slippers, the ones the old lady had made for her in a frenzy of knitting that had started on Remembrance Day during the one-minute silence. Laura-Marie recalled hearing the click of the knitting needles precisely when the CBC's announcer at the cenotaph said, "And now a minute of silence. . . ." Laura-Marie had never seen Olivia knit before that. The wool came mail-order in twenty-four different colours.

Laura-Marie paused beside the fan and touched the steel mesh. She turned the dial to HIGH, then to LOW, then to OFF.

In the kitchen the old lady stood at the sink, looking through a shiny saucer-shaped colander at a half-risen sun. Laura-Marie watched her turning the colander. The perforations were arranged in the pattern of a daisy flower, which now, in the pale kitchen, had the sun as its centre.

She saw something last night, thought Laura-Marie, maybe more than I did. I'll be able to tell by her eyes when she turns around.

But the old lady did not turn. She flung a mass of frozen chicken parts into the colander and ran water over them.

"Livia?"

The old lady's shoulders jerked, her skirt trembled.

"Livia?"

"I'm making noodle soup."

"Have you. . . ?"

Finally she turned. "What? What?" She had a dead cigarette in the corner of her mouth. Eyes like cold stones gazed from beneath the bandanna she twisted around her head every morning.

"Have you seen anyone today?" Laura-Marie wondered if the angel of death had assassinated everyone in the village.

Olivia rotated like a doll on a stick. Water gurgled through the holes in the colander. "Satan hauled all the hypocrites away at 7:43 A.M. I watched 'em climbing a giant fishermen's net to the sky."

Laura-Marie slumped onto the leatherette seat of a wooden chair. "Have you seen anyone?"

"Hah! More than usual. Zoop-zoop-zoop!" Olivia shouted.

Laura-Marie half expected to see ripples in the coffee the old lady had left on the table.

Bones rattled in the colander. "When I saw the flashing light I thought they were coming to pick me up. Went right by. Not meant for this old hen!" The partially thawed bones flew into a kettle squatting on the counter. "That boy with his gun was on the road a while ago."

The boy with the gun would be Aaron Lindner, thought Laura-Marie, but what did she mean by flashing light?

Laura-Marie used to believe that all Olivias were like the Olivia de Havilland she saw on the late movies on TV, with heart-shaped faces and secretive smiles and graceful manners. Then Olivia Schellenberg had moved in with Laura-Marie's mother, Isabel, and then Isabel had died, and Laura-Marie inherited the old lady. Olivia Schellenberg had a lumpy face and seldom smiled. The people of Silvercreek thought she had Alzheimer's disease. Laura-Marie did not try to set them straight—the villagers understood disease, but they would never tolerate a witch.

Laura-Marie said, "I think something happened last night."

"Something happened, all right. Them hypocrites got the call and now they're all on fire."

With a soft *foof* a circle of flame leaped from one of the burners of the gas stove.

Olivia used to be the cook at the Bible college in town where Laura-Marie's mother had been a secretary for thirty years. One night in early spring, as Olivia was locking up, a man—they never found out who—dragged her behind the chapel, then raped and beat her in the dirty snowbanks. She'd been carrying a basket of laundry, and when one of the students from the dorm found her, she was crumpled up in a pile of crumpled-up, soiled, white kitchen linen. She was seventy-two then. She had no family and was not sick enough to take up space in the crowded hospital. So Laura-Marie's mother, Isabel, took Olivia to live with her, since she had a large house to herself—Laura-Marie had by that time moved to the city. Isabel kept an eye on Olivia at the Bible school, for Olivia had spells sometimes, though Laura-Marie had not asked what kind of spells. She was not much interested at the time, what with her love affair with Willie.

Isabel was gentle and iron-clad. She loved gardening, and, having been widowed early, had managed to construct an independent life for herself. By the time Laura-Marie and Willie moved out of the city to Silvercreek, Isabel and Olivia's lives had fallen into a pattern and people forgot who Olivia had once been.

Willie left Laura-Marie. And then her mother died of a bee-sting in the garden while Olivia baked cinnamon buns in the kitchen. Laura-Marie had a job making boxes at the box factory in town. She didn't move to town, though. Taxes on the property in Silvercreek were low, and there was lots of space between houses in which to conceal the Olivia that Laura-Marie inherited from her mother.

It was all temporary, of course—the old lady would die and Laura-Marie would find another Willie. But the old lady didn't die. Wouldn't.

Olivia switched on the radio. The local station carried funeral announcements at 9:05. Della Goosen, an old friend of Isabel's, read them and Olivia never missed them. She always smoked a cigarette while she listened, and sometimes nibbled on a hard-boiled egg. "I hope the old crows are watching," she'd say. "I'm immune to tar and fat. Broken heart's what I'll die of."

It was not quite 9:05. The news was on. Laura-Marie waited to hear about the strange lights over Silvercreek during the night. Wouldn't someone have seen them? Someone coming home late from a party?

The radio carried no news of unexplained phenomena. Laura-Marie was startled to realize that she might have been the only one to have seen and heard the thing in her woods. She had really hoped someone else would spread the word. She herself had not thought of telling about what had taken place.

Olivia chopped vegetables for the soup on a wooden board and sang snatches of "Fuchs du hast die Gans gestohlen" throughout the newscast. ". . . mit dem schiess Geweh-eh-ehr!" pinged off the hard surfaces of the kitchen, punctuated by the thunk-thunk-thunk of the blade on the cutting board. Olivia specialized in stews and soups. Dormitory food. Laura-Marie sat stiff in her chair watching the loose ends of the bandanna wag, and said nothing, but she knew at the conclusion of the news that no one had phoned in about the lights. Or perhaps had and wasn't taken seriously.

"I'm going for a walk," said Laura-Marie.

"A walk? A walk? The traffic will toss you in all directions. Like a paper bag."

"What traffic? I'm not going on the road."

"Not on the road?"

Laura-Marie had once read that cats were the familiars of aliens from outer space, that cats collected Earth-data in their queer little brains and were regularly beamed into some kind of fifth dimension and the data siphoned out into alien computers. The old lady, like the cat, could be an alien spy. Perhaps her assault at the Bible school had not been an earthly one, but a visitation of some sort. And last night they had come to collect information.

The snow at the edge of the oak stand was soft and thick. Laura-Marie stood there with her hands in the pockets of her parka. Her feet were in Willie's old suede Mexican boots. And as she stood at the brink of a search for burn marks in the trees, for melted snow, it was Willie she thought about. Naked except for his long brown beard, he had chased her through these woods at sunrise one spring morning. And this was where she had gone to look for him first when she came home from the box factory to find his wheel idle and the clay half formed. His letter to her had been tacked to one of the oak trunks.

And then her mother had died, and almost immediately Willie was replaced by Olivia. The two women lived abandoned in the old house. Laura-Marie was certain her mother had arranged it, penance for having lived in sin with Willie.

She stared into the woods. Something stirred, but not in the trees. She caught a flicker in the corner of her eye of something moving along the row of evergreens that formed the back border of her property. Something human.

He had a rifle cradled in his arms. His army coat was a light patch against the dark pines. He wore nothing on his head. What was Aaron Lindner hunting for today, Laura-Marie wondered. Magpies and jack-rabbits and partridges? Or burn marks in her oaks? She deliberately walked into the bush while he watched, so he would not take her for wild game and shoot her down.

Animal tracks led through the woods. Laura-Marie dipped her No.12-blue mitten into one of the depressions. Older folks in Silvercreek claimed to have seen cougars in and around the village over the years. Laura-Marie did not believe the stories, even though her wildlife handbook listed cougars as a provincial resident. This was flat farmland. The river was not far off, but mountains were a lifetime away. The oak bush itself was a freak. People feared the woodticks, which the oak was rumoured to conceal, more than they did clawed beasts, and Willie and Laura-Marie had never thought about cougars while they were conducting their private garden parties in these woods. The tracks were probably the spoor of Silvercreek's rampant Irish setters. The depth and softness of the snow made it difficult to tell. Even if there had been cougars at one time, there'd be none left now.

Tree trunks cracked with cold. Beside a graceful, newly

fallen twig, a magpie lay with its claws lifted towards the sky. A round black eye stared hypnotized upwards past the crooked tops of the trees.

Olivia was not in the kitchen. Something white and whipped and creamy had taken the place of the potful of icy chicken flesh on the counter. Do-gooders in ankle-high pointy-toed boots and dark grey coats were always bringing food to Olivia and Laura-Marie. Hardly a day passed that someone didn't deliver a pan of lasagna, or leftover Shake 'n' Bake, or crumbly matrimonial cake to their door.

The cellar stairs creaked. "Sex-in-the-pan!" cackled the old lady to Laura-Marie, who had just dipped her finger into the thick topping.

"What?"

"SEX IN THE PAN!" Olivia scooped up a ladleful and held it high in front of the window, and wheezed at the layers of gooey chocolate and pastry and whipped cream.

"Who brought it?" Laura-Marie hadn't realized she'd been gone that long, wondered why she hadn't heard voices coming from the front of the house. "Who brought it?"

"The Queen."

The Queen was Katherine Schultz. Olivia had noticed that the Schultzes' car had crowns beside the rear windows. "So," she said, "not all the hypocrites have been taken up into the sky." The Schultzes were the wealthiest and churchiest people in the village.

"Did she say, 'Here, I brought you a dish of sex-in-the-pan'?"

"No, no! She said, 'I brought you a pan of better-than-Robert-Redford.' That's what the hypocrites call sex-in-the-pan because they're not allowed to say *sex* out loud."

"You talked to her?"

"No, no! She talked at me through the crack of the door." Olivia dried the colander with her apron.

"Who calls it sex-in-the-pan, then? *Why* do they call it sex-in-the-pan?" said Laura-Marie through a mouthful of sweet, sticky cream.

"If you eat it you get pregnant!"

Laura-Marie felt drowsy in the warm kitchen. She lolled over the table sucking on a spoon coated with Robert Redford chocolate. The chicken broth steamed and gurgled beneath its lid on the old stove. Olivia hummed a slow, low version of "Fuchs du hast die Gans gestohlen," and the radio percolated at low volume with a variety of voices. Laura-Marie remembered the vibration in her breastbone and the green light searching in the woods, and its sparkle on the snow.

Olivia stood in front of the fridge, her woolly figure bent forward a little, the ladle cocked beneath her chin. The stone eyes glittered for a moment, then she made a doll-on-a-stick turn towards Laura-Marie and said: "Did you hear? Dead at the other end! Dead. In the snow. DEAD! DEAD!"

"Who, Olivia? Are you sure?" Laura-Marie got out of her chair and lurched towards the radio. She turned the volume up high, but the announcer was talking about a break-in at the Co-op store. "What did he say?"

Olivia sucked up the broth in the ladle.

"What did he say?"

"A lady. Dead."

"Where? Here?"

"Zoop-zoop-zoop!" Olivia reached into a cupboard and pulled out a coil-bound cookbook published by the church women in town. She flipped through it and slapped it down in front of Laura-Marie. "See?"

BETTER-THAN-ROBERT-REDFORD
(Sex-in-the-pan)

"How did she die? Did they say how she died, Livia?"

"FOWL PLAY! Killed by chickens!"

Laura-Marie went back to her chair at the table and sat staring at the floor. Either the green light had brought about someone's death, or Olivia believed she herself had died in that dirty snow behind the Bible school chapel two springs ago.

Every Saturday afternoon she invented a new life for herself from the classified pages of the city newspaper. New *lives*. The ads were promises. All she needed to do was make a phone call, write a letter, ring a certain doorbell at a certain house, and a fresh, safe little world would be hers. She could choose whatever she wanted: a widower with a coin collection; a wealthy, middle-aged playboy ready to settle down; a free trip to Leningrad as a travel companion; a real Rolex watch, cheap. Silvercreek was, after all, only temporary. Laura-Marie would hover over the densely engraved pages for an hour or two, and then Olivia would come in trailing yarn and instruction booklets and hold strips of weaving against various parts of Laura-Marie's body. "You got enough money to go to Leningrad?" Laura-Marie would ask.

Today Laura-Marie's mind couldn't stay focused on the offers in the classified section. Something was different today. The weather wasn't unusual—crisp and bright, like last Saturday and the Saturday before. It was as though today for the first time Laura-Marie wasn't waiting anymore, waiting for changes, waiting for Willie to come back, or for Olivia to be— *gone*. The searching lights had done something. Perhaps she'd been impregnated with a cosmic cell from another galaxy. Perhaps she would be the next Big Bang.

Laura-Marie heard people talking outside the back door. Olivia had gone out to put sunflower seeds and bun crumbs in the bird feeder she'd ordered from the Sears catalogue for Christmas. When Laura-Marie scraped the hard white frost from the back-door window, she saw two figures in the yard. Olivia had on a man's black overcoat and mukluks, and held an empty bread bag in one hand and a half-filled sack of seeds in the other. Aaron Lindner, wearing snowshoes on his feet, stood beside the feeder and pointed into the woods. His rifle was strapped to his back.

Laura-Marie had first seen Aaron Lindner on a winter dawn a year ago, about six months after the death in the garden. That morning the planet had had no horizon. An ice-mist whitened the sky. Several days of snow had levelled and eventually obliterated terrain like a soft brushing of white paint. Even the feather ridge of pines at the back of the yard was absorbed in a thick shroud of hoarfrost. After leaving the nestling gables of Silvercreek and the various patterns of trees, Laura-Marie, on her way to the box factory in town, found the road and the sky and the fields around her all a silvery-white cloud, as though she were floating through the atmosphere of Neptune. The road had no edges, the low skyline of town had disappeared. She began to feel disoriented and dizzy, like the first time she had fainted, in her mother's bathroom, when she'd discovered secret blood in her baby-doll bottoms. In a panic, Laura-Marie had turned around on a farm driveway marked with two poles. As she pointed the car to her oaks, which were a black smudge in the distance, the boy had suddenly materialized on the road in front of her. He held a dead white rabbit slung over his shoulder.

Laura-Marie had told Olivia about it when she got back to the safety of the Silvercreek house, though Olivia at that time was still in silent mourning for Isabel, and hadn't responded.

Katherine Schultz informed them a few weeks later that he was Lindners' boy, come home from a botched attempt at private school in the city. A no-good kid—hot-tempered, given to violence, mindful of no one. The Lindners lived on a farm just outside the village, just beyond the creek and only about half a mile from Laura-Marie's.

"What did the kid want?" Laura-Marie asked Olivia when she came back into the house with a swoop of smoky-smelling coat and frosty air. "Why was he talking to you?"

145

Olivia put the bag of seeds into the closet, and her coat. "Something hiding in those woods. He's *verrückt*, like me. Pop-pop-pop, he goes." She slapped her cheek three times, a habit she had when she was in a good mood.

"What in the woods?"

"DEAD AT THE OTHER END!"

"*What* in the woods?"

Olivia stood still in the middle of the kitchen with her hands folded in front of her at the waist and said, as though reciting, "In India when a native walks through the mangrove forests he wears a mask on the back of his head."

Laura-Marie had spoken to the boy only once. Her cat had disappeared in early spring. The cat had belonged to Willie when he'd lived there. After it had been missing for four days, Laura-Marie had seen Aaron walking way out on the field with his gun. She'd stalked him for several minutes, caught up with him, and asked him if he'd seen the cat. He'd thought she was accusing him of killing it. "I'm not like that," he'd said. And he'd turned and tramped off across the muddy furrows.

"I just want to know if you've seen it," she'd called after him.

He had not answered. After that she left him alone. Left alone, he hunted and prowled and kept his distance from society.

Laura-Marie was confused—had Aaron told her that? Or was it something she remembered from somewhere else? "Why does a native wear a mask on the back of his head, Olivia?"

But Olivia was taking mixing bowls and measuring cups out of the cupboards and wasn't paying attention.

Laura-Marie went back to her classifieds.

At three o'clock they listened again to the news. Still nothing about the lights, nothing about a death in Silvercreek. We were both imagining things, Laura-Marie thought. Except that I'm supposed to be sane and she isn't.

146

Olivia had rolled out great flat sheets of yellow dough and was cutting them into plump coiled noodles with Isabel's special sharp butcher knife. She stopped and looked at Laura-Marie. Her smile showed the gap in her teeth in the left-hand corner of her mouth. "Maybe there are mountain lions in the bushes, eh?" She poked Laura-Marie's shoulder with the point of the floury knife.

Laura-Marie jumped away. "Where's that Robert Redford stuff?"

"Sex-in-the-pan!" Olivia went to the stove and stirred the pot of chicken broth, dredging up soggy parsley stalks and rattling the chain of the spice ball hooked over the lip of the kettle. "Double-double-," she moaned. "Double-DARE-YOU!"

"Dare me what?" said Laura-Marie as she scooped a spoonful of goo into her mouth directly from the pan.

"To go walk with the mountain lions!"

"Have you ever seen one, Olivia?"

"Seen what?"

"I mean seen one here."

"Maybe." Olivia began to beat the side of the pot with her wooden spoon in a clock-like rhythm.

Laura-Marie got up from the table and went into her bedroom to find her wool hat. The sight of the fan jolted her, and she pressed her fist into her breastbone. Sunlight glittered on the fan's metal parts. Its blades had gone slower than they could and faster than they could.

She skirted it and confronted the closet door, a door which did not go right to the floor but was more like an opening cut into a box. She looked back at the fan, then at the small white enamel doorknob that stared at her breast like a Martian's eye.

The beating of the spoon on the soup kettle stopped. As Laura-Marie carefully arranged her hair under the brim of the hat, Olivia crept up to the open bedroom door. "Let's lock the doors," she whispered.

"I'm going to the store at the other end of the village," said Laura-Marie.

"Murder!"

The store had no name. The various signs out front advertised Coke and Pepsi and 7-Up and Sprite, but no name for the store. The owners lived next door to it, in a trailer, as though they would be leaving any day. The Gleasons had come to Silvercreek three years ago to open a store with a coffee shop. People referred to the store as Gleasons', and winter mornings and Saturdays the little coffee shop was full of men.

Laura-Marie shuffled around the three aisles that made up the grocery section and read labels on cans and bottles and boxes. She was hoping to hear rumours about the lights and the noise last night. She listened especially closely when a new customer came in and sat down at the coffee bar, because the topics of the day usually started fresh when someone new came in. People came into the grocery part, too, but most of them hurried in and out—the only things Gleasons stocked were conveniences.

Laura-Marie strained her ears towards the windowed corner where Gleasons had put the coffee bar, the corner she'd never paid much attention to before. Some of the men were sitting in pairs and mumbling too softly for her to hear. She tried to catch half a sentence, a word. No one spoke about something weird happening in the woods during the long, cold night.

Carrying a bag containing a raisin pie baked in a city bakery, Laura-Marie stepped cautiously down the snow-packed wooden stairs in front of the store. When she got to the ground and looked ahead to the road, she saw Aaron Lindner coming towards her. As they passed on the small parking-lot, behind the many vehicles facing the store, Aaron and Laura-Marie glanced at each other, but he lowered his eyes quickly. Laura-Marie wanted to talk to him, but, since she couldn't hold him with her eyes, said nothing.

The only people Laura-Marie had ever seen speaking with Olivia, besides her mother, were the do-gooders and occasionally a lay minister from some church or other. The idea of Aaron Lindner having a conversation with the old lady in the back yard earlier that afternoon was suddenly intriguing. Laura-Marie waited behind a half-ton truck for him to come out of the store. Inside her mittens her fingers got cold and she held them one at a time to her mouth to breathe on them. The fuzz of the No. 12 wool tickled her nostrils and she twitched her nose while she watched the aluminum storm door for a sign of Aaron. The mittens began to get damp.

At last he came through the door and down the steps. At first he didn't see her there behind the truck. He had a small paper bag in his hand.

"Aaron," said Laura-Marie.

He turned his head sharply in her direction, but his eyes remained cool, unsurprised.

"My—uh—my—the woman who lives with me—her name is Olivia—said some odd things when she came in from talking to you at our house before. . . ."

The boy stood completely still while Laura-Marie spoke. His expression didn't change. The rifle poked up over the back of his shoulder and the little paper bag hung from his folded leather mitten.

"It's just that Olivia is not easy to—you know—really communicate with," Laura-Marie continued. "She sort of forgets to mention the important bits when she tells things. She said something about—something in the woods. She's altogether a kind of unusual person. . . ."

"What did she say?" asked Aaron Lindner. He had a soft voice, low-pitched.

"Oh, well, something about tigers and masks. . . . I'm not

149

even sure if it's anything you said to her—she could have pulled that bit out of anywhere, I guess. Actually, I don't know her very well."

"We did talk about tigers and masks."

"Pardon?"

"We did talk about tigers, masks, the mangrove forests. And I know that she's one of the few people who's seen a cougar here."

To go walk with the mountain lions. . . .

"Did she say that?" asked Laura-Marie.

"Not exactly. I had to piece it together. They could come up here from the river to hunt in those woods."

"Well, I don't know. . . ."

"She seemed afraid to talk about it. Afraid of the cougar. I told her that many people have been attacked and killed by tigers in the mangrove forests of West Bengal. That's in India."

"I see," said Laura-Marie. "Now she'll be scared even to take the breadcrumbs out to the birds."

"But remember the masks," said Aaron.

"Yes, what was it?"

"The tiger experts told the Bengali people that they should wear masks on the backs of their heads when they walk through the mangrove forests, because a tiger always attacks from the rear, where people don't have eyes. She thought it was funny, and I guess it is funny."

Laura-Marie felt chilled and confused and the pie seemed oddly heavy. "I see," she said, and she started to turn away from the boy, to head back to her house. "Thank you."

But when she'd walked only a few yards she stopped and called to him, "I heard something last night. Something strange."

Aaron Lindner, who had been walking in the opposite direction, turned to her, and this time his face showed more. "Did you see anything?"

"So you heard it, too. I was sure I was awake, but no one else seemed to know about it. . . ."

"Lights," said Aaron. "Over your woods. More like a bright glow. I saw it."

"And a low hum. . . . Have you seen anything around the village?"

"Not yet."

"What should we do?"

Aaron shrugged and looked out into the fields beyond Gleasons' store. "Nothing. It was ours. Just—ours, I guess."

The hand-cut noodles lay scattered like thousands of question marks over the brittle linoleum floor. Tea-towels were slit into ragged pennants of surrender and lay crookedly draped over chair-backs and the edge of the table. A fine white dusting of Robin Hood flour over the whole kitchen reminded Laura-Marie of a castle room unlocked after a hundred years of sleep. Olivia was not in the kitchen. Laura-Marie looked about for the knife. She did not see it anywhere. The red bandanna hung over the lip of the counter, unknotted.

Laura-Marie could not move for several seconds. All those towels slashed into limp strips. The knife missing. She was overcome with dread, and did not know how she would dare to walk into the other rooms of the house to look for Olivia. Perhaps there was even someone else in the house.

Then, as though the shock of the kitchen scene had temporarily blotted out her other senses, her hearing returned, and what she heard was a soft ticking sound coming from the living-room next to the kitchen.

The old lady sat in her rocking chair with her knitting needles. The chair was covered with an afghan that had been Isabel's. In fact, the chair had been Isabel's. Laura-Marie had never found it comfortable, but somehow Olivia's body fit. The whole room was not quite comfortable. Laura-Marie and Willie had not spent much time in it, had not furnished it properly. Olivia liked to knit there.

"Livia?"

A new colour of wool hung between the needles. Olivia's eyes were closed—she seemed to be knitting with her eyes closed.

"Are you all right?" Laura-Marie asked, afraid Olivia would shriek out one of her absurd answers. Or hoping she would.

The eyes remained closed. Laura-Marie ached to see those cold stones. What had brought it on, this *spell*, as her mother had called it? Olivia had said *murder* just before Laura-Marie had left. Perhaps she'd actually been terrified at being left alone that moment, terrified of being murdered, or of murdering.

"Where's the knife?"

A smile opened at the corner of Olivia's mouth. Her eyes flew open and she laughed. The eyes became small with laughter. "Did you think I'd swallowed it, girlie? Eh?"

And then Laura-Marie laughed, too. For the first time she laughed with Olivia. They laughed together until Laura-Marie, standing between the two rooms, saw again in the corner of her eye the question marks strewn on the kitchen floor. She went and sat across from Olivia on an old piano stool that had no piano. "Livia, what did you see last night? Did you wake up?"

The eyes closed again. "I had a dream. I was dying and going to heaven to see Isabel. Heaven was a bright light and I could see that there was no one else there, except Isabel. And me. That bee should of bit me. I wouldn't have died. And even if I had, it wouldn't have made so much difference to anyone."

Laura-Marie had never thought about Olivia having guilt before. It's all right, Olivia! she wanted to say. That wasn't heaven, it was only a flying saucer from a far-away planet!

"It wouldn't have made so much difference to anyone," Olivia said again.

And that other guilt, too, of having been violated all those years ago. Isabel had once whispered to Laura-Marie that she,

Isabel, suspected that Olivia's attacker had been someone Olivia knew, someone she knew and trusted, a so-called Christian person, because Olivia had turned against Christians after the assault, although she had not turned against Isabel.

Olivia felt worthless, Laura-Marie realized, and had invented a batty invalid to replace the original Olivia so she couldn't be held responsible for her fall from grace.

But what had brought this all on today? Laura-Marie began to sort through Olivia's jumbled pictures of the world, which in Laura-Marie's mind were white and billowy like kitchen linen. Memories of Isabel dead among the daisies in the garden. Olivia's own body between dirty snowbanks and dirty towels behind the Bible college. And the dream last night evoked by the moving lights in the snapping January cold.

"Did you wake up?"

"I don't think so."

Laura-Marie began to understand why Olivia expected to die of a broken heart. Someone who had loved her, and whom she loved, was gone. It's taken me too long to look into the witch's heart, thought Laura-Marie to herself as she tiptoed among the coils of dough.

Tic-tic, went the needles.

As Laura-Marie began sweeping up, she heard Olivia talking to herself in her rocking chair. "What, Olivia?"

Olivia did not look up from her knitting. "Should have worn a mask on the back of my head."

Or maybe there is still time, thought Laura-Marie.

Laura-Marie lay awake most of the night, waiting. Sometimes she was in a half sleep, with disturbing half-formed dreams snaking through her restlessness, dreams about the slashed tea-towels and blood and Olivia stabbing. She wished, in her wakeful moments, that the greenish-white light would come again. When Olivia's morning noises began with the dawn, Laura-Marie felt disappointed. She wanted to believe in the lights, but the blades of the fan never faltered.

Most of Silvercreek had emptied into the churches in town by the time Laura-Marie and Olivia were finished their many coffees. Most Sundays Olivia liked to watch all the cars go by on their way out of the village. She became almost merry at the idea of being one of maybe a handful of people left behind by the church-goers. But today Olivia looked withered and listless, and she said little, just sat in her chair in the living-room in a sort of stupor.

Laura-Marie sat wondering how to touch Olivia. A loud banging at the back door broke the Sunday silence. Not a mittened knock. This was wood against wood. Laura-Marie could see no vehicle out front on the driveway.

Aaron Lindner stood at the door, rifle in hand. Up close his eyes were wide and staring, hazel-coloured and shiny even in the shaded rear of the house. His long hair covered his ears. He looked like a child, except for the gun.

Before he said anything, Laura-Marie heard Olivia. She called faintly from her chair in the next room, "Ask him if he'd like some sex-in-the-pan." And then a soft chortle.

Aaron gave Laura-Marie the missing butcher knife. "This was lying out near the bird feeder," he said. "And I found something in your trees a couple of hours ago."

Laura-Marie pulled the edges of her V-neckline together. She took a step back into the porch, because of the cold and because of his eyes. "Something in our trees?"

"I found the cougar."

"You found—the cougar?"

"Dead, though. Not long dead. I mean, maybe a day or two. It's at the far end of the bush."

"You killed it! You shot Olivia's mountain lion!" Laura-Marie kicked the barrel of the rifle, which was pointed down at the doormat, with her slipper.

Aaron rested the gun on its butt in a corner of the entryway. "What do you think I am?" he shouted. "What does everyone think I am? I hardly ever fire my rifle. I used it to put your cat out of its misery a few months ago—someone set a leg-hold trap down by the creek. And I kill partridges now and then for my mom to roast. I didn't kill the cougar. I came here to tell you about it because I thought you might want to see it before the conservation guys come out from the city to pick it up. That's all."

Laura-Marie rubbed her forehead with her fingertips. "Who killed it, then?"

"Not a mark on it."

Laura-Marie's fingers froze on her brow. She lowered her hand and looked intently at Aaron's face. "So," she said.

He shrugged. "Could be an old cougar, dying a natural death."

"DEAD!" Olivia shrieked suddenly from the kitchen behind Laura-Marie, startling her so that the butcher knife jerked in her hand. "Dead at the other end!"

Laura-Marie went into the house and found Olivia pacing in front of the kitchen window. She had lost her earlier withered appearance and her face was lively and pink. She slapped her cheek in excitement.

"So she's dead! I knew it!"

"How did you know it, Olivia? How did you know about the mountain lion?"

"There's a wind coming up," said Aaron Lindner from the doorway. "And see those clouds up north? If we get a storm tonight everything will get all covered up. I may have to drag her out of the bush before it hits."

"I have to see," said Olivia, and she got her black coat and her mukluks from the closet.

"Olivia, there's a lot of snow. . . ."

"She can come," said Aaron. "She has to."

I've lost control here, thought Laura-Marie. They know more than I do. That's why Willie left. He knew more than I did, too.

Aaron was waiting for them at the bird feeder, waiting to lead them to the body of the dead mountain lion in Silvercreek, where mountain lions didn't belong. As they started out, Laura-Marie called, "I'll walk behind Olivia. We'll keep her in the middle." *I'll be the eyes on the back of her head.*

They stumbled steadily through the changing textures of snow in the oak stand. Aaron made a track for them to follow with his leather hunting boots. As they passed through a clearing in the trees where some of the snow still sparkled, Laura-Marie remembered the old lady holding the colander to the sun, making the light dance through the daisy petals as she turned it round and round.

PLAYA CARAUNA

Mother prepared to walk the walk of the killer bees by covering her varnished hair with a filigreed shawl. Every morning at ten the sun shone into the narrow passage between our casita and the next, a passage lined with flowering lantana shrubs, and when the sun arrived, so did the bees. Within an hour, the corridor was in shade again, and the bees were gone. "Could they be killer bees?" Mother had asked the first morning.

Her carmine-coloured nails fluttered along the hem of the shawl as she adjusted it on her hairdo. She'd already been to breakfast at the hacienda, on the patio. She'd returned to our casita to touch up a troublesome nail, and was on her way back for more coffee and a chat with Frau Sondheim, or perhaps Laszlo himself.

"Are ya comin'?" she drawled in fake Texan.

I had not slept during the night. Roosters crowed, cats squabbled, and Laszlo's servants had babies whose cries from the women's quarters mingled with the roosters and cats until I could not tell them apart. At times I believed that the wailing and squawking and whimpering was coming from the ancient air-conditioner roaring beneath our window. The full light of the morning had silenced the cries, and I had dozed while Mother was at first breakfast. The roosters were only phantoms from an earlier time.

The last time I'd been to Mexico was on a beach holiday, a cheap package where they stuck you in a small, naked room on the tenth floor and fed you continental breakfasts and deadly margaritas for a week. Now I was in a different Mexico, though still in a tourist town. Nothing this time was wrapped, or tied with string.

I sat up on the edge of the bed. Mother leaned over and positioned her face in front of mine. "Are my eyebrows even?" She tried to relax her face muscles, letting her chin sag and the corners of her mouth droop.

"No," I said. She tottered towards the bathroom. The high heel of her sandal snagged in a throw rug placed arbitrarily between the beds and the bathroom.

"The mirror in here is—you know—wavy."

Warped, I thought. I was sorry I'd told her her eyebrows were crooked. They weren't, at least not any more so than usual, and now I'd have to wait for the bathroom.

I dressed and browsed through the old books Laszlo left in the casitas in case a guest needed something to read beside the pool. The books had been left behind by past guests who had spent the winter at the Playa Carauna before discotheques found their way through the Mexican jungle. The copyrights were dated in the '20s and '30s and '40s. Hard-cover books without dust-jackets, but with startling titles on their spines: *The Curve and the Tusk, Yankee Pasha, The Lure of the Dim Trails, The Leather Dog*. I picked up *Yankee Pasha*, but Mother's shadow fell on the page. I washed my face and we walked to the patio, among lantanas and killer bees and a dozen or more cats.

The patio was covered by a splendid thatched roof attached to the hacienda and supported by many slender beams. The terrazzo beneath was polished and spotless. We sat at a linened table on wicker chairs, and while Laszlo's boy served me fruit, and eggs with orange yolks, Mother drank coffee and filled me in on what she'd learned that morning.

"Laszlo came here in 1941. His parents were Hungarian Americans. He left his wife and children and took mules through the jungle to get here. It was just a fishing village then. I think he's a homosexual."

I squinted into the bright lawn and across it to the pool at the far end of the compound. Someone new was sitting beside the pool. Drops glittered on his skin like chain-mail.

"Frau Sondheim said they used to have to hack their way through virgin bush just to get to the beach. About two blocks, would you say? When his patrons started having children, they all chipped in and built the pool. You'd look so much nicer with a little eye shadow and some colourful clothes. I don't know why you always have to wear black."

"Who's the new guy?" I asked. As we looked at the stranger, two little boys emerged from the shrubbery beside the pool and chattered in Spanish to the fair-skinned swimmers sitting on the deck. In a moment, striped T-shirts and knee-length pants lay in heaps and two small bodies hurtled through the air above the water.

"IIee-hah!" cried the real Texan reading the *Wall Street Journal* on a wicker settee in a corner of the patio. "Look at 'em little Mexican boys cannon-ballin' into our swimmin' hole!" He was the one who'd watched Mother and me play crib last night by lamplight, and had said, "Y'all must be Canadian—I'nt seen nobody but Canucks play cribbage."

The clientele of the Playa Carauna were not the customary tourists. The hotel had once nestled in the jungle beside the town's only street, which ran parallel to, but several hundred feet from, the curved bay, separated from it by jungle. As time passed, developers cleared away the jungle, built a new street closer to the water, and sold beach-front property to American innkeepers. The Playa Carauna ended up on a rectangular lot hemmed in by high-rises and surrounded by a steel fence.

I'd noticed that the Playa was out of sync the moment we'd walked through the wrought-iron gate, from the old street into a brilliant, jewelled yard, an expanse of lawn bordered by exotic flowering plants, presided over at one end by the grand hacienda with red tile roof and at the other by towering coconut palms. Nestled in a corner behind the main building were twelve small, tidy casitas, each with its own patio. The patios used to overlook tropical forest, but now fronted bluntly on the fence that separated them from the garish hotel next door.

When we'd arrived, two languid yard-keepers were trying to revive a chipped marble fountain near the gate. Antiquated statuary lurked everywhere among ferns and hibiscus, and when I looked closely, some of the vegetation itself resembled the house-plants in my apartment back home—spindly, sparse, forced to stay alive when they'd rather be dead. Gliding about here and there were Laszlo's boys, smooth-skinned, inscrutable. They served the meals and clipped the grass, and unlocked the gate if you came in late and had to ring the bell to be let through.

To my surprise, the idea that we had entered a time warp did not escape my mother. "Where's Ava Gardner?" she'd whispered to me as we waited on the main patio for Laszlo to process my credit card. We were surrounded by *New Yorker* magazines, *Wall Street Journal, Vanity Fair, Atlantic, Der Spiegel*. "Have you noticed there are no mosquitoes here?" Mother had said as a boy showed us to our room.

That first night at dinner, Ava Gardner had materialized in the form of Frau Sondheim, one of the Argentinian Germans who'd been coming to Laszlo's since the late '40s. She was voluptuous and regal, beautiful and aging, and had high cheekbones, like Laszlo. I could tell that my mother admired her, but resented her, too, a little. If it had not been for Frau Sondheim, *she* would have been the Ava Gardner of the Playa Carauna.

The new guest ambled across the lawn, towel draped over his shoulders. His dark, thinning hair was swept back from his forehead and behind his ears. At the back of his neck, the hair was long and straight. His face was not young, but neither was it old. As he approached he regarded us through almost oriental eyes, narrow and cool.

"He's here to buy leather," Mother murmured over the rim of her cup.

"Leather?"

"Good morning again, Mrs. van Thiesen!" The man smiled and looked wicked.

VAN Thiesen?

"This must be your sister."

"Well. . . . "

"I'm her daughter."

"Why, you didn't tell me you were here with your daughter. My name is Mike."

"This is Gracie. She's an assistant at Manitou College."

"What's your field, Ms. van Thiesen?" He pulled up a chair from another table and sat down, tugging the chair nearer between his legs as he did so. I was aware of a pair of white thighs covered with black hairs.

"Biology," I said.

"She spends a lot of time looking at dead shrivelled things in jars," said Mother. "Even on weekends."

"I hear you're in the leather business." I was usually reticent among strangers, but we had crossed several borders to get to the Playa Carauna.

The demon smile again. "Into leather. Yeah. They've got lots of cheap cows down here."

"But not right here."

"No, not right here. I met a girl on the plane to Mexico City who's got a condo on the bay. She asked me to come down for a few days."

"But not to her condo."

"No, not to her condo."

Mother was glowing. She liked men, and she liked me liking men. I could see flirtation beginning to flash in her eyes. Her carmine lips parted. I'm not sure whose leg moved, his or mine, but our knees touched, mine clothed, his bare, and though I could not see it happening, I had the feeling that his other knee had met my mother's.

Frau Sondheim floated up the three steps that joined the path with the patio. A large butterscotch cat I had named Head Honcho Cat, because he was the only one we'd ever seen on the patio, came up with her, mingling with the silken billows of her floor-length sarong. She clutched a large, round sun-hat to her breast. Mike straightened up as she got nearer. He pulled the towel closer about his chest, as though to protect his virility from her splendour, from the earthiness of her bare shoulders and the way the fabric of her dress draped and clung to her body. The Texan, whose name we did not know, jumped to his feet among much rustling and flapping of newspaper, and nodded and smiled.

"Good morning," came the low voice, rich in its blend of accents. "Once again," she added to my mother.

Everyone settled in at the table and we talked about how you could spend your day at various stages of holiday. I noticed that Mike had a way of tilting his head back when he talked, so that he looked at you over his cheekbones, which was what made his eyes half closed, calculating, but at the same time defensive and cautious. When he listened, his face was lively—the wicked grin could change to a childish frown and back again, instantly. The speaking Mike and the listening Mike were two different characters. Perhaps he was not like the other fun-seekers on the beach, the ones I'd met on my package tour the last time. Perhaps he was more dangerous.

162

More guests drifted in for late breakfast: the honeymooners from California; the family from Venezuela; the chic couple from Manhattan, who seemed to belong more in a swanky beach-front hotel, like the Hyatt or the Ritz, than in the Playa Carauna.

Frau Sondheim clasped her topazed fingers together and said to me, "So, you've come to retrieve your uncle."

A crackling of seashells drew our eyes to the door in the stucco wall at the opposite corner of the patio. Laszlo stood in front of the strings of shells that curtained his office. He was dressed in khaki walking shorts and a white silk shirt, and had in his left hand the walking stick with onyx cougar's head. At the table, everyone put on smiles of greeting, but before any "good mornings" passed our lips, Laszlo was striding towards the swimming pool. Spanish words cut the sunlit yard like gunshots. Straight-bodied, straight-legged, with a smooth, cat-like face, he thrust the stick in the direction of the illicit swimmers and they fled the pool. Their bodies shone like brass as they ran to hide between the bushes and the wire-mesh fence that ran along the street. Laszlo continued his scolding in the nasal-gutteral tones of the local dialect, then, when he turned back, was met on the lawn by a man in a suit, carrying an attaché case. They went back to the gate behind the hacienda and left the Playa.

The Texan folded his paper and left the patio. "Shoot," he said through a wide smile as he passed the flowers growing beside the walk.

Frau Sondheim leaned back. "Our host has business in town this morning." She watched me cut into a wedge of pineapple with my fork, and I wondered if her comment about my uncle still waited for a reply.

"Fella looked like a lawyer to me," said Mike in a satisfied tone, as though a liaison with a lawyer brought Laszlo down to a common level. Mike put on sunglasses and bounced the heels of his palms on the arms of his chair. He's thinking about the Mexico City girl and her condominium, I thought.

"We haven't walked on the beach," said Mother. "You want to do that today, Gracie? Anyone else interested?" She meant Mike.

"This isn't the best part of the bay," he said. "Further up's where the beach bars are. More action."

I tried to see his eyes through the black plastic. "What sort of action?"

Again the staccato shouts of Laszlo, this time from the corner of the compound near the pool. We could see his face on the other side of the fence, between two hibiscus shrubs. The intruders were dressed now, and, driven by Laszlo's warnings, serpentined towards the gate under cover of trees and bushes.

"Wonder what he promised to do to them," Mike drawled.

The opening of Handel's *Messiah* burst through palm leaves and thatching. Our group was snagged in a sudden web of tragedy, Mother in a yellow jumpsuit and red loop earrings, Frau Sondheim with her hat held like a shield for her breast, bare shoulders showing above the brim, Mike cloaked in the white guest towel and sucking on a strawberry from my plate, Laszlo's dark-skinned boy hovering near one of the white pillars. "One forgets it is almost Christmas," said Frau Sondheim.

The music came from the Sonesta Massage Salon across the street. Madame LaMotte-Fouqué had large stereo speakers on her private balcony upstairs and had been playing classical music since we arrived. Not Mike's idea of action.

"When will you see your uncle again?" There was the question at last.

I swallowed a sweet shard of pineapple. *Tröstet, tröstet,* came the voice of the tenor from Madame LaMotte-Fouqué's massage salon.

One thing I remembered was that he had an ear missing. He'd gone to Panama one autumn and when he came back it was gone. I was a little girl then, and though I knew he looked lopsided and comical, I don't think I realized it was because of the ear. The stories about it came later. He left again, this time to live in Mexico, and I hadn't seen him since. He came back sometimes to visit, but once I discovered Manitou and got involved with DNA and tipis, I did not connect much with home.

Piranha, machete, airplane propeller. "Pooh," my father, whose brother he was, would say. "Some bruiser bit it off in a brawl. Now he can hear the buggers sneaking up behind him. Could have been useful to him in Italy."

Uncle Alvin had gone to war for adventure. He returned gaunt of soul, an exposed nerve. He'd spent hours talking to my mother in her little house in Granton, while Father worked at his office-workshop bringing life to dead pickerel and owls and black bears and bobcats. He was the only taxidermist in Granton.

"We did not have an affair," Mother would say about Uncle Alvin, although I never implied that she had. "But his mother was dead and his sister was a creep, so he came to me."

"What did he talk about?"

"I don't remember."

But there was more. The family album had several pages of photographs of my mother in winsome poses, and she'd told me Uncle Alvin had taken them in her back yard one summer before I was born. No other photos of her were like those. And I remember a party at Aunt Doreen's farm one Sunday afternoon when I was very small, where Uncle Alvin had wrestling matches with some of the young cousins and neighbour boys, in the barn, in the hay. The boys attacked him with war whoops, and he fended them off with agility and gentle strength. The other men at the party ignored the game, but the women, looking flushed, watched quietly and did not try to stop it.

Uncle Alvin spent the rest of his life pursuing get-rich-quick schemes in foreign countries. "He's selling refrigerators to Eskimos," said Father, who never went anywhere. (Father finally left Granton after he died. He was buried on the family plot at his parents' farm, now owned by the creepy sister Doreen and her common-law husband, Boris.)

But now the Mexican government was cracking down on foreign residents in their country and Uncle Alvin wanted to come home. He was seventy-two. "He can't stand our winters!" bristled Mother when she read the letter he'd sent to his sister. "This is nonsense." Boris and Doreen elected her to fetch Uncle Alvin from Mexico, who had asked to be "taken home," the way my father had asked to be "taken home" when his pain was unendurable. We decided to go at Christmas, make a holiday of it, seeing as how Doreen was paying the fare. Mother thought my company would be useful, since I'd been there once before. Because I could toss a few Spanish phrases around, she considered me fluent in Mexican.

The day after we arrived, a taxi driver took us to the address Uncle Alvin had written on the letter. We zig-zagged up the hill along short, narrow streets, past houses without walls, and food markets cloaked in bluebottles. "Feliz navidad," Hector, our driver, called to neatly dressed men and women on the sidewalks. "Are you sure this is where your uncle lives?" he asked as we played snakes-and-ladders on the crooked streets. "Last week we had a big shoot-out here. Drugs. What does your uncle do?"

We did not know. He lived with a woman who had a child. That was all we knew of the current Uncle Alvin.

At last the driver stopped the car and pointed to a lopsided pink building that had a sagging wooden door and no windows facing the street. A rusted yellow Volkswagen was parked out front. "This does not look good to me," said the driver.

"It doesn't look good to me, either," whispered Mother. She got out of the taxi. The driver leaped out and motioned for me to come along. As we crossed the street, the Volkswagen suddenly came to life with a clatter and spurted down the street like a startled frog. We had not noticed anyone in the car when we drove up, but now we could see a child, a light-skinned, dark-haired boy, sitting at the wheel.

The driver knocked on the door and shouted in Spanish. In a moment the door opened a crack and someone asked a question. "He wants to know your name."

"Alvin?" cried Mother, and she yanked on the door. It was held firmly on the other side. "It's Bill's wife, Marge." From where I stood I could see a wide leather belt and a hairy belly.

More questions, mingled with some familiar words. "He wants to know, what is the name of the Granton ladies' slow-pitch baseball team," said our driver.

A brown dog slunk up behind my mother and grinned and licked the perfumed hand that rested on her shoulder-bag. The dog brought with it a cheerful gang of flies. "For god's sake, Alvin!" Mother snapped. She tried to pry the door open with her red fingernails.

"Your uncle is not here," the driver explained to me. "He has moved."

"The name of the Granton ladies' slow-pitch team is the Buttons and Bows!" I yelled above my mother's clamour, though I wondered why my uncle would know that or care about it.

"Buttons and Bows is the mixed team," Mother said through clenched teeth. "It's the RAIN-bows!" Then to me, "I wouldn't expect you to know that!"

Two pudgy fingers poked out, between them a slip of paper torn from what appeared to be a pharmacy bag. The taxi man took it and managed to glance at it before my mother snatched it from him. The hairy belly inside the door growled more instructions, and the door drew shut. A latch fell into place.

"Where is this?" said my mother as she squinted at the address printed in pencil on the bag-paper.

"Oh, oh. It is in a bad part of town."

My mother rolled her eyes and with her free hand swatted

the dog and the flies away. She began mincing across the street to where the taxi was parked.

"You are to go there the day after Christmas. You are not to go until then. I will take you. This does not look good to me."

As we drove away, we saw the Volkswagen parked in front of a fruit stand. The boy looked straight ahead, only the top of his head showing above the lower window-frame.

As Laszlo's boy cleared away my sticky plate and rinds of fruit, I said to Frau Sondheim, "He's packing. We will pick him up the day after Christmas, and the day after that we go home."

"Does he have a ticket?"

"We have his ticket."

"What does he do here?"

"Ladies," said Mike, "please excuse me, but I think I shall begin the day." I looked at him and thought about the belt around the waist of Uncle Alvin's messenger.

Mother and I went through the hotel gate and then turned to admire the stone pillars on either side of it, as we did every time we left the Playa Carauna. A bronze plaque on the pillar displayed the name. On top of each pillar was a modest but striking cougar's head, carved from yellow onyx. "What does *carauna* mean?" asked Mother.

"Cougar," I guessed.

"Stupid name for a resort."

We were on our way to the beach. We would walk the two miles to the strip of high-rise hotels, have lunch in a patio bar, and take a taxi back so Mother could have a siesta before cocktails. She wanted to stop somewhere to buy some of Mexico's famous vanilla. She never baked.

An old Vega was parked on the street just outside the Playa's fence, two wheels on the sidewalk. Two naked little children tugged on a piece of nylon rope attached to a fat puppy, and a tired-looking young woman squatted in front of a brazier on which she was grilling blue shrimp. We skirted the picnic and nearly stepped into a fresh pile of excrement, which at first we thought belonged to the puppy. But in a second we realized otherwise. My mother swatted the air. "Should have brought one of those pooper-scooper things along."

"Them or us?"

"I hope this isn't what the beach is like. You're all covered up."

"I don't want to burn."

"You don't want anyone to notice you're a woman, you mean."

She didn't know about Fred. Fred was 73 and lived in the block next to mine near the college. I'd met him while taking a stroll after dark to cool off. He was strolling, too, and eventually began stopping at my apartment during his nightly walks. We'd watch the late news, and he'd put his hand under my kimono and stroke the top of my thigh. The *top* of my thigh. Then he'd walk home. But I had not told my mother about any of the men I'd fooled around with. My mom did not seem to know anything about what lay between flirting and marriage. "Are you going to study lizards all your life?"

If the old pictures in the album told any truth at all, my mother had had other possible identities, but they'd slipped away around the time my Uncle Alvin moved to Mexico for good. Nowadays her time was spent in the fashion corridor of the Granton Mall, and at hairdressers, and going to luncheons with other women in hairdos and chunky jewellery. She'd made an effort to include me while I was growing up, but I was stubborn and stand-offish and didn't want to fit into her society. Now our relationship seemed to be based on the mutual need to make each other more real. Here she was, wearing a halter-top and fuchsia shorts and a fuchsia Frau Sondheim-style hat. She still had beautiful legs and an unlined face. She looked like everyone else on the beach. To her, I was as dull and toady as a rusted Volkswagen.

"Mother, I like men. I just don't see myself as bait."

"You look like a sardine."

"You mean a minnow."

"Do what you want." She clutched my shoulder with one hand while she bent over to remove her sandals, a silky hand that had turned brown after only one day beside Laszlo's pool. Sand sprinkled out of the shoes onto the beach. She put them into a tote bag slung over her arm.

"I think we should talk about Uncle Alvin," I said. "Don't you think there's something pretty weird going on?" She hadn't mentioned the Granton ladies' slow-pitch team or the Boxing Day rendezvous since the day we'd journeyed up the hill. She seemed to have brushed it so cleanly out of her mind that I'd been afraid to spoil one of her few vacations by asking her questions.

"Of course there is," she replied. "There has been since he came back from Italy."

"What's he going to do in Granton?"

"Doreen expects him to live in that dingy little summerhouse on the farm. Ha! Even if he lived with me in Granton, it wouldn't be big enough for him. It's too late. If you'd at least have interesting hobbies. How can I tell people you make *tents* in your spare time?"

"Maybe you could tell them we're part Cree and I have a recessive wigwam-making gene." I remembered the bolts of new fabric I'd left unfurled and scattered in my living-room so that when I came home the vision of the patterns and colours as I opened the front door would begin to create pictures in my mind at once, so I could spin new patterns around a cone of bent saplings. Mother had come from Granton to the city to see my first installation, in the foyer of a new elementary school, and though it was fine for children, she hoped I'd "get out of tents" and into video dating or perhaps long lunches.

We padded along the flat wet sand where the beach met the surf. We noticed as we went that the inhabitants of the beach were changing, from dark-skinned Mexicans dressed in conservative bathing suits, to blondes and redheads wearing strips and strings and sun-tan oil. Where the natives had played in quiet family configurations, the jet-setters made desperate pursuits of pleasure with stereo tape-decks and hysterical games of volleyball. Soon we saw no children at all.

High above the bay, stick figures attached to strings floated under silvery-pink parachutes, pulled around in giant circles by motorboats on the water below. I stopped to watch the parasailors. From this distance, it looked as though the cables stretching from the boats to the harnesses would cross one another and tangle up and cause some hideous accident.

"You want to go on one of those things?" asked my mother. She squinted upwards from beneath the pink hat-brim.

But I only wanted to watch them, people wafting in the sky, held up by silk umbrellas. How did they feel when they came back to earth and walked on their own two feet? Bound to the earth or released from the sky?

We put our shoes back on and walked up the steps to the beach bar of a big hotel. Mother had brought an issue of *Vanity Fair* from the Playa and I had taken *Yankee Pasha*. We ordered beer and chicken salad. I tried to read but my eyes were drawn to the beach and the water and the parachutes and the perfect curve of the sea gulls' wings. Mother looked at the pictures in her magazine. "Look," she said. "This is a picture of Bette Davis when she was twenty-four years old. 1932. That was when I saw my first movie. I was twelve. We had to go to North Dakota to see it."

"What was it called?"

"I don't remember. This picture could have been taken yesterday. Just looking at her hairstyle and her dress."

We ate our chicken salad. Mother found a piece of cellophane in hers and wanted to leave, but we saw Mike come in from the hotel side of the bar. His hair was wet and slicked back and he had perched his sunglasses on his widow's peak. Fresh from his dip in the condo pool, I thought. But he was alone. Creases darted out from the corners of his almond eyes as he smiled at us from the doorway. He came to our table.

Mother forgot about the chicken salad and gave him a flirty wave. He sat down beside her, across from me, and flashed the wicked smile. "So you found the action," he said, watching my face.

"Oh, was that it?" I said, thinking about the kerfuffle Mother had raised over the cellophane. "Where's your friend?"

"She has a lot of other friends. The apartment was getting crowded."

The way he said *friends* and a sharpness in his usually slow voice made me think he'd been a victim of the racy beach life. The action went too fast for him. Perhaps they like leather, too, I wanted to say, but then Mike asked, "What are you doing this afternoon, ladies?"

"I'm going back for a nap," said Mother. "We had a long, heated morning on the beach."

I gathered up my book and our check.

"No, I'll get a taxi out front. You stay." She reached over and put the fuchsia-coloured hat on my head. As she stood up to leave she peered at the check. "Y'all can pay that," she said in Texan, and she dismissed it with a loose-fingered swat of her hand. "Tell the waiter about the you-know-what. And try to find some of that vanilla."

"Your mom's kinda wild," Mike said in his slow, lazy voice. "Unlike me."

"Well, you got a way of smouldering quietly in a corner. I wouldn't say you're like your mom there, no. But I'd just as soon sit in a patio bar with someone like you as with someone like her."

Someone *like* me, someone *like* her. "So, what are you doing this afternoon, Mike? Taking in the action?"

"Want to go to a movie?"

"A *movie*?"

"For fifty cents we could see *King Kong* just up the hill a little ways."

"Why not?" I said. I took off the pink beach hat.

He picked up my book. "Huh. What's this about?"

"Pirates. Lost love. What do you do with your leather?"

"Motorcycle accessories."

"You drive a motorcycle?"

"Get myself killed? You looked good in the hat."

The movie was not the second *King Kong*, it was the old Fay Wrey *King Kong*. They were out of raisinettes. After, I wanted to walk back to the Playa—we hadn't gone very far up the hill—but Mike offered to pay for the taxi. He didn't look like the walking type to me.

Frau Sondheim's pale fingers stroked the stem of the glass of cold California wine in front of her. "What is it like in the part of Canada where you live?" She looked at Mother, who had changed into a melon-coloured sun-dress and saucer-sized green earrings. Strains of *Swan Lake* accompanied the early evening breeze off the bay.

"Well, where we live, it's more like—well, more like a big garden, wouldn't you say?"

I looked sideways at her. She hated gardening, which practically made her a pariah among her age group in Granton. But I nodded.

"Lots of farmyards with lots of trees and bushes, and, in between, great big flat fields of plants of all colours, some in rows, some just thick carpets, you might say."

"Is it so very flat then?"

"Well, yes, but not that you'd notice. In Saskatchewan, it isn't really terribly flat, it's more rolling, but it's so dry and empty in places, it feels a lot flatter than Manitoba."

Everyone took a sip of wine.

"Now, that's in summer. In winter, it's all covered in beautiful white. Everything—trees, roofs, everything."

When we'd left Granton, only a little snow had fallen, and winds had covered the bit of snow with dirt from the naked fields. An ice storm in November had broken a lot of the trees. Mother's *garden* looked like Frau Sondheim's bombed-out Dresden.

Laszlo came out of his office and made his rounds of the guests having cocktails on his patio. He asked what we'd all done in the afternoon. I did not answer. Mike had disappeared after we got out of the taxi. I had not seen him for the rest of the afternoon. As Laszlo passed Frau Sondheim's chair, she reached up and held his hand for a moment, and I saw her eyes soften though she did not look up into his.

"What about Argentina?" My mother's voice was tart. Laszlo's hand slid away and he went on to the next table, tall, straight, dressed in silks.

"I live in the city. I do not see Argentina except when I fly over it to get here at Christmas time. My city is like any other city." She sighed. "I am a true porteño, you see." Frau Sondheim spoke in Spanish to the boy, who refilled the glasses, though none were empty. She continued, "I believe Argentina is much like Canada, turned upside-down. If you could fold the world along the Equator"—she put her wrists together and gently closed her hands like two halves of a marbled oyster— "we would match. We have icebergs and mountains and rivers and forests. And the culture of Europe is strong. We could have gone to Canada—perhaps. . . . " She smiled. "And we worship our steaks."

"What about your husband?" My mother leaned forward with her chin on her knuckles and waggled her nails.

"I lost my husband many years ago." Frau Sondheim looked

into her wine. She wore no jewellery tonight and reminded me of one of Tchaikovsky's swans.

Mother and I had dinner at the French café around the corner on the main strip. Most of the patrons spoke what sounded like Quebec French and we saw many packages of Rothmans cigarettes. The women were chic. These Canadians were foreign to us.

"Listen," said Mother softly during the *canard à l'orange*. "Do you think Frau Sondheim is a Nazi?"

"She might be a Jew. What does it matter? She's sad."

Mother sat back and tapped the breast of the duck with her fork. "I have not seen one real Mexican restaurant here. Even Granton has a Mexican restaurant. We must try to find one before we leave."

"I'm sure Uncle Alvin can recommend one."

She held the duck with her thumb and forefinger and tore a bit of meat away with the fork. "I haven't told you. Alvin can be a difficult man. He's sour and tough and stubborn. I'm afraid he's going to want to take his señorita along. And the boy."

That was not what I was afraid of at all.

When we'd finished our meal, I put the check in front of Mother and said, "Your turn to pay."

In bed I read *Yankee Pasha* after my mother had fallen into her quiet way of sleeping. To my dismay, I was falling a little in love with its swashbuckling hero—I'd always been attracted to those more confident and aggressive than I was. But Mike and the pink hat floated between the lines on the page, and I finally put out the plaster Venus de Milo lamp and fell asleep with Jason Starbuck on one side of me in the narrow bed, and my leather-hunter on the other. I woke up only once during the night, when a baby, or a cat, or a rooster, called out from the lamp-lit yard.

Then, my mother's laughter, mingled with a man's right outside my window. 10:30. I'd slept through the huffing and puffing as she wrestled with her bra, the clinking of her jars, the rattle of her wooden bracelet and her beads. She and Laszlo, talking and laughing among the lantanas, among the killer bees, her head bare, though once I saw her hand come up to shoo away something that was not there.

By the time I got to the patio, she had left, and I saw no sign of Mike or Laszlo or Frau Sondheim. I ate quickly. I wanted to walk by myself today, to translate the vignettes of the street in my own tongue.

We were all together for cocktails again at six o'clock. Mother had had a massage at the Sonesta Massage Salon, from Madame LaMotte-Fouqué herself. Laszlo had introduced them, and when he paid his pre-dinner respects, he and Mother babbled and laughed so much about it that he forgot to ask anyone else what they had done during the day. Mother seemed to think I had spent the afternoon with Mike. Frau Sondheim was quieter than usual and seemed tired.

Mike whispered in my ear that he thought the Texan was a bounty hunter. I whispered back that he was undoubtedly an oil millionaire.

"Look what I got myself this mornin' on the beach," said the Texan, "from a little girl wearing a little white dress." He reached down and pulled up a crucifix made of rough wooden slats. Dangling from it on white cords was a wooden mouse dressed in a Mexican costume. The mouse had floppy wooden feet, and as the Texan jerked the strings, the feet clattered on Laszlo's tiles in time to the polonaise filtering through Laszlo's thatched roof. "Shoot," said the Texan. "I'm gonna take it home for my little girl."

Out on the beaches and streets along the bay, children danced their marionettes for the customers to see while the father of the children chanted the price; teen-aged boys offered tours of the red-light district; women sold flowered caftans and shawls and ponchos; and the men promised to find you any sort of action

176

you desired. Grandmothers put the puppets together and sewed the garments. Babies slept on cobblestone as the tourist rabble bartered and heckled and jeered around them. Earlier in the afternoon, I'd seen an American college student selling football jerseys to Mexican boys, and I'd been flattered and courted by American real-estate agents offering free cruises to luxury condominiums. Society at the bottom of the hill was as flat as the dancing mouse's floppy feet. Even the sea gulls drank piña coladas from hollowed coconut shells tossed aside by sunworshippers.

"How about going to see those cliff divers tonight?" said Mike. "We could have dinner."

The cliff divers would be handsome charlatans, but I raised my eyebrows at Mother. She waved the idea away. "I'm having Mexican food here tonight. Laszlo's cooking. Gisela says it's the best in town."

Frau Sondheim smiled and nodded.

"Wear something that shows off your waistline," Mother called when I was halfway to the casita.

Trumpets, torches, a parade. A rocky precipice lit up by greens and reds and blues, a drum roll and a crash of cymbals. The divers in their sequinned capes were attended by the same fanfare as their compadres in the bullrings. Mike and I sat at our table on a terrace cut into the rocks and watched the ritual unfold at the striking of each hour. The construction of our cavern shut out the sounds of the other diners and all we heard was the orchestra, though faintly, the hissing of the tide on the rocks below us, and the pomp of the cliff-divers' parade. We fell into an enchantment, I think, for we spoke little, but stared out into the darkened ocean, and after awhile, the bodies twisting and arching in the narrow gorge leading to the ocean became little more than birds diving for herring. I felt as though I had been in this cave watching gleaming bodies fly by for all eternity.

Every hour Mike and I created our own ceremony by choosing a different drink, always one made with tequila, thinking we would be less sick in the morning. We ordered doubles so we would not have to rely upon the promptness of the waiter.

Once we were a little drunk, I said, "Anyone can sell anything here. All you have to do is stand on the street and call out. Or just stand on the street. What would *you* have to sell, Mike?"

He leaned forward holding his glass under his chin and his smile made his face turn devilish. After a moment in which we heard the trumpets sound down below, he said, "I'd sell all the Mexicans a one-way ticket outta here and let the gringos have it. I'd show every man, woman, and child the golden spirits of their past haunting the jungles and I hope they'd build a kingdom of their own, carved right out of their own souls and their own spiritual riches. That's what I'd do."

"Exactly!" I cried, and raised my glass, except that my *exactly* sounded more like *ksaakly*, and I realized my speech was beginning to crumble.

"And then I'd build a huge condominium hotel at the edge of it and whistle for the Americans." He beckoned the waiter. "I bet you thought I'd say motorcycles."

"It wasn't a test."

"What do you say we start back at the beginning with the margaritas?"

"No!" I said. "There must be more! Let's not start over. How about—tequila, vermouth, and grapefruit juice?"

"Did you get that, mesero?"

The waiter shrugged. A little later he brought us margaritas. I slid forward in my chair and put my knees between Mike's, mine bare, his clothed.

"Your mom keeps talking about tents. 'You should see Gracie's tents,' she says. Are you an inordinate camper, Gracie?"

"In between checking pickerel for mercury, I make—tipis." I licked the salt off the edge of my glass. "Surrealistic wigwams."

"To hell with wigwams. What have you got up there, fish for thermometers?"

"What?"

"You said you checked pickerel for mercury."

"Fish for thermometers." With our laughter we shattered the cliffs and the perilous rocks below, and our voices echoed on the cavern walls around us.

"I've got some Cuervo in my room," said Mike after the last diver had been trumpeted into the receding tide. "That's one way we haven't had it yet—straight."

Outside the restaurant, the press of the street vendors and tourists was at its usual midnight peak. Mike bought a long braid of leather and tied it around my loose white shirt. "There, that'll make your mom happy."

Where we were, where the cliff divers were, was far away from the Playa Carauna. I wanted to walk back, through the crowded, older part of the city, but Mike offered to hire a taxi.

Someone on the patio spotted us coming through the gate. We'd had to ring to get in, and the bell attracted attention. From a distance I could see my mother leaning out of the lamplight into the courtyard. Her silver bracelet flashed on her forearm. "I've taught them how to play crib!" she announced, and she gestured to the card-table in the corner, where I half expected to see hotel guests chained to the table legs. Frau Sondheim still looked tired, but more relaxed than before; the Texan beamed at us through the smoke of a half-burned cigar; and Laszlo sat elegantly in a straight-backed bamboo chair. He looked softer than usual. At first, I thought perhaps they'd all had a massage across the street, but then it occurred to me that they, too, had been drinking all evening.

Mike and I were invited to sit, and so we did. Within seconds, I realized I could not form sentences without my face and the words disintegrating into giddy heaps. I looked at Mike and attempted to make a subtle gesture towards his casita with a nod of my head. His sunglasses covered his eyes. When he did not move for several minutes, I concluded he was asleep.

"I'm not waiting a minute past eleven."

"It's a minute past eleven now."

Mother's impatient toes curled upwards out of the sandal she was tapping on the curb outside the Playa Carauna. "All right, I'll give him five minutes, but there's no doubt in my mind he's forgotten. He flies around day and night, why should he remember this?"

"You're unforgettable."

"I feel like I'm ninety-nine years old!" she snapped. "This heat's really starting to get to me."

We were waiting for Hector, our taxi driver, to take us to pick up Uncle Alvin. "Why doesn't he just meet us at the airport tomorrow?" I said to the sidewalk. "Why does he want us to get him exactly today? Where's he going to sleep tonight?"

"He's bunking with Larry." The answer came from Mother's lively toe.

"Larry?"

"The man from San Antonio."

"Oh, *that* Larry."

"He has a gun."

"Uncle Alvin?"

"No, Larry."

"Good. Let's take him along with us to Uncle Alvin's."

Her shoe became still. "He really is lost, you know."

"Larry?"

"Gisela Sondheim's husband. I thought she meant he was dead. She actually lost him." She turned and stared at the cougar's head on the gatepost, as if it held the secret of the missing souls.

"Here's Hector," I said.

The taxi flew by, made a reckless U-turn in front of Madame LaMotte-Fouqué's, and stopped finally at our curb. We saw our taxi-man's cheery face through the windshield. "Feliz navidad!"

"Feliz navidad," we replied together, and got into the back seat.

We were just about to pull away from the sidewalk when the door of the passenger side of the front seat jerked open and Mike flung himself into the taxi. "Going my way?" he grinned.

"No, we're going the opposite direction," I said.

"Me too," he said.

"We'll drop you at the zocalo if you like," said Hector.

"What's up?"

"We're going to fetch my Uncle Alvin."

"Let me tell you—" Hector leaned way back and took his eyes away from the busy traffic along the beach drive. "Before I came, I went to the house of your uncle." He looked at us over his right shoulder. "To my surprise, stopped in front of it is a Greyhound. There is no one in it."

"A greyhound?" My mother raised her pencilled eyebrows.

"A bus, Mother."

"They have those here?"

"It is empty, of course," continued Hector. "I ask the bambinos playing in the street—"

"Maybe he's a bus driver."

"—if an old gringo is driving this bus, and they say, no, it is a young mexicano."

Mother said, "What's so weird about a bus on a street?"

"It is a Mexico City bus." With his thumb and index finger Hector shaped a rectangle in the air above the steering-wheel. "A Mexico City bus is never in that part of the town where your uncle is. The children say the driver brings packages." I could see Hector's eyes watching me in the rear-view mirror. "It does not look good to me."

"Maybe they're"—Mother pulled a compact out of her

handbag—"flower bulbs or something." She checked her lipstick.

The traffic got thicker as we neared the zocalo. "The day after Christmas," explained Hector.

I had not seen Mike the day after the night we did not have the tequila straight. I stayed in my casita with my hangover and drank bottled water and watched our one solitary cucaracha make her daily sweep of the dresser and Mother's make-up bag. Mother said she'd seen Mike going into the Sonesta late in the afternoon, probably for a steam-bath. On Christmas Day, Laszlo and his boys set the patio and the lawn with large tables covered with pink linen and white poinsettias. He invited his guests and all his friends for Christmas dinner, and Madame LaMotte-Fouqué played carols about snow and sleigh rides. In the evening, we drank black Russians and listened to Handel again, while the Texan danced his mouse among broken piñatas. We were all friends suspended from the thatched roof of the Playa Carauna, and none of us ever wanted to touch the earth again.

Late that night, I sat down beside Mike on the wicker settee and said, "You don't really buy leather for saddlebags. You came here to wrestle crocodiles and lasso killer bees, didn't you?"

His eyes, here under the slanted roof of straw with only two lamps burning on the patio, were the colour of the Kahlua in our glasses. "Tonight, I wrestle crocodiles and lasso killer bees. Most of the time, I'm just a lonely boy. And I haven't had a mom in a long, long time."

My mother, her filigreed shawl on her shoulders, sat playing gin rummy with the honeymooning woman from California, who was also missing her mom.

"There's something brave about her," Mike said. "Have you noticed it?"

Something brazen.

"I think about how I spend fourteen hours a day in a leather sweatshop in Caroline, Vermont, full of old moms, and I think, maybe they're like her and I treat them like strangers day after day. I'd like somebody to make me braver now and then. Not to wrestle crocodiles, just to think about who I could be, think about possibilities." He stroked Head Honcho Cat, who had jumped onto the settee between us. "And you're not really a biologist, Gracie. I'll bet you kiss those fish and turn them into Indian princes."

"Yes."

We both looked at the Texan. The dancing mouse had crumpled at his feet and tears streamed down his cheeks.

Hector stopped on the street in front of the old plaza that teemed with Mexicans carrying straw bags bulging with market goods. The shoppers and the street pedlars raised a clamour that would not be drowned out, as it would be on the beach, by the noise of the surf. Hector held his cupped hand out towards Mike, but Mike folded his arms and drawled, "I think I'll see a little of the real Mexico. Mind if I tag along?"

Neither Mother nor I spoke. I was afraid the situation with Uncle Alvin would become tricky, and be embarrassing for Mike. Mother probably assumed I wanted Mike along.

" 'S that okay with you, Mom?" he called out.

"Fine, fine," she replied, perhaps thinking Mike was tough and could be useful in case we ran into any more hairy bellies. She waved Hector to drive on.

We turned away from the flash and sparkle of the bay and started up the hill, and wove our way along the familiar crooked path that led away from the beach and hotels and markets. About halfway up the hill, we came to a street that followed the contour of the hill. We stayed on the long narrow street fronted by broken-down buildings and half-walled hovels for about two kilometres. At last we saw the yellow Volkswagen parked in front of a shop on the right-hand side of the street. But across from it was a shiny white Cadillac with a Texas licence plate. Leaning against it was an extremely large man wearing a large cowboy hat and sunglasses. He seemed to be watching the Volkswagen. The Mexico City bus was gone.

Mike was sitting up straight in his seat. "God, that guy's built like a brick—"

"This does not look good to me," said Hector. He drove by and stopped half a block away from the Caddy.

"This is where your uncle lives?" said Mike, looking at the dilapidated scrap-lumber fences on either side of us.

Being careful not to point, Hector said, "Your uncle lives in a butcher shop," and he jerked his head backward to the store we'd passed. I had seen sausages and limp chickens hanging in the small, square windows on either side of the door.

"Well, let's go." Mother began to get out.

"Wait!" Hector reached over as though to grab her arm. "I will go first." He put the taxi in reverse and backed up till we were just in front of the Volkswagen.

"Mike, why don't you go with him?" suggested Mother.

"The street is very quiet," said Hector. "Where are the children?"

We saw no one, though we'd come through a mile or so of bustling sidewalks, no one except the man wearing the cowboy hat. I turned and made sure no young head was hidden behind the steering-wheel of the Volkswagen.

"I don't like the looks of the guy with the hat there," mumbled Mike, and he slid down in his seat.

Hector walked briskly to the door of the butcher shop. I saw Mike watching him in the side mirror. Someone spoke sharply in Spanish, then words began to fly in a variety of voices. The large man across the street threw a cigarette butt onto the pavement. Some sort of argument seemed to be taking place. People spitting short, nasty phrases.

"Oh, for heaven's sake!" Mother swung open her door and unfolded her brown legs into the street. I saw the Texan shift his weight to one foot, and though I could not see his eyes, and he did not turn his head, I knew he was watching my brightly coloured mother march to the butcher shop.

Hector beckoned her on. "Señora. Señora."

"Alvin? Alvin?" I heard her chirp as she disappeared into the shop.

Silence. The view of the bay was blocked by meaningless fences. We had nothing to look at except the cowboy and his car, and that did not seem like a good idea.

"I can't let her go in there by herself." I slid over to the door.

"Shouldn't someone stay with the taxi?" said Mike. But I heard him behind me as I walked to the meat shop.

"It is not looking good." Hector shook his head. He stood just inside the door. The room behind him was unlit except for a bit of sun filtering through the two dusty windows. In front of a display cooler full of blue-tinted shrimp stood two Mexican men and a woman. Their skin was shiny with perspiration. "Your uncle and your mother are in there." An unpainted door led to a back room. I could hear a muffled conversation. One of the voices was high-pitched like a child's or a young woman's.

One of the sweating men moved to the door and stood in front of it.

"I'm her daughter," I explained.

Hector said something in Spanish. But the other man did not move, and then the staccato shouting began again, with all four Mexicans talking at once. Finally, Hector said to me, "Please wait for your mother, señorita."

Mike hovered in the doorway leading to the street and looked out against the bright sun. Hector went over to look out with him, and so we all waited. I watched the flies crawl on the chicken carcasses hanging in the window. The voices droned on in the room at the back of the butcher shop.

"Vamose! Vamose!" a man shouted on the sidewalk out front. I couldn't tell who he was talking to. Hector came in and knocked on the inner door. "Señora, señora, we must go. It is looking very bad."

I heard Mike say in a faint voice, "Mr. Big there's got a shotgun in his Caddy."

Texans and their guns.

The unpainted door flew open and Mother, looking angry and brisk, came through. I moved towards the back room.

"Señorita . . . ," Hector implored. Mike took my arm. The door swung shut.

"Let's get out of here!" Mike hissed through his teeth.

"Let's wrestle crocodiles," I hissed back.

But I had seen, for the fraction of a second that the door had been open, three faces: a boy's, with serious eyes and black hair falling over childish creases in his forehead; a woman's with eyes like the boy's and the cheeks and brow of the Mayans; and Uncle Alvin's. Deep lines I didn't remember cut across it like the face paint I used to make from red beets in other children's gardens in Granton, and he looked more lopsided than I remembered because he had hardly any of that sandy-coloured hair left to make up for the missing ear. He was in a wheelchair, leaning forward with his hands clenched on the armrests. In fact, the whole scene had been clenched, Uncle Alvin's lifetime taut and frozen before me in that one glimpse through a closing door. The boy had held something in his small hands, but I could not summon up what it had been. I believed it was a dancing mouse dressed in Mexican clothes and dangling with its feet off the ground from a tangle of white string.

I followed Mother out of the butcher shop. A man in a white suit and American running shoes stood in the middle of the street with his hands in his pockets. We did not hurry to the taxi, my mother, the driver, Mike, and I, lest like cats passing a dog we enticed a chase. We sauntered in a half urgent, half nonchalant sort of way past the butcher shop window, past the absurd yellow Volkswagen, past the Cadillac on the other side of the street where the giant rummaged for something in the back seat.

"Isn't he coming?" I asked.

"No," said Mother.

"But he's an invalid!"

"He is not the least bit ill."

"He's in a wheelchair."

"It's a fake. He also has a false I.D. And he intended to leave his son behind."

"*His* son?" A dog barked behind the fence. We pulled out into the narrow streets, and though we left the curb slowly, Hector drove faster and faster as we got further away from the butcher shop. As we'd climbed into the taxi, I'd seen the Mayan woman and the child walking quickly across a back lot. They carried nothing and I saw no sign of Uncle Alvin.

"Who was the man in the suit?" I asked. "Was he a policeman?"

"We're not sure," said Mike.

Hector said, "He told us he was a federal agent and there was going to be a bust-up. But—" He shrugged. "He did not show us his badge."

Mike, in the back seat with me now, kept looking through the rear window. His glasses were askew atop his slick hair and his eyes were narrowed to disguise his apprehension. He held tight onto the door handle as the taxi swerved and lurched its way back to the safety of the crowded zocalo.

"It wouldn't work, Gracie," and I heard a sadness and weariness in my mother's words that she seldom allowed. "He's in deep here. He's in trouble. Immigration will let him stay if he marries that girl, so that part's all right. It's the trouble he wants to get away from. . . . "

"I didn't get a chance to talk to him!" I cried. "That kid is my flesh and blood!" My cousin. I didn't even know his name. "They're in danger. What are we going to do?"

"I don't know, Gracie."

Mother sat very still for a moment, and I knew by the way she'd said it that she was rethinking it all, getting ready to explain, or change her mind.

"Gracie, I was . . . afraid of him, his life. And when I think how we used to sit at that ugly little chrome dinette table and talk, and how he had such dreams, always those warm, tropical dreams, and nightmares about the war. . . . His life—has just become so much bigger than we could handle now. I am afraid of him."

A tightness in my stomach hardly let me breathe. "He's old now. He'll settle down. He can send a little money to the mother for the boy."

"They're a family. Let them face it together here." She let out a deep sigh. "I don't know what will happen to him."

A family—an old scoundrel with one ear, an Indian girl less than half his age, and a fair-skinned boy who prowled the streets in a rusty Volkswagen.

"He gave me something to give to his sister."

Mike leaned forward. "Mrs. Thiesen, I suggest you open it up and see what it is before you take it through customs," he said slowly.

The back of my mother's hairdo remained frozen, and I realized how much her head bobbed and danced in normal times.

"He is right, señora," said Hector.

"I'll do it now."

Had my mother been carrying her floppy tote bag, the situation at the butcher shop might have escalated, if the Texan or the man in the white suit, or whoever the bad guy was, had suspected a transference of contraband. But she and I had both taken small clutch-bags adequate for fetching Uncle Alvin. Now she slowly opened hers and pulled out an envelope. After some hesitation, she lifted the flap. Wrapped in a hand-embroidered handkerchief were some photographs and a thick, folded document—a will, perhaps. "He took these out of his suitcase." Mother flipped through the photos with the flat bottoms of her fingertips, and we saw Uncle Alvin at different stages of his life, many of them in jungle landscapes, some with women, but most of the pictures were of his family.

I heard another sigh, long and deep, my mother engulfing her swashbuckler's spirit, or releasing it for the last time.

Hector, to be polite, asked Mike if he would now like to get off at the old plaza with its holiday crowds, but Mike answered that he would prefer to accompany us back to the Playa. On his broad, tanned hands, still clutching the handle of the door, his knuckles remained pointed and white.

I looked at the photos again. No one smiled, suspicion haunted their eyes, and though Uncle Alvin always turned his missing ear away from the camera, the photographs still looked off-balance, somehow. I held one of the photos close and stared at Uncle Alvin's creased, weathered face. An old lonely boy . . . a Yankee pasha.

"Stop!" shouted Mike. The wheels of the taxi squealed on the cracked pavement. We all tumbled forward and our eyes flew to Mike, who was braking with his canvas beach shoes on the taxi floor. "We'll walk back." He grabbed my hand and pulled me into the street.

"Bring vanilla!" I heard my mother call as Hector eased the car into the noon-hour traffic.

Mother was on the patio. She had been swimming. No—not swimming, for she never allowed water to touch any part of her hair. But she had walked in the pool. I could see that by the way her bathing suit creased on her belly. She sat at a table spread with fruits and salads, and talked with a red-haired child about winter in Granton. I took the pink hat from her head and put it on mine.

"They still haven't got that old fountain going," she said. Laszlo's boys stood with their hands on the edge of the white marble like faith-healers. The fountain was clogged. They did not know how to use tools to unclog it.

"I got the vanilla," I said.

"What will I use it for?"

"I don't know."

"I've thought of going back to get him, but—"

I patted her bracelet. "Another time. We'll get him another time."

Mike and I had walked home slowly, and as *feliz navidad* echoed in many voices on the street between the hill and the boy, we had reinvented Uncle Alvin. We gave him a legendary life and gave his son a name. I cried, we laughed. We watched tipis flying like spirits over the water and the frail human bodies flying along. Mike held my hand. He did not get tired from the long walk.

"Isn't this book from our casita?" asked Mother. "You left it here."

I hadn't finished it. It would stay in our casita for the next guest, or until I came back.

Mike came from the pool.

"Tequila. Straight. Your room," I said.

He walked gingerly on the hot cobblestone path. "Where are those bees?"

"The time for the killer bees is long past," I said. I was aware of my mother, still holding the book, standing very still, watching me go.

A baby cried in the women's quarters, women who worked in the kitchen and cleaned the guests' rooms, but were seldom seen. Just outside the office, the Texan stood surrounded by suitcases and shopping bags and boxes, and I imagined the dancing puppet coiled and folded inside one of them, its big flat feet hugging its body, perhaps concealing the gun. "Larry," I said to myself. One of Laszlo's boys stood behind him to carry the bags when the taxi came. I could hear the crisp, walking-stick voice of Laszlo himself coming through the seashell door. Frau Sondheim, with dark tendrils of hair lying on her shoulders, walked slowly across the lawn, her head bent as though she were searching for remnants of Laszlo's Christmas in the grass. The orange cat tiptoed slowly behind her. Whatever it was these travellers had lost or found, they would all cease to exist when my mother and I walked past the onyx cougars' heads for the last time.

Mike ushered me through his door just as a smooth green gecko on the casita wall disappeared like a ghost behind some vines.

Madame LaMotte-Fouqué played Mozart on her balcony. A canopy of trumpets covered the bay.

"BRIDG OUT"

They discovered the bisected Leona Berg watercolour near Baffle, Saskatchewan. Half the painting. Leona Berg was a friend of April's family. The painting was worth about five hundred dollars, unframed. Leona had been at the wedding, but she'd presented the gift to April and Sam a month earlier.

"This is so unbelievable."

"Oh, shut up, Ape. You've said that five hundred times."

"This is a tragedy," said April Heppner, not yet knowing about the swollen, leaden clouds waiting for them far to the west. "It's a death. We killed—*you* killed a piece of Leona."

April and Sam sat in a cow pasture beside the No. 1 Highway and stared at the half-painting on the easel. They'd stopped there so Sam could paint a distant potash mine. The sun was low, the colours of the air and the prairie just right. April had brought a book and didn't mind leaning back against a fencepost and reading while Sam worked.

He'd opened his easel and his paints and set up the Canson paper, which he'd halved with the company paper cutter the day before the wedding. Sam had started painting in smaller dimensions lately and the new cutter at the jeans factory where he was plant manager sliced cleanly through several layers.

The half-painting had fluttered out onto the stubble and quack grass when Sam had opened the pad of watercolour paper, just fluttered off the easel and landed at April's feet, upside-down. "What's this?" she'd said. She looked at the painting. "WHAT'S THIS?"

"What? Oh-oh . . ."

"Sam!"

"That's the picture from Leona—thing."

"Berg! Leona Berg. What happened? Where's the rest of it?"

"How did it get in there?"

April reached up and grabbed her ponytail, as she often did when surprised or distressed. "This is unbelievable!"

The RVs rolled by on the No. 1. The ones from Ontario usually honked when they saw the plates on Sam and April Heppners' Mustang. There was a lot of honking.

"Where's the rest of it?" said April.

"Back in Kenora in the other half of the Canson pad, I suppose." Sam began to feel an uneasiness, a sudden weight that had come out of the sky.

"This is unbelievable. I happen to know she gets about five hundred bucks a painting."

"Well, who put it in there?"

"I told you I put it there, to keep it flat and clean."

"That was so long ago." Sam folded up the easel and closed the paint box. "What does it matter how much money it's worth? She made it for us."

"What are you doing?"

"I can't work now."

"Well, what are we going to do?"

They looked at the painting for a long time. Mountains, trees, part of a lake, a winding trail cut off by the evil paper cutter. Sam said, "What was on the other half?"

"Something. Something important, more. . . . I just can't remember."

Sam took the painting from April's hand and held it at arm's length. He had to know what was in the missing half of the picture. "Maybe this is the whole thing."

"No, I remember it was bigger. Exactly twice the size, Samoo."

Both were thinking about the double irony of the scene Leona Berg had chosen for them. They were on their way to the Rockies for their honeymoon. Sam had never been to the mountains, though he'd almost made it once before. He had taken the train. The train crashed in Alberta, and many people had been killed. Sam had narrowly survived the crash because a microwave oven, thrown from its moorings on impact, had flown against a window and broken it. Sam and a few other passengers managed to escape seconds before a tanker car exploded and destroyed the car he'd been in. It had taken a long time for Sam to recover from the horror, and for his mind to leap beyond the crash to his original vision of glaciers and valleys and alpine meadows. For Sam now, getting to the Rockies was nearly an obsession.

His mother had worked shift at the mine at Red Lake when he was growing up. Sam hated the mine. He hated the shift work and he hated his mother looking tired, dressed in drab work clothes, next to his many aunts who were more glamorous and well dressed. When he was very small, he hadn't even known what a mine was. One day when Sam was about nine, his Aunt Nettie had hung a glow-in-the-dark picture of mountains on the wall over his bed. Parts of the mountains, and the frosty lake in the foreground, were silvered and shone softly when the lights were out. Late at night, Sam would lie with his head at the foot of the bed so he could gaze at the picture and pretend his mother was crossing the lake to get to those mountains, where she could pick nuggets of silver right off the glittering fields of ice.

The scene sorted itself back into its earlier arrangement, with

Sam seated before his low easel, brush poised, and April reading her book and leaning back against a fencepost, shifting now and then when a point of stubble got out of hand. The RVs continued to honk on the No. 1 and ground squirrels whistled in the ditches.

In Baffle they gassed up and picked up Cokes, and April decided to call her mother.

"We're almost in Regina!" Sam cried as the Coke cans tumbled out of the machine. "Call her from the hotel."

"She might be sleeping by then."

"Don't call her at all. You just want to tell her what big bad Sam did with his big bad paper cutter."

April slouched back to the Mustang. "I wouldn't do that."

The Cokes made their skin feel sticky and they felt grimier and grimier as they approached Regina at sunset. Sam's potash mine lay safely on the back seat. He was particularly pleased with his clouds, though back in the pasture April had been unenthusiastic. The dry farmlands on either side of the highway disappeared into the dusk like Cheshire cats.

April wondered whether it was appropriate to phone a mother on one's honeymoon. Her mother had been very particular about traditions and etiquette when they'd planned the wedding. April was envious that Sam never worried for a moment about where to put his stepfather's stepmother in the receiving line. The problem was that April's mother took social blunders seriously, and she did not talk about her family's lapses to her friends. She kept it all in and suffered from anxiety attacks.

So April decided not to call her mother until perhaps the night before they returned home, maybe from Bismarck, North Dakota, and she would not tell anyone about the painting.

Then April thought about the microwave store she owned in Kenora. Sam believed it providential that he'd met, and been attracted to, someone connected with microwave ovens. But April was worried about the store because it was not in the mall.

A lot of shoppers bought microwave ovens on impulse after they'd gotten their paycheques from the jeans factory and were strolling around the mall on a Friday night while their children bobbled ahead, in and out of every shop. Children were good scouts, from the merchants' viewpoint. "Making Waves" was in a business complex next to the dry cleaners, across from Kenora Realty. No impulse buyers, no kids cruising for gadgets. She'd have to talk to the mall manager about getting display space somewhere.

The lights of another potash headframe in the lavender dusk made April think about the painting again. Whenever Leona came from Winnipeg to visit April's mother, the two of them would visit April. What would April tell her about the terrible accident? "The first time she comes," said April out loud, "we'll tell her it's being framed."

"What?"

"If she comes soon we'll tell her it's being framed, and if she comes months and months from now we'll tell her we didn't like the first frame and we're having it reframed."

Sam's glasses had been sliding down his nose since they'd left the filling station. In the summer, glasses always slid down more after sunset, as though all the natural oils of the body collected there at the end of the day. He'd push them up over and over again, rub the sweat away from the bridge of his nose with his thumb and index finger, screw up his cheekbones so they lifted the bottoms of the frames a little higher. Now his lenses were smudged and blurry.

He'd stopped thinking about the painting and was thinking instead about riding with his cousin Betty through dried-up dike-bottoms in her dad's '63 Chevy pick-up, how the scented cardboard Christmas tree hanging from the mirror had danced when they'd hit the ruts, how Betty had worked the stickshift and the clutch, how they'd laughed. A lot of girls were like that at sixteen—half boy, half woman, making a young man aware for the first time of his feminine side. Betty had gone to Toronto to school when she was seventeen and Sam hadn't seen her since. But he wondered if she'd stayed that way—a thin, confident rough-rider who could be a good friend to a man. Most girls evolved out of that, but maybe she hadn't.

Then he thought about being married. He wondered if it would be better than what they'd been doing—taking turns spending weekends in each other's apartments. Kenora had a new condominium development and that's where he and April would live when they got back from the Rockies, if she would be able to tear him away from the mountains, and if they could ever agree on where to put the dank old upright piano April had hauled up from her parents' basement.

So when April started talking about framing and reframing, what was on Sam's mind was listening to April plod through grade five Conservatory pieces, listening to her improvise Beatles songs in the key of C on a piano that would never be far enough away. She was saying, "Then we have to keep a space open for it on a wall somewhere."

"Why don't we just frame the two halves separately, put them in different rooms, play find-the-matching-piece?"

"You're jealous. You don't want someone else's art in your house. You want to fill it up with your own."

"Yeah. Sure. April, what's done's done. I don't want to worry about it till we get home."

"Listen: what would you do if it were yours? What if you'd given one of your pieces to someone and it got damaged? What's the right thing to do from your point of view?"

Sam took his foot off the accelerator. The outskirts of Regina twinkled up ahead and traffic was heavier now. He opened his window to let in the sound of the city. "Well, I don't think I'd want to know about it, to tell you the truth."

April crackled the walls of her empty Coke can. "Ha! Then we have to make up lies."

Regina turned out to be a short city. Nothing was very tall or very far away. From their hotel room on the fourth floor, they could see the edge of town, fields, tractors, grain elevators. The streets were dusty. "We're in the middle of a drought," said the hotel clerk.

In the dimly lit dining-room of the hotel, Sam and April had a late supper. He ordered a steak sandwich and fries, she spinach salad and an item the menu described as "poached chicken breast in multiple mustards." The other guests sized them up as honeymooners because they looked a little worn out and a little uncomfortable with the silence that lay between them on the linened table. When they spoke they bickered about what colour of wine to order.

The hotel was designed in such a way that some of the rooms overhung the street below. At first April was exhilarated by the sounds of the movements of the city at night, of young girls laughing, shouts and whistles of boys, souped-up cars, sirens, a drunk in aria, a dog barking on its leash, horns conversing in code. Sam stood on the balcony for awhile and told her that his mother had taken him to a hotel in Winnipeg once, and he'd nearly fallen from their eighth-floor window when he'd tried to touch the pigeons that were floating on updrafts from the hot streets. He had never told his mother he'd almost gone over the ledge. He'd never told anyone until now.

After Sam had turned off the last talk show and had installed himself in the bathroom, April closed windows, closed heavy drapes. The noise still came in. She looked for some sort of knob that would control the air-conditioning. It wasn't in any of the usual places. "Samoo, it's hot. Is there a thermostat or something in there?"

No gurgled through toothpaste. When he came out, Sam said, "Open the window."

"It's loud. Don't people ever go to sleep in this weird town? I thought they rolled up the sidewalks here at 10 P.M."

April was always short-tempered when she was hot. Sam knew that. Hot summers were not good for her. To cheer her up, Sam said, "We could tell Leona that my brother is using the painting as an example in his art class."

"He doesn't teach painting, he teaches graphics."

"I know. But does she know?"

"I don't think so. That's a good one, Sam." April looked cooler for a moment. She stood in the lamplight and brushed her springy brown-gold hair. "That's a good one."

Sam sprawled on one of the double beds and skimmed the newspaper he'd found in the lobby. He was still wearing his jeans, the ones his factory made.

"Phone down about the air-conditioning, will you?" said April.

"They're having a lot of rain in Alberta," said Sam. "Before I call, tell me why you said what you did about me wanting to fill our house with my own paintings. You never thought I was egotistical before we were married."

"Well, all artists are a little egotistical, Sam. It's okay. I don't mind." April turned and blew him a kiss along her manicured fingers.

Sam's glasses were sliding again. "No, they aren't. I'm not. And don't make like that painting was such a personal treasure to you. You can't remember what was on it, either." He reached for the telephone receiver.

"I know it wasn't a nude," said April under her breath.

Sam waved the receiver in triumph. "You're mad because I saw someone else's breasts, is that it?"

"It was a nude I knew."

Sam put his hand over the mouthpiece. "Oh my god . . ."

"What?"

"The guy at the desk heard me. It's one of those phones where you connect with the desk as soon as you pick it up."

"Well, tell him about the air-conditioning."

"I can't now. We'll open the window. I haven't even seen Joanne Lowry on the street since then."

"She works at the realty office. I see her every day." Sam had dated many girls and women before he met April. He spoke fondly about all of them, as though they were all his friends. April turned the television on again and stood in front of it with her hands on her hips. She, too, wore factory jeans.

"Take off your pants."

"Oh Sam!"

"You won't be so hot."

Another train crash. No one had been hurt, but April stiffened and fought back the instinct to turn and see how Sam was reacting.

On the bed, Sam looked at pictures in the newspaper of Albertans frolicking in huge puddles, celebrating the long-awaited rain. When he heard the news report of the train accident in Quebec, blocked by April's soft curved shape, his mind did what he had taught it to do: lit for a thousandth of a second on bodies in flame, then leaped to the mountain peaks beyond. "Well, I didn't pick her."

They quarrelled about Joanne Lowry until April took off her jeans, and their yawns took the edge away from their sarcasm. Before they fell asleep, Sam said, "Maybe we should move to Baffin Island. We wouldn't have to tell any lies. Leona Berg wouldn't come up there to visit us, would she?"

"Leona Berg could be anywhere," said April into the nape of Sam's neck. "She could be right up there in that water sprinkler. Do they need microwaves in Baffin Island?"

The clouds in the morning were a seamless, unchanging slate grey, and the air was very still and humid. April talked a lot that morning as they drove. She was somewhat animated because she hadn't slept well. Noises had erupted all night on the street below their room. She talked about convection ovens, browning units, sales schemes.

Sam grew tired of it and switched the topic to the wedding, which they had not really talked about much the previous two days. That worked all right until they got onto Sam's grandparents, who were Mennonites and had refused to stay for the dance after dinner because of the liquor.

Some of April's friends had warned her not to marry a Mennonite, even though he wasn't a real, practising Mennonite, that their differences would catch up with them sooner or later. April thought that Sam secretly wished her parents hadn't gone ahead with the dance, so his family didn't have to be embarrassed, and it had caused April's mother no end of anxiety about the right thing to do. So when under the grey sky between Regina and Swift Current Sam began to talk about what a good sport his mom had been, April changed the subject. "I want to look for an antique piano lamp. I hear Saskatchewan is good for antiques."

"The only antiques in Saskatchewan are the roads. I'm not leaving the No. 1."

"Well, I don't mean trails with ruts in them. We'll stick to the—you know—pavement or asphalt or whatever."

"You never told me this was going to be a shopping trip. The prairies don't have any real antiques, only queer junk that takes up valuable space in tourists' trunks."

April opened the glove compartment to get her nail kit. "My corsage! Look! It's a wreck! Didn't you see it this morning when you put my nail kit in here?"

"Yeah, but it was a wreck already."

"My going-away corsage! It was an orchid. How did it get in here, anyway?"

"You can't keep flowers forever, Ape."

She held it lovingly to the place above her breast where Sam had pinned it in the Kenora Best Western while everyone waited in the ballroom for their return at midnight. She had planned to press it in her bride book. It was not supposed to go along on the honeymoon. In fact, her mother was probably frantic looking for it. She had to call her. . . .

"I'm sorry about your orchid," Sam said to April.

She put it on the dashboard and wondered how she might resurrect it.

A wall of rain hit the Mustang without any warning. April's emery-board made quick, nervous movements in the corner of Sam's eye as he sat bent forward, trying to see turns in the road and sudden taillights in front of them.

"I read they were having a lot of rain here," said Sam.

"Maybe you should stop."

"I think it's letting up a little."

April could find only country music on the car radio.

By the time they got to Swift Current the rain had quit, but the clouds were still heavy-looking, and the atmosphere remained humid and oppressive. "I can't wait till we get to the mountains," said Sam. "Rain doesn't seem so endless when you can't see the whole sky, like you can here."

"Look, Sam—'Mel's Kitchen.' Let's stop here."

"I'm getting gall bladder attacks from greasy food."

"I'm sure you can get a salad and a tuna sandwich here."

Mel didn't have many customers. Sam and April had seen about twenty vehicles in the parking-lot, but when they asked the waitress where everybody was, she jerked a thumb over her shoulder and said something about a skeet-shooting range behind the diner. A man in a 'Mel's Kitchen' T-shirt and a bright red beret bit little pieces off a raw foot-long wiener he was holding in his right hand, while with a lazy left hand he rolled a bottle over a slab of dough.

April insisted that they sit at the counter, "to be kooky," and Sam said to the dough-roller, "I wonder if I can get a salad."

"Salad bar's around the corner," Mel replied without turning.

April said, "I want one of those foot-long hot dogs with the crunchy skin. I love those." Although she spoke to Sam, the man they hoped and believed to be Mel reached up to a shelf and slapped a wiener on the griddle next to where he was working the dough. The wiener crackled immediately. "You better get your salad," whispered April. "My hot dog will be ready before you can say wilted lettuce."

When Sam came back with a platter full of leaves and sprigs and wedges and jello-y blobs, April was just making her first notch in the over-sized frankfurter. "The salad bar is a work of art!" said Sam. "They must be expecting somebody."

"Maybe all of them over there will come over here later," said April through a cloud of hot-dog bun. "This is great. I bet there isn't a microwave in the place."

"But Ape, can you imagine the type of people who shoot skeet and then eat salad bar? I mean, the pick-up trucks in the parking-lot say skeet, but the salad bar says racquetball or bird-watching or something."

April patted her lipstick with a napkin from the bulging dispenser in front of her. "Mel says Kindersley is loaded with antiques."

"What's a Kindersley?"

"A little town north of here."

"Where is Mel?"

"He went to draw a map."

"Sounds like trails with ruts to me." The sheet of pie dough lay on the board where Mel had flattened it. A small fly exploring its surface reminded Sam of a snowmobile on the Columbia Ice Fields. "I don't want to go to Kindersley."

"What is the matter with you, Sam? Is something eating you? You used to love wandering on funny wilderness trails and old logging roads looking for weird things and getting lost."

It was true. Sam did like to explore backwoods roads. He liked finding little mysteries alongside the trails and thinking about what kind of people might be attached to them. He was glad not to have anyone with him who could explain the mysteries. But on this trip he seemed to be storing up the wandering for when he reached his destination.

"Well, you're not the way you used to be! You used to be loose, never took anything seriously. Now I'm hearing about antiques, which you've never mentioned before, and trousseau teas, and microwaves, which you used to think were a joke."

"Microwaving is my career now, Sam. And what about you?" April hesitated. They were getting nearer the crash site, nearer the mountains. He was tense. "I just think you could be a little more sensitive. You're not making this trip alone this time. I saw a picture in *Western Living* of this piano lamp that would be perfect on our old upright. . . ."

Mel came through the saloon doors that led to the kitchen. "Here you go." He put the neat ink drawing in front of April. Both Sam and April glared at the i-dot on the belly of his shirt. They ate quickly and Sam laid the money in front of his plate on top of the yellow check left there by the waitress.

Mel was back at his pie dough. "Newlyweds," they heard him say softly, as though he were talking to the fly. They never got to see the skeet-shooters at the salad bar.

The weather report on the radio featured more rain to the west. April said, "It seems silly to go on, doesn't it?"

Sam knew that she meant there was no point pushing their way through intermittent showers and downpours, especially since he got aggravated with adjusting the wipers to suit the accumulation of water on the windshield. But the question became one of the dull clouds that pressed down on them as they passed Swift Current and the Kindersley junction.

Sam hit the brakes at a town called Chimneytop. They approached it from a hill to the southeast, and as they looked down at the town nesting in a few acres of dry, rolling grass, they saw that a section of the town consisted of old two-storey houses with chimneys in the centres of their steeply pitched roofs. The shingles and the chimneys were colourful, and, against the dull sky, strangely bright as well.

"Who needs antiques?" said Sam as his eyes leaped from chimney to chimney. "The prairies are full of these bizarre little scenes that nobody's bothered to exploit. It's like Disneyland, except there's hundreds of miles between attractions." He rummaged in the back seat for his paints. "You don't need to go pay money for an oil lamp someone bought in Chicago at a five-and-dime in 1953. Why don't you take some pictures?"

"I'm not used to this cynical side of you. Is it your gall bladder?"

April snapped the glum serenity of the village while Sam worked away at his easel on the hillside. She wished she were on one of the rooftops looking down at the sea of grass. "Bet you wish you hadn't guillotined your paper."

"No, it's perfect on here."

"I know! Let's tell Leona the painting was stolen. It was stolen from the condo while we were on our honeymoon. I mean, that would be high praise to an artist, wouldn't it? Like getting an award."

"What else would we say was taken? She wouldn't believe anyone would want just the painting. Other things have to be missing."

"We can make up the rest."

"More lies," said Sam. "The problem still remains, April—what do we do with the actual pieces?"

Lightning crackled so near that Sam's brush jerked on the idle chimney tops and nearly spoiled the work. A second later the thunder broke into an uproar above their heads. April tore off to the car, calling to Sam, who hunched over the painting to add the last twist of the brush.

Large cupfuls of rain assaulted him just as he closed his paint box. Through gathering streams of water on the windows April watched him run around the front of the Mustang, paints and easel tight under his arms like giant splinters piercing his body. He made a face at her. She reached over and threw the door open. The smells of ozone and wet cotton came in while Sam fitted the box and easel into the back seat.

"Let's go back to Swift Current," said April when Sam was sitting damply behind the wheel. He did not answer but made a U-turn on the highway and headed east.

The rain was torrential by the time they reached Swift Current, as though it had raced ahead to meet them at the Blueberry Hill Motel. The kidney-shaped swimming pool next to the office seethed with the downpour, and April watched the surface of the pool water rise like thousands of small wet mouths to kiss the relentless drops of rain.

Inside the office, Sam tapped a desk bell and waited for sounds of a response from beyond the open door behind the desk. He turned to gaze out the windows and saw a woman dressed in green garbage bags running past.

In a second she was inside the front door, stripping off the bags. "Had to turn off the lawn sprinkler," she drawled.

An American, thought Sam. They chatted while he signed in. The woman was about forty and pretty, to Sam's mind. She was muscular, perhaps from lifting weights. Her voice was strong and she looked tough in an attractive sort of way. He noticed an erotic snake tattooed on her left arm. Her breasts were large and solid, but her hips were thin like a man's in boot-cut jeans.

"Do they have women in the Marines?" he asked April when he was back in the Mustang.

She reached for the room key. "Huh?"

"Nothing."

"Let's order in Chinese food and watch TV," said April. "I wonder how many channels they get here."

"I saw a satellite dish on the roof."

"Wonderful."

"I'm hungry for pizza."

Late at night, during humid, ginger-scented love-making, April suddenly lowered herself to her elbows, raised Sam's eyelids with her thumbs and said, "We could tell her the damn painting is on loan to a little gallery in Medicine Hat."

Sam let his eyeballs roll back. He'd been dreaming of Betty and the motel manager twined together naked on a mountain meadow of ice.

"Let's leave it there forever," he said.

The weather channel's morning satellite photograph showed a stationary mass over the North American plains, with some clearing in the Rockies.

Sam was sorry he'd paid the motel bill the day before because it meant he had no reason to go into the office where he might see the tattooed lady dance her snake across the Chargex machine.

"Samoo," April's voice tinkled as they stowed their luggage. "Maybe it isn't raining as much up north. I mean, we could just drive up, come right back if you don't like it. . . ."

"Kindersley," said Sam. "Okay, listen. I'll go in and ask the manager. And if—they say it'll be a worthwhile trip, we'll do it."

She wouldn't know a butter churn from a chamber-pot, thought Sam about the woman in the office. His hand was tentative on the bell. He half expected a burly husband to come through the inner door. But it was her, in a red-striped rugby sweater that enclosed her body like a fine glove.

"The only thing ah know about antiques is that one of mah guests recently bragged about a real good find at a place called Wagner's Barn. Here, ah'll show ya."

And Sam did get to see the snake dance, across a map of Saskatchewan. The smell of the thick blue felt marker she used to chart his route mingled with a fragrance of cinnamon which could have come from her private rooms, or could be her natural smell, the smell of the Far South.

"But ah wouldn't go there if ah were you. They're talking about flash floods on the radio. You might find yourself up a crick without a paddle."

"We're coming right back to the No. 1," drawled Sam.

"Keep the map." She smiled. Gold flashed in a distant crevasse beyond her cinnamon lips.

Sam folded the map slowly and carefully, and regretted that he would probably never see the Blueberry Hill Motel again. When he left the office, he saw the green garbage bags hanging from the coat rack as though they were real clothes.

April sat in the drizzle and remembered how, as children, she and her sister Lillian had run into the yard barefoot after a shower had passed, had run through puddles and squealed over the earthworms they dislodged. Rainworms they called them, believing they'd fallen with the raindrops. April could see many rainworms right now, shaping alphabet letters on the parking-lot, as if trying to spell a message for her.

Sam seemed better this morning. Still, it was odd that he needed to ask someone if the side-trip would be worthwhile, as though the unknown suddenly frightened him. He probably thought the side-trip to Kindersley was her idea of retribution for the wrecked painting. She had not intended that, but perhaps letting him think it was the best way to resolve the issue, though his words came back to her through the sound of the drizzle and the traffic on the wet highway behind her: what will we do with the pieces?

Things would be better when they got to the mountains. Their relationship had been smooth in Kenora, where they were on their own turf and they each had their own boundaries and definitions. Or at least, *she* did. April thought about her mother—should she call her? She looked at the rainworms.

They'd twisted and reshaped themselves; the message had changed.

When she lifted her eyes, they met Sam's as he came out of the office and paused in front of the aluminum door. He's got a map. We're going to Kindersley, thought April.

And Sam thought, I've got her lines and circles on this map. I wonder if I'll remember her when I look at it twenty years from now.

April said nothing when Sam got into the car. He laid the map on the console between them with the blue lines facing up.

They crossed old bridges that spanned swirling creeks and coulees. The vehicles they met threw up sprays of clean water from the washed highway as they rushed by. April did not try to find any more stations on the radio. The country music burbled on low volume just beneath the shuh-swap of the wiper blades and the swish of rubber treads on the film of rain covering the road.

After they'd driven in silence for thirty minutes or so, April felt the need to be celebratory, to show her enthusiasm for the trip to Kindersley. She turned up the radio.

> Listen to the story 'bout the man who tried
> To drink from the river but the river ran dry.
> He drank so long and he drank so hard,
> The river ran dry and he broke his heart.

April sang along and at the same time she scanned the blue lines on the map, though she did not pick it up. "Where did she say to go?"

Sam hit the brake as if she'd awakened him from a trance. April gripped the armrest and clenched her teeth, fearing a crash. But the Mustang continued beneath the tumbling skies.

"Who?" said Sam.

"The manager."

"Oh. She—uh—said to go to a place called Wagner's Barn. There."

April picked up the map and studied it as the wipers and hiss of tires and the song played together.

> River of love, river of love,
> Drink from the river, fly like a dove.
> The river runs long, the river runs free,
> But the river of love never runs
> To me.

Sam was on the train. The clicking of the windshield wipers had become the clicking of the metal wheels on the railway track. Someone was walking on the track ahead of the train. The car swerved to the centre of the road and then back to the right again as an orange pick-up truck bore down in the other lane.

April's body jerked hard against the car door and then left across the console. She steadied herself by pressing on Sam's thigh. "What's that child doing walking on the road in this rain?"

"It wasn't a child, it was a small guy."

April looked back at the receding figure. "Just a kid!" she cried.

"It was not. He had a moustache."

"Oh! He didn't. We should have given him a lift." April kept watching over the seat-backs to see if another car would pick the boy up.

"Given him a lift? There's no room in our back seat. Look."

"Oh, your precious paintings."

"All right. All right, I'll stop and chuck them out and make room for the puny juvenile delinquent."

"You could put them in the trunk."

"The trunk's too dusty. The rubber thing is worn away. It leaks."

April reached down and cranked open her window. "See

that? Feel it? It's rain, Sam. I don't think our trunk will ever see dust again."

"He's too far behind us now," said Sam. "It's too late to stop."

"Did she say how far it was to this turn-off?"

"Who? Oh. The turn-off. We should be just about there."

> River of love, river of love,
> Drink from the river, fly like a dove. . . .

Stark white clapboard flanked by salt-and-pepper-coloured tombstones caught Sam's attention just as he'd begun to believe they'd missed the crossroad. The weather had worsened as they headed north. Instead of leaving it behind, they'd followed it into the centre of Saskatchewan's farmland. Sam slowed the car and he and April peered at the white building through the blur. Black windows stared back like eyes in a skull.

"Evangelical Mennonite Mission Church," April read out loud.

"She said there'd be a church here," said Sam. "I think our Wagner will turn out to be a Vawg-ner."

"It's so plain. No belfry or anything."

A quarter mile further on they discovered the intersection. A man in a see-through plastic raincoat stood in the middle of their turn-off road and pounded a wooden sign into the mud with a sledge-hammer. An old station wagon rested on the shoulder of the main road.

"We're looking for Wagner's Barn," said Sam through his open window. "Uh—Vawgner's Barn?"

The man pointed with an awkward thrust of the hammer. "This way."

Sam and April stared at the gravel road and saw that it disappeared into a grey sea.

"Bridge's out." The man stepped away from the sign. BRIDG OUT. Then proudly, "My boy made it just a few minutes ago."

Sam put the Mustang in reverse, but April called, "Is there another way we can get there?"

The man lowered the sledge-hammer to the ground and let its handle lean against his leg. He began pointing and making circles in the air with his muddy hands and giving directions.

"I want to go to the mountains," said Sam without moving his lips.

"What?" said April while the farmer chattered and gestured beside his son's sign.

Sam's teeth were clenched. "Let's get out of here."

April waved to the man. "Thank you," she smiled, though he was not finished his instructions. As Sam backed onto the main road, he and April saw the man still pointing and shouting.

"We'll catch the No. 10 west of Kindersley and link up with the No. 1 at the Alberta border," said Sam.

"I guess we will," said April through clenched teeth.

In Kindersley they bought saskatoons and cheese for lunch, and April found opera on the car radio. The saskatoons reminded Sam of the Blueberry Hill Motel and he jiggled each small handful of berries on his palm before placing them one by one on his tongue. The mountains were finally within reach, and even though the rain poured down, he regained some of his composure while they sped west along the No. 10.

The opera made April drowsy. She took the elastic band out of her hair and slept curled up in the bucket seat next to Sam. A vision appeared in the darkness inside her eyelids, a vision of the two halves of Leona Berg's watercolour neatly fused in the centre. A shadow fell across the half of the painting forgotten in Kenora and April still could not see what was on it.

As they hurtled west and a little south along the narrow asphalt highway, away from Kindersley and towards spires of rock, certainty in Sam became stronger and stronger, despite all the little uncertainties that had sprouted on the prairie around them as they'd travelled. Sam knew that the rain would end, that it had an edge. And he knew that edge was in the mountains, neon blue and icy white, and that they lay just ahead. Now he only had to drive. He shut out the drowning fields and the urgent comings and goings of tractors and bulldozers, of trucks and vans filled with haggard men and women. He shut out the sleeping April. He drove as fast as he dared, and each mile stripped away a layer of doubt.

A few miles before the intersection with the No. 1, bright orange and black barricades funnelled the traffic into a maze of pylons and signs and flashing lights. ROAD CONSTRUCTION— DETOUR. April's eyes opened. She shifted, stretched out her legs and drifted back into a half-sleep without knowing what had slowed them down.

Sam was not daunted. The detour road was chipped and cracked, worn out, but it was high and followed a steady course south. He'd have to meet the No. 1 eventually, and so he began eating the remaining saskatoons out of the paper basket tucked in beneath the ashtray near his knee. He hummed softly in harmony with the aria bursting from the four stereo speakers.

At last Sam realized that there was no one else on that road and a worry crept up the back of his neck, because the rain was coming down very hard and all around them the prairie was a grey turbulent sea. He picked up the map but kept driving. Oblivious now to the wide bright lines painted on the map by the dancing snake, he tried to get some bearings, but with no point of reference could make only vague guesses about where the detour had led them. He would have to stop at a farm and ask for help.

He began singing, his tune cutting into the soaring operatic melodies.

> Listen to the story 'bout the man who tried
> To drink from the river but the river ran dry.

It became a chant, a talisman to help them find the No. 1.

The chipped, cracked road went through a grove of oaks and on the other side turned abruptly and dipped into a valley. Before him, a hundred metres ahead and a little lower, Sam could see the parallel railings of a bridge. Most of the bridge was under water, but beyond it the road rose out of the water again and continued up the opposite slope. Through the mist and rain Sam could see a car climbing the rise on the other side, on its way, no doubt, to the No. 1, having just crossed the flooded bridge.

The Mustang dipped its wheels into the brink. Slowly Sam guided it towards the middle of the vanishing bridge. Water lapped and gurgled at the car's bottom and the wheels churned up small torrents.

April sat up tall and rigid. "What are you doing? Where are we?" She reached for her ponytail, though there was none to grab.

"Detour."

"Detour! Go back, for god's sake, Sam!"

"I saw somebody go through." But he hadn't seen it cross. It may have been themselves climbing the opposite bank, spirited across by his desire, by his will.

The car stalled halfway across the bridge. The water seemed higher than it had been when they started across. Sam could not get the car started. April did not speak. The orchid was in her hand and she squeezed it and squeezed it.

"Someone will come along," said Sam.

But no one came along.

"Let's push it back to the road."

"No!" said April.

He opened his door. Instantly the floor of the car was awash. The berry basket drifted for a moment, then sank. "Get out and push!"

April's face was white. She took the orchid with her and

clutched it in desperation as she leaned hard against the hood of the car. The hem of her cotton skirt, the skirt that had been stylishly draped and pinned, along with its matching blouse, on her mother's living-room drapes at the trousseau tea, sucked up the flood water and clung to her knees. Goose bumps crept up the insides of her thighs. Her feet slipped inside her sandals. The Mustang went crooked and its fender grated against the hidden concrete abutment of the bridge.

"We'll never get it up the grade!" cried Sam. "Let's go!" He took April's hand.

"Your paintings!"

But Sam started walking, pulling on April as he went. He was cold from the rain and the icy flood waters lapping against his bare calves, but he followed the silver railing with a slow, steady swinging of his legs. They waded on ahead to the side of the valley in which Sam hoped to find the No. 1.

The road took a dip as it left the bridge. The water was deeper and swirled and eddied in beautiful, horrible patterns. Sam had not turned off the car ignition and they could still faintly hear the soprano singing sadly behind them.

"No!" shouted April, still holding the orchid to her chest. "No!"

"We have to."

"Why is this happening?" she sobbed.

Sam wanted to tell her it was because they hadn't picked up the boy on the road to Kindersley, but April would have thought he was being sarcastic. And yet Sam believed it to be true. The boy might have known where to go. And Sam would not have attempted to cross the bridge with a stranger in the car. He had lied to April—the hitch-hiker had not had a moustache.

They stepped into an undertow. The weight of their bodies pulled by the current of spilled river water separated them. Though April could no longer hold onto Sam, she kept her fingers clenched around the orchid as they slipped down the raging valley like dolls. April imagined leaping among chimneyed rooftops, Sam saw only the neon blues and icy whites of his mountain skies and smelled cinnamon.

When the car was retrieved, the luggage and the easel and the manicure kit, and the paintings of the potash mine and the chimneys, were returned to April's and Sam's parents. The watercolour pad was destroyed, along with the soggy berry basket and the maps, by an autobody man from Milner, Alberta. And though April's mother had nightmares about Sam and April's last moments on earth, she never thought about the picture of mountains Leona had given them for their wedding. Sam's father put the other half of the Canson pad in the attic with Sam's old toys, and there the flowered alpine meadow surrounded by neon blues and icy whites remained flat and clean.

April's naked body was found snagged in an oak tree only a mile down the valley from the bridge. Sam's was never found. But it may have drifted as far as Medicine Hat, where a little art gallery faces the river.

GLASS FLOATS

"Sooner or later there will be only one of us left, Jilly. What will happen then?"

"She'll walk into the sea. Or him. He. That's why we're here."

Jilly began her systematic punching of the five or six pillows that surrounded Kat and propped up her frailty. Each pillow four times—fump-fump-fump-FUMP!

"I don't think it will be a he. Men don't live as long as women. And that's not why we're here." Kat pulled on the loose skin of Jilly's upper arm as Jilly struggled to snare the mattress into the fitted corner of the sheet. "Stupid thing always pops out like a goat's phallus."

"You roll around like a bottle on a wave."

"Where are the dogs?"

"With all that wiggling, you could be out with us on the beach."

"I haven't seen them today. Or are they dead? I always forget."

Kat hadn't really forgotten whether or not the dogs were dead. *Or are they dead* was a game she played with everyone left at the lodge. Jilly was the only one who saw through it. Many dogs were dead. Kat had owned six pairs of purebreds since she was a little girl in Lido Plage, Manitoba, matched sets she liked to walk on matched leashes along the trails beside the river. Kat and her husband Ricky had lived in her parental home near the river until the last set of dogs, silver schnauzers, had been laid to rest, and the house had practically fallen on their thin-haired heads. All Kat's dogs ran together in her mind in a pack. She called out their names in her sleep. The current dogs, Lear and Lady Macbeth, were drifters who'd found a haven with Kat at the lodge. One was lab-ish, the other collie-ish. They were not matched and had never known a leash.

"Come outside," said Jilly. She ran an old cloth over the bedtable, under the tinny transistor radio, under the vitamin bottles, up and down the tree-shaped lamp, along the contours of the empty vase. "The dogs are on the beach with Ricky and Nadine. Sonny is coming today to strut with Ricky."

Kat's head turned towards the shaded window. "I may get up to watch them wiggling. Have the whales gone by already?"

"Yes, last March." Which March, when was March? So many dogs dead, so many whales gone by. "I said, Sonny's coming today. On the ferry."

Kat wrote something with her fingertip on the coverlet Jilly had smoothed for her. Jilly knew she was writing *Katrina*. When paper and a pen were around, Jilly used to find dozens of sheets of stationery, filled with *Katrina*, stacked up neatly on the bedtable. For a long time now, Kat had been writing it only with her finger, on the bedcover.

"What else is new?" said Kat. "Besides Sonny coming. I heard you the first time. What else is new?"

Jilly went into Kat's bathroom to rinse out her cloth and get fresh water in a glass. "We start daylight-saving time today."

Ricky and Kat had the master bedroom with the private bath. They had been the only couple who still slept together when they first came to the lodge, and they were accustomed to a big bed, because of the dogs. But after Wendy died and went to 'Billy Graham's stadium in the sky,' as Kat called it, Ricky had moved into Wendy's room. He said Kat had stopped sleeping at night and kept him awake. But Ricky had always loved Wendy. He'd never forgotten her younger beauty, her perfumes, her buttocks on the porch railing of the old Lido Plage house. Kat said she supposed that Ricky was finally making love to Wendy now, night after night, in the single, narrow bed in the room next to the kitchen.

"Daylight-saving time?" Kat warbled from her huge pillows. "What do we want to save time for? They'll bury us no matter how much we've saved. I say let's ignore it."

"Well, we have to pick up Sonny at the right time."

"Oh, let him strut over here by himself. It's too late, anyway. Besides, he won't show up—isn't he dead?"

Kat's bathroom was cluttered with souvenirs from the tidal pools beyond the beach. The first thing she'd done when she arrived at the lodge was load up her vanity with starfish, seashells, kelp, barnacles, sand dollars, smooth stones, and driftwood. She'd needed to bring the ocean into her room, into her private space, to save it like a keepsake. She watched the creatures as though she expected them to do tricks, maybe lick her face, take bits of food from her hand. Jilly and the others had already been there for a long time, and they toured her menagerie respectfully before telling her that starfish were living animals and that she was slowly killing them on her vanity. She allowed them to take the starfish back to the rock pools, but she kept the barnacle because its snapping beak reminded her of a begging dog.

After a few months of daily beachcombing, Kat got used to the idea that this would be her last home, that she didn't need to pack up for some future trip back to Manitoba. But she gave the starfish names and looked for them after high tide to see if the ocean had carried them away. She didn't seem to mind if they were gone—a starfish didn't care where it was, she said.

Now Kat hardly ever left her bed. Shells and twisted wood still lay strewn among her jars and bottles and combs. And one dead barnacle on a rock. The strange thing was, Jilly heard the barnacle snap its beak every morning after she brought Kat her breakfast and cleaned up her room. Jilly would pass the bathroom door on her way out and hear a hard click from the shiny, tiled darkness.

When Jilly came out of the bathroom, Kat was holding a denture in one knobby hand and looking at it with an expression of pity. "Do you think it pays to get new teeth, Jilly? These don't fit anymore. I can't bite the way I used to. Are Nadine and Eckhardt out there?"

Jilly raised the venetian blind to look out onto the beach and the bay. "Nothing between us and Japan," Wendy and Leo had written when they'd chosen the property twenty years earlier. A huge, simple, square house with a veranda on two sides and several bedrooms of various sizes, situated on a snug bay on the Island. "Perfect for our retirement home." Four couples who'd grown up together on the prairie, and who'd remained friends over the decades because they were all, for one reason or another, childless, migrated to the house Wendy and Leo had chosen for them on the West Coast. A fifth couple, Sonny and Linda, who'd only loosely belonged to the group of cronies because they'd had five children, did not go to live in Prairie Lodge with the others. They stayed with their family in Winnipeg.

What was peculiar about the group of ten, and difficult for Jilly to endure, was that despite the camaraderie among them and all the *times* they'd spent together, all the playing and inventing, and the madcap efforts to be outrageous, they had never shared inner feelings, never confided, in twos and threes, about the dark sides of their private lives. One time Leo had had drinks with Harold, and had told him *something* about Wendy, about some sort of obsession or fetish, but Harold had not said much about it even to Jilly, and it never came up again. A mutual acquaintance of Kat's and Jilly's had hinted once to Jilly of an affair or near-affair Kat had had while Ricky was in Ottawa for a few weeks on business. There were times when Nadine and Eckhardt would not answer their phone for days—Jilly would leave messages on their machine and wait for return calls, but none would come. Or one of the couples would fail to show up at a dinner party with no explanation. Then the next time they all met, everyone pretended it hadn't happened.

Jilly believed the others in the group all had closer friends somewhere, sisters, brothers, neighbours, with whom they whispered confessions. But Jilly had no other friends. The group was all she had.

Only after they moved to Prairie Lodge did the survivors finally begin to measure out, slowly, so slowly, all the fears and regrets and angers that had shaped their lives. Except for Jilly. The configuration of the three couples and the widow that uprooted and went to the Island had her in the position of listener. Always and only the listener. Still, she was grateful. It began with Kat saying to Jilly, one morning on the veranda, "Do you think all the men are in love with Wendy the way Ricky is?"

The lodge was almost in town, the hospital was adequate, and Doctor Mazlit lived three properties over. Wendy and Leo were gone, Jilly's husband Harold had died before he even got to the ocean. And five were left: Jilly, Kat and Ricky, Eckhardt and Nadine, all clinging to the last vestige of autonomy afforded them by Prairie Lodge. The paint was peeling from the house. No one cared about that anymore, except Jilly. While puttering around the flower-beds, she'd start smoothing the wrinkled surface of the wood siding with the flat of her hand, and try to push down the curled-up edges of paint, until someone or other called her in (someone was always calling her) and she realized she'd let half an hour slip away, and no work done on the flowers.

The sun had cleared the interior mountains and the cedar forests, and was shining full on the bay and on the beach. The tide was on the way out. Rocks at the ends of the half-moon shore glistened with sea water.

"Yes, Nadine and Eckhardt are on the beach with Ricky," said Jilly. "I expect Nadine doesn't know she's there, though." When Nadine had first started to lose her mind and say all those strange things, Kat had said, "She's remembering ahead, like in *Through the Looking-Glass,* what the Queen says."

"And she's probably cold," said Kat. "I hate old people who are always cold. Always old."

"And Eckhardt will be complaining about the saltwater corroding his wheelchair."

"That's why I don't like to go out anymore."

"Why?"

"Because of the bitching."

"You mean theirs drowns out yours?"

" 'Let's fight till six, and then have dinner, said Tweedle-dum.' " Kat stared at the hazy blue between the slats of the blinds. A gull flew up from the shore and intersected the strips across the window. Jilly raised the blind. She turned a crank and a panel of glass swung open. A breeze had rushed into the bay to replace the departing seas, and it carried with it the cracked voices of the three old beachcombers tottering at the edge of the sand.

"What did you mean before?" said Jilly. "About Sonny. 'It's too late'?"

"Well, I didn't mean it's too late, exactly. . . ."

"What then?"

"I meant, it doesn't work anymore. You know how mad he could get me."

"You loved it."

"Yes, he made me think. He was so outrageous. Nobody else in our group was outrageous, Jilly."

"You were in love with him."

"He's an old fart!"

"No, he's still got the wild boy in him."

Kat shivered and brought the coverlet to her chin. "Jilly—Jilly, what if I'm the last one left? I don't think I'd have the courage to walk into the ocean. All by myself. And I don't really think that's why we're here."

"The last one must take our souls into the sea so that we can all become marine animals living at the bottom of the sea where time passes much more slowly, and where we can evolve into all sorts of lovely colourful fish. You don't want to become a prairie creature again, do you? All that cold and dust and mosquitoes?"

"You'd make a terrible starfish, Jilly. You hate clams. Close the blind. You know the light bothers me."

Jilly cranked the window but left a small opening. Music came from the beach. A man singing, a man who could have been Ricky or Eckhardt, were it not for the harmonica neither of them knew how to play.

"Oh, that's that Brownie McGee Sonny and Ricky always listened to," said Kat. "Ricky's starting to strut already, old fool."

Jilly could see him standing as straight as he could beside a sodden log, with his back arched inward and his buttocks raised, taking short steps in time to the music on a beach littered with kelp and wet seaweed and empty mussel shells. And she could see Sonny, too, strutting like he used to on Ricky and Kat's lawn in Lido Plage, with the summer sun setting on a clean, flat horizon. A tape recorder lay in Eckhardt's lap. The dogs darted after sea gulls.

The telephone rang.

"That will be Sonny, calling to tell us which ferry he's catching," said Jilly. "Here's your blood pressure pill. Take it right away while your water's fresh." She heard the barnacle snap as she passed the dark and empty bathroom.

Even on the prairies they'd heard that sometimes you could find glass floats from Japanese fishing boats lying on the Pacific beaches. You would be very lucky to find one. So that was the treasure they always looked for. Jilly felt sure she'd find one someday. Kat didn't care about Japanese floats. She turned it all around and threw bottles, corked and bearing slips of paper on which she'd written notes, into the ocean whenever they took a trip on Dr. Mazlit's yacht. "What do you write on them?" everyone asked. "Just my name," she'd answer. "I imagine that's pretty titillating to whoever finds them." Kat's joke. Her way of thumbing her nose at Jilly's preoccupation with glass floats.

With the sun so bright this morning, the hunting on the beach would be very good, because whatever was shiny would sparkle. Jilly set out with the dogs running ahead chasing stocky, scruffy ravens that scavenged the bay. She wore Harold's wellingtons and a fishnet sweater pulled over several layers of shirts and turtlenecks, and Wendy's pink sweatpants. Wendy had left a legacy of sweatsuits and jogging outfits, in nursery pastels, with matching headbands. Jilly had borrowed the outfits, though never the headbands, even before Wendy had become so suddenly and perilously ill, and she kept on taking them from the closet in the room Ricky had stolen. Jilly told Kat she felt Wendy's warmth in the fleece-lined cloth, for Wendy had been the sweetest and most generous of them. Kat told Jilly that when she wore Wendy's outfits she looked like the flavoured popcorn you could buy in shopping malls.

Jilly heard Eckhardt's voice like a raven's squawk behind her. She turned around and saw his mouth open in a wide O, his lower lip sagging out and wet, his tongue waggling like the scarf fluttering around his neck. His wheelchair glittered. Ricky waved her on. Keep on going.

Lear and Lady Macbeth trotted in and out of the curves of water spilling quietly onto the sand and tossed large stones back and forth with toothy smiles. "That's what my shepherds always did," Kat would say. "The collie must have shepherd blood in her. She taught Lear that game." It was Nadine who had actually named the two stray dogs, just before she'd spurned reality once and for all to put on her deathcloak of peaceful hallucination. She'd been an English teacher, but Jilly suspected she was harbouring some monumental sin, and that the dogs had become, with her naming of them, her sin-bearers, since she clearly could carry it no longer.

The tender moment of low tide. A softer, more distant rasp of surf, a whiteness of sea gulls, the sand a Lilliput of marine society. Jilly watched her feet press shiny wet dents into the naked sea bottom. Sometimes on these outings, she'd go backwards so she could see each footprint disappear in front of her. Then she'd go forward again. Some days, she'd stay in one place for the whole walk, never getting very far forward or very far backward.

The dogs did not warn her about the strangers with the pails. Jilly saw the webbed colours first, bright purples and corals in pails that hung from scaly, short-nailed fingers. The two men had wispy brown beards and moustaches that covered their lips, and though their eyes were friendly, Jilly took a step back in the sand, out of surprise and an old-womanish fear she hated. One man wore a pony-tail, the other had puffy, curly hair that jumped around on his head with the breeze playing in the bay.

"This is a private beach," said Jilly. "Where did you get them?" She thrust her jaw towards the pails.

"Rocks on the other side of the point," said the man with the pony-tail, and he jerked his head back over his shoulder. He had a long pointed nose and enormous ear lobes.

Jilly looked at the beds of rocks on the point, then back at the pails. *A starfish doesn't care where it is.*

"We just want to go back to our truck," said the other, taller man in a low, slow voice that boomed like a cartoon giant's. "We thought we'd walk on the beach instead of the road."

Jilly turned. Ricky and Nadine and Eckhardt were huddled over the tape recorder. She could hear that the music had stopped. "I can't tell you to put them back," she said. "And I don't mind you walking here this time. But I don't like to see that." Again her chin pointed down at the stars in the pails. She knew what they did with them—poisoned them in formaldehyde, coated them with lacquer, sold them in souvenir shops. "You really should put them back." The metal pails were coming alive now as the starfish began to twist and writhe like eels, trying to get out.

"We don't hurt them," said Pony-tail, as though he were talking to a kindergartner.

The men just stood there. The dogs came bounding out from behind a pile of derelict logs pushed up against the trees bordering the shoreline. Lear barked first. Lady Macbeth dropped the gnarled branch she carried and joined in. Then everyone was on their way again.

Jilly disliked intrusions by strangers more and more. The others didn't mind. Company, they called it, not understanding how vulnerable they were to thieves and salesmen.

But Jilly didn't want to think about that now. Whenever she walked at low tide she tried to discern, in the smell of the air, the flatness of the ocean, the thickness of the forests, the flight of gulls and eagles, just why it was that prairie people were also sea-lovers. She would close her eyes and pretend the wind came off a billowing grain field and the cry of sea gulls was the trill of horned larks as they rose and fell in the wide, blue, prairie sky. And she could almost do it. But even with her eyes closed, she knew that there was nothing permanent on the horizon, and that beyond that horizon lay more nothing, and more nothing. The nothingness was not emptiness, however—it was mystery, a mystery that prairie dwellers did not know. Their horizons always held outlines of towns or escarpments or shelter-belts. Mystery was a missing element. And the forests here were a mystery, too, the way things disappeared into them. . . . Even with your eyes closed you knew all that, felt it.

Jilly had not walked far when she stopped and turned around to look at the strangers' backs. They wore plaid shirts as brightly coloured as the starfish. "You can pay for your passage here!" she shouted.

The men looked over their shoulders at her but kept walking. They thought she was ranting. Ricky and Nadine and Eckhardt stopped fiddling with the tape recorder and watched.

I mustn't alarm them, thought Jilly. So she followed the men. "Wait!" she called. "You can pay for your passage on our beach today." Why did she give in? "Just bring me—one—when it's—ready." Jilly expected them to sneer, but they only frowned. "I know somebody who'd like one."

They nodded. The Giant put down his pails and picked out two brittle starfish. He held them in front of his chest. "Which colour?"

Jilly picked one that was soft orange like a spring sunset. But no sooner had she pointed to it than she saw her folly: Kat didn't keep starfish anymore—she'd been trained not to. Jilly had told her to let them go in the tidal pools so they could stay alive until they died nature's death. Why did she, Jilly, now want to see one of those creatures, a star the colour of a spring sunset, preserved on Kat's vanity?

The wind was colder than Jilly had first realized. She kept on towards the others on the beach, where the harmonica was howling again and Nadine was tossing soft pellets of dog food to the sea gulls. The tide would go out again just before dark.

"I can't find my glasses."

"You never had glasses, Nadine," Jilly said. "She never wore glasses, did she, Eckhardt?"

"Lo," Eckhardt moaned.

They sat before Jilly's lunch of soup and biscuits and fruit. Kat had hers on a tray in her bed.

"Do you want glasses?"

"Your carrot soup is better than this junk," Nadine continued.

"It is my carrot soup."

Nadine put down her spoon and stared into her lap.

"And you're right. I have made better. I seem to be losing my touch." Jilly reached into Nadine's lap and squeezed her hand. Then Jilly tasted the soup to see if she'd accidentally salted it twice. It had no salt at all.

Nadine slowly raised her head and looked into Jilly's eyes. "I couldn't find the chocolates this morning."

If it were the truth Nadine was telling, she had lost everything she'd ever had as well as things she hadn't had or wanted. Sometimes it was glasses or non-existent chocolates, other times it was a certain dress or photograph. The worst times were when she couldn't find her doctor's phone number. Her doctor back home. He'd died before she came to the Island. She insisted on calling him because he would make her better. "It would be considerable long distance to phone him up," Ricky told her.

Eckhardt's soup dribbled into the white Corelle. So many crumbs of biscuit lay scattered around his plate it seemed unlikely any had gotten to his mouth.

Nadine watched her husband scooping the carrot soup into the basin formed by his lower lip. She began sliding crumbs to the edge of the table with her hand. "You should break your crackers into your soup," she scolded, while with her other hand she adjusted the modified turban she always wore to cover her white hair.

Eckhardt flared, something about bad manners. Jilly said, "There's no one to see now but us."

Ricky dropped his spoon into his empty bowl. "What's

Sonny coming all the way out here for? It's too long a trip for him. He's blind as a bat, for god's sake!"

The last time Sonny had been there, a summer fifteen years earlier, Linda had come along. She was an Oshawa girl, and had always stood off from the group, jealous, the men thought, of their friendship and the beauty of the Manitoba women. They all danced on the veranda and went sailing with Dr. Mazlit, and just before sunset one evening, Sonny and Kat ran into the woods, laughing, martinis in their hands, to look for mushrooms to go with the steaks. They got lost, found the trail again at daybreak, and emerged from the woods laughing still. Linda did not take to the ocean, hated the Island. She never returned.

Amazing that they'd all stayed together this long. Jilly meant to keep it that way—she had to see them through to the end. Wouldn't it all fall apart, what was left of it, if she didn't?

Nadine tore at the collar of her blouse. "They make me wear this hideous nightgown! She gave me this ugly, stifling gown to wear. They don't believe me here. Listen, Jilly! They don't believe me!" She fixed a claw-like hand around Jilly's wrist.

"Nah-een! Nah-een!" scolded Eckhardt. With his good hand he banged the fruit knife against the edge of his bowl.

Jilly loosened Nadine's collar. "It's all right, Eckhardt."

"That fool Sonny," Ricky went on. "He'll get Kat all excited again. Who do you think it was gave her the idea for those crazy bottles? How a blind man could get an old lady so flittered up, I'll never know!"

"Maybe Sonny can get her out of bed for a change," said Jilly. "And I thought you were looking forward to listening to the old music and dancing. . . ."

"I done my dancing!"

"Listen! They don't believe me! They took my chocolates!"

"Nah-een! Nah-een!"

"Blind idiot!"

"Shut up, shut up!" Jilly cried. "It just needs salt!"

The dogs barked at the screen door that looked out over the beach into an approaching tide. At least the sea gulls were quiet.

The door on the landward side of Prairie Lodge seldom got knocked upon. Most callers, including strangers, automatically followed the inlaid cedar-slab walk around to the sea-front, and then stood with their hands on their hips and stared at the bay waters for awhile before mounting the veranda steps. So the knocking from the unused part of the house caught everyone off guard. Eckhardt, in a futile slump on the toilet in the kitchen bathroom, thought he'd left his cane in the sitting-room and that Ricky was rapping the furniture legs with it. But no, there was the walnut stick leaning up against the sink, next to the aluminum one sent over by the hospital after his stroke. Ricky was certain it was Sonny playing some sort of knock-out-ginger trick on the veranda. "Can't find the door and he rattles around on the walls of the house!" Ricky muttered as he pulled the pages of his newspaper closer about his head. Kat heard the knock and guessed that a raven was slamming a closed clam against the ridgepole on the roof. Jilly, like Ricky, thought Sonny had come early to surprise them, though he'd said he would be on the late ferry. She took off her apron and smoothed her hair before she went to answer.

Nadine, whose bedroom was near the landward door, got to it first. When Jilly came along the hall, she heard a man's voice. "Bed and breakfast?" it said, as though it had been saying it all morning long. He was a wide man wearing a short wide jacket that appeared to be inflated with sea air. His eyebrows were raised in question and they remained in the middle of his forehead as Nadine answered.

"Yes, come in." She was as gracious as a queen.

Jilly squeezed past her and smiled at the man. "Sorry, actually not," she said.

"Jilly, he's come for Wendy. We'll get Ricky and Eckhardt to bring out the body."

"Nadine, Eckhardt found the chocolates," whispered Jilly. "He's in the garden."

"Who wants chocolate?"

"Don't mind her," said Jilly. "No, we're not bed-and-breakfast, never have been. Sorry."

"Isn't there one around here somewhere?" The eyebrows were still up there under tanned, beefy wrinkles. He did not look to Jilly like a bed-and-breakfast type. She pictured bed-and-breakfast people to be small and pale. The man at the door looked like a police detective or a quarry worker. "Could I use your phone to call around a bit?"

But Jilly hadn't been born yesterday. She knew what "casing the joint" meant, and she knew what a *scam* was. Harold had warned her about those things through a maze of tubes in intensive care. "Why don't you continue on into town and stop at the Lindleys'? They're right on this road. Big sign. You can't miss it. They're B-and-B. Very popular. They'll know of all the homes in the area."

Out on the little driveway, next to the mossy lawn that covered the space between the holly hedge and the house, was a car that looked as though it could hardly have fit through the approach in the hedge. A long, shiny, pink car, with a perky blonde head in the passenger's window. Something Wendy would have called a designer dog bounced around the interior, from the front seat to the rear seat and back again. Jilly decided they were Americans playing around at touring Canada, customers for plastic-coated starfish. But she could not let them in . . .

"My wife's dying to get a good look at the ocean. From the road it's. . . ."

"Just a bit further on the view is quite lovely," said Jilly. "There's even a place to pull off, and—I think—yes, one of those pay telescopes."

Now I suppose he'll ask me for change . . .

But that was the end of it. The stranger trotted back to the pink automobile where his family waited. He wore high-topped runners.

"That Sonny?" came Ricky's impatient call from Wendy's bedroom.

"No, not Sonny," Jilly replied as she shut the door. She knelt down to brush up the carpet with her hand. They'd always tried to save the carpet here at the front entrance, as though someday a queen would visit them through that door. The nap was still thick and erect. Jilly erased the impressions of the soles of her and Nadine's shoes. Then she turned and took that hated step backwards when she discovered Nadine still standing right behind her in the hallway.

"He wants me, doesn't he?" Nadine clutched at the collar of her blouse.

"No, no. He's just looking for a—view. He says his wife is dying for a view."

"Well, she should come and stay with us, we're all dying. The view isn't helping."

Nadine went into her room. Jilly watched her as she sat down on the edge of her bed. Nadine folded her hands in her lap and stared at the paisley pattern in the carpet. Jilly supposed pictures ran through her mind unconnected, like an animal's thoughts.

Kat was asleep. She'd closed her window and the blinds and left a tap dripping in the bathroom. Jilly began to pick up the lunch things dumped onto the floor beside the bed and heard the creak of wicker from one grey corner of the room. Ricky sat there wearing his beach hat and his fishing vest.

"I came to tell her it wasn't Sonny," he said. "She's asleep. She can sleep during the day, not at night, it seems."

Jilly hurried to get all the lunch things onto the tray so she could leave and allow Ricky and Kat their moment together.

"She's alone so damn much, you know? She can walk. It's not as though she can't walk. Hell, Eckhardt can barely walk, for a good reason, and he gets around like a gopher."

"Shhh!" Jilly held her finger to her lips. "I'll bring in some daffodils," she whispered. "Maybe that'll get her interested in coming out." No, no—Wendy liked daffodils, Kat liked finding slugs in the wet, spongy grass.

"Oh, Sonny'll get her up, I expect."

"You want her to get up, don't you? Sonny's only staying for two or three days."

Ricky nodded. "As long as they don't run into the bush again."

Jilly did not like the way Ricky always called her fairy-tale forests "the bush." She picked up Kat's vase from the night table. "I'll put the flowers in here." The dark, smooth, cool of the vase matched the atmosphere Kat had arranged in her room for her afternoon nap. The enamel sides were decorated with weird, long-legged dogs running among blossoms and butterflies. A gentle rattle slipped up through the graceful neck as Jilly set the vase on the tray. She shook it. Something was inside, something that sounded like pearls.

Afraid to pour its contents into her hand in the dark, Jilly took the vase into the bathroom and closed the door. Fluorescence glared along the tile walls, and she spilled the pearls onto the vanity next to the barnacle.

Pills. Dozens. The blood pressure medication. What was it doing in the vase?

Jilly pulled open Kat's vanity mirror. Behind it on narrow glass shelves stood the many varied shapes of vials and tubes. Jilly found the capsules she brought to Kat every morning with her breakfast. The vial was nearly full, as it had been earlier that day.

"She hasn't been taking them," Jilly whispered. "She hasn't been taking her medicine."

She picked one up and rolled it between her fingers. "Just a spoonful of sugar . . . ," she sang. With a flick of her wrist, she popped it into the dark mouth of the running-dogs vase. Its snap as it hit the bottom was amplified by the cavernous ceramic interior.

Snap. Like a barnacle's beak.

The sound Jilly heard every morning when she left Kat's room, not the barnacle's resurrected snap, but the sound of Katrina's longing for release.

When Jilly turned out the bathroom light and opened the door, she saw that the wicker chair was empty and that Kat was still asleep, though she'd shifted her position a bit so her face was partially covered by a corner of lace shawl.

"I don't want to be the last. Worse, left alone here with Nadine. Or is she dead?" A shred of paper napkin stuck to Kat's upper lip where a little egg from supper had made it sticky, only she kept brushing the tip of her nose with her hand as though that was where the foreign object had lodged. Her lamp illuminated the fresh daffodils on the night table. "You can't throw me back. I'm like that barnacle."

"Then eat pretzels and do cartwheels on the rocks!" Jilly thrust her curved hand towards Kat's face, making Kat flinch and raise a forearm in self-defence, but Jilly peeled away the paper shred, then grabbed Kat's bony shoulders. "Make it quick so I don't have to stumble around this house six times a day carrying your tray! Get it over with instead of lying here trying to snag little bits of last-minute purpose from the outgoing tide!"

"No, you're doing that! There's nothing left for me!"

"Isn't this what we lived for? We lived and worked so we could come here and do nothing but comb pools of sea water for anemones and pearls."

"You did! I spent my life walking on the riverbanks. I found all those things and I'm tired of it!"

That was true. Kat had never held a nine-to-five job, and, though not wealthy, she'd managed to live in leisure while her friends complained about their jobs and put money away for retirement.

"I looked into those pools of yours, Jilly, and all I saw was myself looking back at me! Is that what I came here for?"

Again Jilly thrust her hand into Kat's face, but this time she placed a pill on her tongue and held a cup to her lips. "Make something up. Just let your thoughts run wild, like dogs. You don't have to answer any questions or plan your passage to heaven. You can just look at a thousand different things a day and let simple things catch in your mind. Patterns. Shapes. Sounds."

Kat drank. Jilly wondered if the pill had gone down or had nestled slyly behind pale guns.

"You don't do that," Kat gurgled.

The window shade delivered strips of sun onto Kat's lap, making fibres of wool and silk shine.

"No, I try. But I'm always so busy. . . ."

"Too many patterns to keep track of."

"I'll be done with it when I walk into the sea. I'll be the one, you know."

Kat flexed her knees under the sheet. "Who was here earlier? I heard a strange voice." *See who's at the door. Tell them the Queen is not at home.*

"A man. Nadine thought he'd come for Wendy."

" 'If you think we're wax-works, you ought to pay. Wax-works weren't made to be looked at for nothing.' "

"A lost man," said Jilly. She gathered up the tray. While she puttered about with the cutlery and balled-up napkins and spills, the bed began to shake.

Kat was laughing. Some sound came at last from her withered throat and her eyes began to water. "Oh Jilly!" she gasped. "A lost man! Who lost him?" Her eyes closed with the effort of laughter. "Did you tell him he could snuggle in here and you'd look after both of us?"

Jilly sat down on the bed with the tray in her lap, for she, too, felt laughter filling her chest like a balloon. The two women shook and gasped and croaked in antique merriment for several seconds, then Kat said in a sort of runaway babble, "Jilly—Jilly, did you know I used to have a pair of leashes that said, 'I heart my schnauzer'? You know, instead of *love* there's that pink heart? 'I heart my schnauzer!' "

Fuller voices emerged, now that their lungs had expanded. Their cries echoed in the salt-scented rooms.

"Turn on the lamp. I'll get out of bed later," said Kat when they were done. "For Sonny. I'll wear one of Wendy's warm things. We'll be popcorn twins."

"I'll tell Ricky to come help you dress."

Now. Exactly the right time. The tide running towards the sun, the winds all past, finally, and flying over forests and channel to the mainland, fogs and mists waiting in the wings for nightfall, darkness approaching from the east like a black, low-slung cat. By the time Jilly and the dogs get to the point of rock far away from Prairie Lodge, the sun is only an inch from the straight edge of the horizon. Jilly is racing with that falling red star, for she saw from a way back the spark in the water beside the rocks. A small orange-red flame, a bit of fire on the sea. Jilly keeps her eyes on the spot and in a few seconds it flashes again in the same place, as a gentle swell lifts it into a weak beam of light.

Jilly stays close to the receding water line, and in veering off towards the point is tempted to dissect the crescent of sea between the beach and the point, wade right into it. But she does not know how deep it is there, or if treacherous stones lie beneath its surface. To get to the shining thing she will have to make her way along the boulder rubble and steep rock faces that shape the farthest limit of the bay.

The sun descends so quickly once it sees the horizon. It touches the ocean and laughs. Jilly must decide: walk into the sea, or scramble among the rocks in waning light. She can no longer see the spark of red glass, but she feels sure the treasure is still caught somewhere along the point. All the way from Japan.

She chooses the rocks. The air is too cold for her to be wet.

Her progress is swifter than she'd expected. She has new agility, and her hands reaching ahead, bracing behind, are like two extra feet propelling her along while her eyes search the water. Almost too dark already. A beer can almost fools her, but then—near the beer can, in the same tiny cove—a prettier thing.

Jilly's shoes slide from under her and she rides down an angle of wet granite on the seat of Wendy's sweatsuit. One foot is swamped in the lilting waves, but Jilly clings to a spire of rock with one hand and pulls her treasure from the sea with the other.

A bottle. A reddish-brown bottle. Jilly's eyes make a desperate sweep of the waters along the point, determined to find yet another thing gleaming red among the rocks.

Nothing.

She's pulled bottles from waves before. Never at sunset, never at such risk. But bottles are the great imposters of Japanese fishing floats, and here is one again. This one has a swollen cork in its mouth.

With wet fingers Jilly raises the bottle level with her eyes and looks through it at the last sliver of sun that watches over the lead-grey sea.

The bottle is not empty. It is dry inside and bears a simple cargo.

Last summer was the last time the Prairie Lodgers had taken a day trip with Dr. Mazlit in his sloop. Kat had flirted with the doctor and made great ceremony of drying the winebottle in the starboard breeze. She'd giggled over the secret message she wrote on a scrap of paper—the label from the bottle?—and with extravagant grace she'd flung the bottle into the ocean. Kat had worn a lacy frill at her throat and a sun-hat with a brim wider than her shoulders. "Call me Kat Hepburn," she'd croaked when Dr. Mazlit praised her costume.

But other people threw message bottles into the sea, and Kat had thrown many since she'd come to the Island. Jilly did not know of anyone ever finding one, and she had no idea what Kat wrote on the slips of paper.

The cork comes out easily, the message does not. So little light left now, though the horizon burns bright red. Paying no heed to the peril of broken glass on rocks where she or a stranger might prowl again, Jilly holds the wide part of the bottle with both her hands and, straight-armed, powerfully, smashes the neck against the granite. The crack of the glass echoes off the walls of quiet and off the metallic sea and off the mass of stone that have enclosed her sin along with the darkness.

Jilly holds the bottom half of the bottle like someone about to take an illicit drink. She is a trespasser. Whatever Kat engraved on that crisp fragment of wine label, whatever secret she'd whispered into that bottle, she'd intended for an anonymous confidant, or for the world, for God, but not for mortal, everyday companions. She wished her wisdom to float beyond prairie, over mountain and shoreline, to a nirvana of loving strangers.

I'll put it in a new bottle and throw it back, thinks Jilly, and I won't tell her. She folds the message into her palm.

The dogs bustle and pant around her. She worries about the glass cutting their paws and begins fumbling her way back to the beach. The shadows deceive her. Her ankles twist this way and that. The dogs find their way easily to the flat sand.

Jilly rests for a moment. She sees Lady Macbeth stop dead in her tracks and look towards Prairie Lodge with her neck straight and her ears cocked. Then Lear. And then both dogs are running madly down the beach to the house, running like horses, flattened out, necks stretched forward. They do not bark. In a second they are black ghosts.

"Kat," whispers Jilly. "No. Kat. . . ."

She leaps into the shallow water beside the point. Her hand scrapes over the barnacles rooted to the rocks. In her head, suddenly, a chant keeping rhythm with her pulse: "I heart my schnauzer, I heart my barnacle." The sound of walking in the ocean is loud, too loud in the soundless dusk. But she cannot move quietly in the water. At last she finds its brink. Her earlier footprints have disappeared. Jilly tries to run like the dogs, but her pace is a futile trot. With each step the water gurgles in her shoes. "I heart my schnauzer. The Queen is dead. The Queen is dead. . . ."

Lights are going on in all the windows of Prairie Lodge. Kat's bedroom light is on bright, the way she never allowed it to be. Her message forms a knot inside Jilly's fist.

Jilly labours up the gentle slope that leads from the beach to the lawn. At the same time, the headlights of a car coming along the road flash in the corner of her eye. At first she thinks it is the big pink car, the bed-and-breakfast man returning to pillage the fortress in disarray. But—it must be Sonny. Sonny.

The car passes the driveway and continues on down the road.

"So that's why you came. You didn't want to strut at all. She didn't want to be the last, and she couldn't remember ahead. You didn't want to strut at all. And when will you be back?"

Jilly staggers across the coarse, spongy grass, mumbling and panting. The dogs are unheeding. They whimper on the veranda, and pound on the door with their large damp paws. Their bodies strain and lunge, as though each is being pulled by an invisible leash.

BETWEEN MOON AND FLAX FIRES

A hurricane in the Gulf of Mexico has pushed a warm wind up from the south. Clear sky and wind make it a night for stubble-burning, for lighting soft heaps of flax straw at the south end of the field and carrying patches of flame on a pitchfork from pile to stubble. You criss-cross the field carrying fire while the wind blows the flames steadily towards the north, to the edge, where a plough has buried the straw and the fire will starve. The smoke from the flax is white, like the smoke from a grass fire, like something pure is burning.

Claire pictures Bruno in the white smoke. He likes the stubble-burning nights in autumn, cleaning up after the messy month of harvest. Carrying the fire is like play, a one-man game. Just before sundown he told Claire he was going to their land out west to burn flax stubble, and she watched him from the kitchen window walking across the yard to his Merc. Holly the lab trotted beside him to the truck. She jumped up onto the seat ahead of him, and Bruno had the key turned in the ignition even before he had slammed the door.

Claire wanted to pick tomatoes before it was dark, but her

garden runners need new laces, have needed new laces for a long time—tonight the second one tore as she pulled it tight. She didn't realize ahead of time how long it would take her to find a new pair. They were at the bottom of her jumbled sewing basket and were probably meant for Darcy or Jonathan. The laces were still in their package. Now they are Claire's.

She sits on the edge of Bruno's easy chair with the runners on the footstool and begins the lacing. Washed underwear lies in a flattened mound in front of the TV. The cat is stretched out on top of the laundry, licking a spotted paw. The children object to folding each other's underwear, so Claire will have to do it. Later. Tomatoes first, although it is nearly too dark already.

Claire does not like to feel hurried, does not allow herself to be rushed. She does not take command of her days, but lets them unfold before her, at whatever pace the plans and accidents and crises and celebrations of others dictate. Claire simply adjusts, adjusts, adjusts as each moment passes. At this particular moment, the weaving of the white strands is pleasing to her. It reminds her of when she used to braid Darcy's hair, when hair-weaving was a fad. The cat comes and tries to hook the ends of the laces with her claws. Claire and the cat play the game together.

And then Darcy is there. She has appeared without a sound, coming from the east side of the house, which is already quite dark. The lamp under which Claire is working on the lacing floods Claire and the shoes with a bright light, but blots out the rest of the room. It is the sheet of white paper in Darcy's hand, hanging at her side, that catches Claire's eye. Darcy dresses in dark clothes in all seasons. Except for the sheet of paper Claire would not have noticed her until she spoke or turned the TV on. Darcy is always working on essays and projects and articles. School has scarcely started. But she wants to go to university next year.

Darcy kneels on the shag rug, half in the light, half out, and begins sorting Bruno's white Stanfields from Jonathan's blues and greens. The lacing of the runners becomes automatic and Claire nudges the cat away. It is not normal for Darcy to sort the men's underwear.

The tasks continue in silence for a few seconds. Claire wonders what is on the paper that Darcy brought in—she can see handwriting in an atypical scrawl in one corner. Not a research paper.

"I talked to her, Mom."

"Talked to who?" Then Claire remembers hearing a far-off voice, someone on the telephone in the den. Darcy went into the den right after supper. . . .

"Carolyn Lanthier."

Claire thinks hard. The name is supposed to mean something to her. A leaf drops from the fig tree behind the easy chair and makes gentle clicking sounds as it touches branches on its way down.

"Mom, Carolyn Lanthier!"

But Claire cannot find the name in the weaving of the laces.

"Mom, Carolyn Lanthier? My—my birth-mother? I talked to her today."

Birth-mother.

Darcy stops folding shorts, but Claire tries to do the second shoe. She can't remember how to start.

Darcy did not say *real* mother. They probably taught her that at the agency. Claire thought Darcy had given up. Claire never asked her about it. That must be why Darcy didn't say anything sooner. Claire never asked. That way, it might go away.

Yes, that's right—Darcy's voice, way off in the den, behind a closed door, talking on the phone. . . .

What more is there to say? "Oh—yes—Carolyn Lanthier. That was her name. I haven't thought about it for a long time. You talked to her. Where is she?"

"She lives in Thunder Bay. In a suburb."

In a suburb. "What did she say?"

Darcy stretches out her legs in front of her, legs in dark green leotards, and winds a white undershirt around her feet. "Well, she sounded—I don't know—nice, you know—decent and everything."

"Glad to hear from you?"

"Yes. She wants to see me."

Claire feels like a child finding a puppy and having the owner show up at the door. All the years Claire and Bruno had Darcy seem now only a season long. "Have you told Jonathan?"

"Not yet."

But Jonathan has known who his other family is since he was ten. He's never wanted to go anywhere near the reserve up north where his mother lives. He was one of the last native children to be given to a non-native family. Becoming Ojibwa has been too much for him to handle up to this point.

"Shouldn't I tell him?" Darcy looks up at Claire with such serious eyes, round eyes behind round, dark-framed glasses. Claire tries to see the woman who is Darcy's mother—how old would she be now—thirty-five? Probably a little plumper, a few lines around the mouth and eyes, straight, straight, chocolatey sleek hair with perhaps a few silver threads here and there, probably cut shorter, maybe curled. Darcy dislikes tight curls. What if Carolyn Lanthier has short, tightly curled hair? The adoption papers said Darcy's father had thin red hair and a stocky build. Darcy is not like that at all.

"Don't tell Jonathan until I've talked to your dad."

"Mom, she—"

Claire does not want to hear any more. She wants Carolyn Lanthier not to exist. Claire herself was abandoned by her mother when she was small. Carolyn Lanthier is not the mother she wants in their lives—the wrong mother is returning.

Jonathan calls from his bedroom, "Is anybody using the car tonight?"

Claire remembers his younger, boy's voice: "Anybody around to take me to hockey practice tonight?" "Anybody teaching me to drive tonight?" Now it is lower, a man's voice.

"Yes," she answers. "I'm going to see Dad for awhile. You can have it later."

"Where is he?" Jonathan's tone is impatient now.

"Burning the flax stubble." To Darcy, Claire says, "Tell him in the morning."

Jonathan says, "Give me the message. I'll go there before I go to town."

"It isn't a message. Darcy, are you going to see her?"

Darcy twists the shirt tighter around her feet. "I think so. Maybe Thanksgiving."

Claire picks up the runners and gets to her feet. The cat makes a lunge at the dangling laces, and Claire slaps her away. It is only a light slap, but Claire would like to throw the cat across the room.

Darcy brings her knees up to her chin. "Mom, she's a lawyer, and she has a husband, and little children. Little children!"

Claire thinks, we'll actually have a lawyer in the family— we'll also have another mother in the family. "I'm going to see how your father is doing."

"She had a name for me."

Claire hurries to the screen door leading out onto the porch. She does not stop to put on her shoes.

"She was going to call me Amber. Amber Maureen."

Claire rushes down the porch steps in bare feet with her runners in her hand, one shoe laced, the other half done, the weaving jumbled, eyelets missed. As she crosses the lawn to the car, she notices that the wind is coming out of the north.

The driveway points south, then meets the east-west road that leads to the hundred acres Claire and Bruno own six miles away. But a bridge under construction between her and that land means Claire will have to go east first and take the highway part of the way. The wind is softer now and the sky has become a dark jewel. As Claire turns left on the gravel road, she sees that the moon is rising out of the distant river. The moon is not yet full, but is swollen expectantly. An almost invisible halo warns of a change in weather, related perhaps to the far-off hurricane. The moon is yellow, as though it has bathed in a river of molten gold. Last night Claire was able to see it from her bedroom window as she undressed for the night.

She drives east half a mile, turns south, and finally comes to the pavement, where she heads west at last. She drives faster on the highway with the fingers of both hands curled lightly over the bottom of the steering-wheel. She must think about what to say to Bruno. She's glad she can tell him about Darcy while he is working. They've always been able to talk about the tricky things, things that frighten or anger or sadden them, when they are working—working on strenuous tasks, like shovelling wheat, rolling up the snow-fencing, digging potatoes, gathering deadfall in the shelter-belts. It's never been good sitting in the kitchen or in front of the late news, and bed is for summing it up, resolving everything, settling things in a moment of peace. Claire will be able to walk with him back and forth, partly hidden in smoke and darkness, and they'll talk it out. Her new shoelaces will turn black in the dust and ash.

Other adopted children have found their natural mothers, people she knows. Last year at the fall supper in Harley, Claire had heard Jeanie Calder telling about how her nineteen-year-old daughter Meg had gone to Toronto to meet her real mother—that's what Jeanie had said, *real* mother—for the first time. Meg had been full of romantic ideas and high hopes, because she and her adoptive parents were not getting along, and the real mother had been delighted to have a companion. But the woman Meg found chewed garlic for her health and smoked cigars, and smelled so much of garlic and cigar smoke that Meg came home, moved out of her parents' house, and proclaimed herself an orphan. Jeanie had said Meg only visits them when she runs out of food.

Tony Lavallee went looking for his natural mother when he was forty-five years old. He traced her to Whitehorse and when he found her house, a run-down tenement in a cold and creepy part of town, he stood outside on the sidewalk across the street until dark, waiting for someone to come out who might be her. But nobody came out at all. Finally he phoned her from a café on the corner, and she told him to get out of town. Tony told Claire and Bruno that what he remembered most was that a little boy had watched him from an open window on the second floor almost the whole time Tony waited on the sidewalk, even though a crisp wind had been blowing out of the north. The child had leaned out on arms folded on the sill and watched. "He might be sitting there now," Tony had said when he told the story, although it had been years since Tony had been there.

Claire sees the moon behind her in the rear-view mirror, still yellow, higher now. And when she gets past a cluster of farms at an intersection of dirt roads, the glow of Bruno's fires appears on a flat line, a little to the north, like a liquid sun rising.

Darcy had decided to look for her birth-mother after reading *Anne of Green Gables*, and after watching a special on television about adopted children finding fulfilment in reuniting with their natural parents. Claire had thought the TV special unrealistic and one-sided, and was surprised when her level-headed daughter fell for it. That had been ages ago. Claire had really believed the moment had passed. Darcy is eighteen now, exceptionally mature and bright. People always say how bright she is—the legacy no doubt of Carolyn Lanthier the lawyer. I should have been prepared, thinks Claire now as she glides along the smooth pavement. I should have kept it in my heart and addressed it up front, instead of burying it.

Before Claire and Bruno moved into the house they live in now, they lived in a little old house a few miles south. That was before they had gotten Darcy and Jonathan. During one of her pregnancies, Claire got involved with Louis L'Amour novels and stayed inside and read while Bruno struggled alone with the farm work. The house had a cellar under the kitchen. To get into the cellar you opened up a trapdoor and descended on a steep, rickety staircase. Claire forgot to close the trapdoor after fetching a jar of Bruno's mother's plum jam from the narrow shelves along the dirt walls down there, and later, with her nose in *The Rider of the Ruby Hills*, on her way to the bathroom, she stepped into the hole in the floor and slid on her rump to the bottom on the worn wooden steps. She didn't lose the baby then, that had happened later—much later. And she never told Bruno—he was already exasperated with the structureless, drifting way she spent her days. It is that incident with the open cellar door that Claire thinks about now as she worries about failing her daughter.

Claire can see a low, crooked wall of flames in the distance. The flax field looks vast, like thousands of acres. The whole horizon is on fire. She wishes she could see the moon and the burning horizon together, instead of being between them. It is hard to concentrate on the driving, on the cars coming towards her, on the dull yellow line that splits the highway. Now she can see the smoke.

The rear-view mirror reflects a bright burst of crimson. Claire can feel the red light flashing across her face. Has the moon exploded? Not quite full, but exploded in blood. A siren whoops, just once.

Claire pulls to the side of the road, expecting the police car to pass her and continue its urgent race down the highway. But it does not pass. It slows down with her. Claire stops on the shoulder. The police car stops behind her. The red light keeps flashing.

Claire has never been stopped by the police before. She's been driving for twenty-five years without getting a speeding ticket or even a warning about a burnt-out headlight. She does not know why she is being stopped. A few seconds pass before she hears the slam of the RCMP's car door. *He's putting my licence number through a computer*, thinks Claire, *to see who I am and check my record. They don't know it's just me.* She rolls down her window and straightens her shoulders.

Another light. This one shines directly on her face. She turns to look at the officer, but he holds the flashlight in front of his own face so she can't see anything except the round beam. She stares at the stripes on his sleeve instead.

"Could I see your driver's licence, Ma'am?"

Of course, she doesn't have it. It is not the first time, but she's never been caught before. She had not stopped to take her handbag when she fled the house. The keys were already in the car. "I don't have it with me," she says in a flat voice. "My name is Claire Decker and I live on a farm with my husband Bruno Decker just a little ways back. I just—forgot to take my wallet with me this evening."

The beam from the flashlight, which seems to Claire to be as bright as a laser, darts about the interior of the car like a cricket in a grain bin. "Open your door, please."

"What? I can show you my registration, if you like. I think it's here in the glove compartment. . . ." But the officer stands back and Claire opens the door. He does not ask her to get out but leans forward into the opening. The flashlight sweeps the floorboards.

"Where are you going? Why didn't you take your licence with you?"

Claire can see his face now—he has kind eyes. "May I ask why you stopped me?"

"You're driving with your brights on against oncoming traffic. We flashed ours at you, but you didn't respond." *And you fell through the trapdoor into the cellar.*

He thinks I'm drunk, Claire realizes. She reaches with her foot for the button on the floorboard and presses it with her bare toes. "I was looking at the flax fires," she tells him. "They're so beautiful. I couldn't help but look at them." Claire is suddenly aware of the second officer in the cruiser car behind her. Someone is waiting, maintaining contact with headquarters.

"Where are you going?"

"My husband is on that field. I'm just going to—to give him a message. I left in a hurry, forgot my handbag."

"Does he own that land?"

"Yes."

"And you came from your house just now?"

"Yes. Just now."

The flashlight beam keeps moving, moving. It travels down Claire's legs to her feet, like a caress. Claire and the officer gaze at her bare feet. No cars have passed for awhile and none seem to be coming. The wind is gentler, just little puffs in the ditch grass. The moon watches. In a nearby sunflower field a bazooka for keeping blackbirds away explodes sharply. Crickets chirp in the field borders.

Two crickets had wintered over in that cellar under the trapdoor. Not long after the loss of the second baby Claire and Bruno had begun hearing their duet beneath the kitchen floorboards. The winter was a harsh one, but the little house gave just enough warmth to the cellar to keep them active. Claire never actually saw the two crickets, but she brought lettuce down to them every so often, and water in the lid of a peanut butter jar. Even so, their chirping turned to a hoarse bleating as the cold days wore on, and in March, their voices became silent. Claire and Bruno had no way of knowing whether or not the crickets ever made it out of that cellar into the thawing spring earth.

"You're driving without your shoes," says the officer.

"No," Claire replies. "My shoes are right here on the seat. Is it against the law to drive barefoot?"

"Put them on, please."

Claire is beginning to feel the way she did when she swatted the cat a while back. That was only a few minutes ago but it seems like hours. She wants to stand on the other side of the fire and see the moon through the smoke while the moon is still large and gold-coloured. She reaches for her runners.

"We feel that you are more in contact with the brake pedal if you are wearing proper footwear." *Proper* footwear? He sounds as though he is reading from an RCMP training manual. He keeps the laser beam on Claire's feet as she ties up her left runner. The right shoe is the unfinished one. She slips it on and does not tie it.

But the officer is watchful. "This message—is it some sort of emergency? Something I can help you with?"

Just let me go. Claire looks out through the windshield into the vast fire two miles in the distance. How comforting the flames are, an unperilous fire, one you can stand in and walk in while shaping it, sculpting it.

She hears a soft click. The beam of light is sucked instantly back into its silver sheath.

Suddenly the second officer is standing beside the first one. "Hello, Mrs. Decker." A woman's voice. Claire can see the woman's face by the glow of the interior car lights. "Remember me?"

When Darcy was sixteen, she disappeared for a day. Didn't show up in school, didn't come home for supper, didn't tell even her friends where she was going. Claire and Bruno, in a panic, called the town police and the RCMP. They told Claire and Bruno not to worry, teenagers sometimes did that, went out on some sort of lark for a day or two—the police wouldn't get involved until twenty-four hours had passed. Except for the woman who stood beside Claire's car at this moment. Though off duty, she had helped the Deckers search, and had done a bit of her own detective work. She found Darcy in a grove of trees three miles south of town, rows of silver maples with large leathery leaves.

Claire hadn't thought of looking there, had nearly forgotten that she and Darcy had had an impromptu picnic in that grove a few summers earlier. Darcy had loved the maple grove, but Claire had not known that she sometimes went there alone on her bicycle. It turned out that Darcy was in love with a boy in school who scarcely knew who she was, or cared. When she'd tried to get a little too close to him, he'd said something cruel to her, and she'd run away to sort it out among the silver maple trees.

Claire cannot recall the woman officer's name.

"Corporal Frame," says the woman. "Cathy Frame."

"Of course I remember you," says Claire. "You were very kind to us."

"How's Darcy?"

Claire does not answer but stares at the stubble fires on the horizon.

The first officer walks back to the cruiser car, but the woman does not. "He made me put on my shoes," Claire says.

"Your name came up on the computer. I couldn't figure out what was going on over here. Is everything all right, then?"

Claire looks towards the fire again, and the moon is there, suspended above the burning field.

The woman sits down on the running-board of Claire's car and stares off into the darkness over the autumn fields. She stares towards the silver maple grove to the south, invisible in the night, but only a few miles away. The night winds breathe across the ditch grass and over the car.

Claire says, "The first time I went to the hospital bleeding they said I'd never been pregnant. The nurses looked for my baby in a bedpan full of blood and said I'd probably had a false test. I'd called that baby Lucinda from the moment she was conceived.

"I didn't dare name the second one. She lasted longer, though—four months. The nurses said, cheer up, you can try again.

"The third baby lived outside my body for one minute. *One minute!* I called her Jennifer Maureen so that there would be a name on her gravestone. I've been pregnant, I've had a living child inside me!"

"Is something the matter with Darcy, Mrs. Decker? Did she run away again?"

"I took the role of The Mother in a play. Bruno took the role of The Father, and a baby was loaned to us to play The Daughter. But now The Daughter wants to go back to the woman who loaned her to us. The play is over. No new play can begin. The curtain has come down and can never go up again. That is not right." Claire turns off the headlights of the car and the orange flames get brighter. And how did the moon get there?

Corporal Frame keeps looking into the deep, empty, silent south. She asks, "How do you make laws about blood?"

"The mother's name should have been burned when she left the delivery room. She should not be allowed to exist on the same planet as me and my child!" Claire hammers the steering-wheel with her fist.

"You know those trees where we found Darcy that time?" asks the officer.

Claire looks south and can almost see them. "Silver maples," she says.

"That's where my authority ends. I have no control over what happens beyond those trees. That's somebody else's territory. Everybody has boundaries like that."

Claire says, "My mother went to the winter fair in Brandon by herself and she telephoned my father to tell him that she wasn't coming back because she'd met a man she loved and he was going to take her to Nanaimo. He was the man who built the horse jumps for the fair. I remember my father on the phone asking her if she wanted him to send her anything—money, clothes. He didn't ask her if she wanted me, and she didn't ask for me. My dad was a lot older than she was and he acted as though he'd expected it to happen. She never came back and I've never tried to find her. We're not quite orphans. We're something in between, between our mothers and the death of our mothers."

Corporal Frame stretches her legs out in front of her. The heels of her boots grate on the gravel shoulder. "Don't you want to see your mother now?"

"Which one?" Claire cries. "I have so many! My daughter's mother, my long-lost mother, the false mother in myself. The mother my daughter will become. . . . Are any of them real?"

"You have to talk this all out with Darcy, Mrs. Decker. I can't believe she wants to abandon you."

"The wind keeps changing—have you noticed that?"

"I've patrolled these highways many years. Fall is a dangerous, emotional time of year. Things seem to come apart the most in autumn." The officer takes a deep breath. "Must be the northern lights, or maybe all those leaves on the ground."

Claire says nothing for some time. She thinks about the hurricane unravelling the order of the universe. The boom of the pretend gun in the sunflower field is louder now, because the wind has twisted around. Claire remembers a day in fall when Darcy was about nine. At that time the Deckers had a huge flock of kittens and mother cats that played and mewed and hunted around the back door, drawn to the smells of the kitchen and to Darcy's affectionate babying. After school that day, she spent the hours before supper sitting among them on the lawn, enticing them with twigs she jiggled under the yellow poplar leaves beginning to blanket the yard. At the table that evening she frowned at her supper plate and said one of the females, the one she called Samantha, who had been missing for a long time, had returned. "But she's acting weird—she's scratching and trying to bite the other cats, and she won't let me touch her—she acts scared of me. And she keeps howling and snarling. You'd think she'd be hungry, but she didn't even go near the food dishes." Bruno asked her quietly if Samantha had bitten her. She said no.

Then he asked her if the cat had bitten any other cats. "No," she said, "they all stayed out of her way." Then without a word, Bruno had gotten up and left the house. Darcy began to eat, thinking her daddy had gone out to make the cat better. Claire kept making up excuses to go to the kitchen counter. From there she could look out the window to see what Bruno was up to. Finally she saw him in a thicket of Chinese elms in a corner of the yard. The twenty-two was raised to his shoulder and his head was bent along the sights. Claire ran to Darcy with her arms outstretched, but before she could clap her hands over her daughter's ears, the gun sounded, and all the birds stopped singing. Long before they started again, Darcy had begun to cry. She cried softly, though, and not angrily. Claire told her, "Samantha was dying anyway, honey. And she could have made you and the other cats very sick."

Hearing the explosion now in the sunflower field reminds Claire of the explosion of Bruno's gun that day in the thicket. Years later, Darcy asked Claire if Samantha had had rabies. "Yes, she probably did," Claire had answered.

"Why didn't you just tell me? I knew what rabies was! You could have just said it!"

That sort of retrospective anger was unfamiliar to Claire at the time—she herself could not remember ever having felt it.

"I have to go talk to Bruno." Claire reaches for the key in the ignition.

"Before you've talked to Darcy?"

The moon is no longer in the sky over the flax fires. Claire looks deep into the fire and believes she can see the black figure of Bruno criss-crossing the field, carrying patches of flame on a pitchfork, and Holly trotting along, keeping a distance from the fire, but keeping pace with Bruno. Then she looks at the back of Cathy Frame's head. The wind has shifted to the south again and ruffles the woman's dark hair.

Suddenly there is bright red flashing again in the mirror. But this time there are many lights, moving very fast. In a moment a fire truck speeds past, followed by a rescue vehicle. At the same time, the first officer comes to where the two women are sitting. "We gotta go," he says to his partner. Then to Claire, before Corporal Frame can ask what's going on, "Looks like your husband's stubble fire got away from him, Mrs. Decker. It just came over the radio. It's threatening a farmyard nearby."

"What. . . ! That's impossible! He's so careful. . . !" Claire fumbles again for the key.

"Don't worry, Mrs. Decker," says Corporal Frame, who is on her feet now. "They'll take care of it. The wind's already shifted back. There's nothing you can do."

He needs me! I should be there. . . .

"Go home."

The next thing Claire knows the RCMP cruiser car is on the highway, its red lights turning and blinking silently like the others, which she can still see above the orange glow of the flames. Claire gets out of her car and stands beside the open door. She stares at the fires for a few seconds, then looks east at the moon. The moon is white now, cold-looking, a sightless eye.

Headlights come out of the east, many cars from town following the fire truck to the scene—sightseers.

In the morning the field will be a mottle of powdery black and dull bronze. The flax-burning clothes hung in the back entry will give off the smell of ash. Usually the smell of smoke and ash in the house is pleasant for awhile, foreign and pungent, until it gets stale, and Jonathan and Darcy complain. Then one of them puts the overalls into the washing machine and closes the lid, and Claire finds them there when it occurs to her that laundry needs to be done. This time, she will not want to smell the smoke—she will wash the clothes as soon as Bruno takes them off.

Claire sits on the running-board where Corporal Frame had been sitting only seconds ago and takes off her right shoe. She holds it in her lap and undoes the weaving, and starts again. This time the white strands find the correct pattern in the eyelets.

Wearing both her garden runners, Claire drives the two miles to Bruno's flax field. But she stops a ways off and watches the flashing lights and the dark silhouettes of firemen and police and Bruno, and probably Tony Lavallee, whose farm it is that is being threatened by the renegade flames, watches them all running here and there, dragging hoses, gesturing. She keeps her window rolled up and hears nothing.

As she drives home, half sentences of what she'll say to Darcy leap and tangle in her mind, only half sentences, which will find their endings when she and her daughter are face to face. She thinks, too, about Bruno and how bad he'll be feeling about the Lavallee farm. The images of the red lights flashing in the night remind her of her unpicked tomatoes.

When she reaches her driveway and drifts slowly towards the house, she sees someone standing near the pond way at the edge of the yard. Darcy, standing in the moonlight beside the pond, her favourite place to go these days when she needs to clear her head. Claire recognizes the cape she herself made for Darcy two autumns ago. The cape flutters and billows in the wind as the girl turns to see who is coming down the road. Claire does not know why, but she is reminded of Tony Lavallee's window child, the little boy on his elbows, leaning on the sill and watching the shadowy man across the street while the cold wind blows through his hair.

Claire walks towards the pond. Above it the haloed moon has turned even whiter in the smokeless depths of the heavens. But the halo means the weather will turn colder. Soon, on the flax field, a scorched, brittle thread of straw will break under the weight of a single snowflake.

Lois Braun is a well-known writer of short stories who lives and teaches school in rural Manitoba. The title story of her new collection, "The Pumpkin-Eaters," was nominated for the Journey Prize in 1989. Her writing has appeared in many anthologies and magazines, including *Border Crossings*, *Western Living*, *The Antigonish Review*, *Grain*, *Prairie Fire* and *Scrivener*.